The scent of new-mown hay—and the smell of death!

Five more terrorists were buried under several tons of hay that tumbled from an upper loft which the shattered beam had supported. Several of the men and women, fearing that other lofts were about to fall, tripped over their own feet in a frantic effort to retreat to the other end of the barn. They had a new fear when two canisters of teargas sailed through the blasted east opening, struck the stone floor and began hissing out clouds of gas. Two brave but foolish Brigadists made a futile effort to pick up the cannisters and throw them back through the opening.

They had not counted on the fragmentation grenade that the Death Merchant tossed in behind the teargas. It exploded in the faces of the two men, riddled them with shrapnel and pitched them up into the air. Concurrently, the third antitank grenade streaked into the barn, struck a Y-shaped brace and exploded. Concussion killed six Brigadists instantly. Flying splinters from the blown-apart Y-brace killed six more, four men and two women.

For a shave of a second, Ferro and Camellion locked eyes through the glass of the gasmasks, Camellion thinking that while some men hunted animals, he stalked the most dangerous game of all—game that could fight back—*man!*

THE DEATH MERCHANT SERIES:

#35 in the incredible adventures of the

DEATH MERCHANT
MASSACRE IN ROME
by Joseph Rosenberger

PINNACLE BOOKS   LOS ANGELES

DEATH MERCHANT #35:
MASSACRE IN ROME

Copyright © 1979 by Joseph Rosenberger

An original Pinnacle Books edition, published for the first time anywhere.

First printing, August 1979

ISBN: 0-523-40478-6

Cover illustration by Dean Cate

Printed in the United States of America

PINNACLE BOOKS, INC.
2029 Century Park East
Los Angeles, California 90067

This book is dedicated to
George F. McAulay II
of Kensington, Maryland,
and to
Tom and Joy Pierson
of
Buffalo Grove, Illinois

Revolutionaries who take the law into their own hands are terrifying, not as villains, but as mechanisms out of control, as runaway machines.

Boris Pasternak—*Doctor Zhivago*

Intelligent people do not try to reason with sadists who slaughter the innocent, with terrorists who murder in the name of "freedom." Intelligent people kill them!

Richard J. Camellion

MASSACRE IN ROME

Chapter One

Big, bold, and bright, the moon illuminated the Italian countryside with a brightness that would permit one to read a newspaper. If Richard Camellion had been superstitious, he would have thought that Earth's satellite hated him. Every time he put his life on the line in Italy, *luna* had stuck her round face into the act, shining with the brilliance of a searchlight.

Camellion was fortunate in that the vineyard, to the east of the villa, was thick with vines heavy with purple grapes almost ready to be picked. By keeping low and staying close to the tangled vines, the Death Merchant did manage to remain in the shadows and to creep forward without being seen by anyone who, from either the first or second story of the house, might be watching.

During the afternoon, George McAulay II had protested. "Us going out there to that villa is a scheme for whacky pointy heads," McAulay had said. "It's as ridiculous as trying to give away ice during a blizzard. Why not grab Camerini as he goes about his daily business? We don't know who and what might be at that villa."

Tom Pierson, another veteran of the CIA's counterintelligence section, had also turned thumbs down on the idea. "I've tailed suspects all over New York City, and even Tokyo. Keeping track of Camerini in Rome would be a snap. We tail him, wait until the right time, then black bag him. But going out there? It all adds up to single trouble and double bad news."

The Death Merchant had overruled McAulay and Pierson.

1

Why? One reason was time. The sooner they grabbed Camerini, the better. The second reason was that Vito Camerini, the man suspected of being a member of the Red Brigades, the dreaded terrorist organization, was a cartoonist who worked at home and never left the villa at any specific time. The Death Merchant didn't intend to waste a week or more of hoping that Camerini would go into Rome and place himself in a position to be grabbed.

The *ponentino*—the westerly breeze—caressing his face, the Death Merchant hurried forward, a .44 Backpacker Auto Mag in his right hand. A noise suppressor was attached to the barrel of the powerful weapon. He paused, listened to the crickets and other insects of early fall, then took a few more steps. Time now for extreme caution; he was getting very close to the house.

Not for a moment did he underestimate the danger. The Red Brigades, the aristocracy of all the terrorist groups in Italy, was the most feared, the most ruthless, and the most proficient in all Europe. Totally brutal and superbly organized, the *Brigate Rosse* had, within the last eight years, murdered over 1,000 people and kidnapped 510 more. In addition, the terrorist organization was responsible for thousands of bombings; another 140 people—police officials, men in government and in industry—had been "kneecapped!" Shot in both knees! The *Brigate Rosse*'s successes were due not only to clever planning and tight discipline, but also to the pathetic inefficiency of the Italian police.

Camellion, moving cautiously forward, felt like laughing out loud when he thought of the three different police forces of Italy. Two were municipal—the ordinary police and the helmeted cops that handled only traffic. The national police force was the well-known *Carabinieri,* who always walk in pairs, with their swords and fancy flamboyant hats. The *Carabinieri* were very picturesque in parades, but against the dedicated terrorists of the *Brigate Rosse* they were as helpless as babies.

When Signor Aldo Moro, the Prime Minister, was kidnaped during March of 1978, many Italians believed that either the Germans, the Americans, or the Israelis had been involved in the snatch because it was so perfectly planned and carried out. For similar reasons of national inferiority, the Italian police had quickly called in foreign intelligence experts to help crack the case, the government confident that the German BKA[1] would find Signor Moro. The BKA, which relies heavily on exotic technology to track terrorists, had failed. Aldo Moro had not been found, not until the *Brigate Rosse* had left his corpse in a red, hatchback Renault station wagon parked at the end of the Via Gaetani in Rome.

All this time, even years before the murder of Aldo Moro, the CIA had kept a careful watch on the activities of the *Brigate Rosse,* most of the talk falling to the case officers of the company station operating within the United States Embassy in Rome. The CIA had hit a partial jackpot during December of 1978, in that it succeeded in recruiting an actual member of the *Brigate Rosse,* an Italian in one of the terror organization's cells in Rome. How far could the man be trusted? No one knew. Marsilio Rigianno was a double agent, selling information not only to the CIA but to the BND, the *Bundesnachrichtendienst,* the West German Federal Intelligence Service.

The violence continued. There were bombings, kidnapings, and bank robberies, not all of these committed by the Red Brigades. There are one hundred fifteen or one hundred twenty known terrorist groups in Italy, some of them fanatics of the Left, others dangerous crackpots of the Right. Members of the Armed Cells for Territorial Counterpower attempted to steal an armored car and were caught in a trap and gunned down by Italian police. Police made raids and hauled in suspects of the Proletarian Armed Formation for Communism, and members of the ultra-Right For God and Cross organization.

Police even managed to capture thirteen members of the Red Brigades. In retaliation, the *Brigatisti* machine gunned the Chief of Police of Milan. An automobile executive in Turin was kidnaped, taken before a "People's Court," found guilty of "crimes of imperialism against the working people," and executed. With utter contempt and unprecedented boldness, the *Brigatisti* dumped his body in the *Piazza di San Pietro* (St. Peter's Square in front of St. Peter's Church).

Ever so slowly the state justice system began to collapse under the crush of trials for acts of terrorism and petty violence. There were proceedings in Cuneo, Genoa, Milan, Bologna, Naples and Rome, and dozens of other cities. There were midnight roundups of all the usual and unusual sus-

[1] The German Federal Criminal Office.

pects, as police swept the communes and crash pads of young activists and dissident workers suspected of forming the flank of the terrorist culture.

Mini-states of siege appeared across the landscape. Airports and bus stations seemed to be under military occupation, with battle-dressed soldiers stationed on runways, at gates and inside terminal buildings. Random roadblocks were thrown up at odd times and at unlikely places. Italian police became widely unmethodical, choosing roads and stopping vehicles by the merest whim rather than any identifiable plan. Their efforts were as effective as trying to empty the Mediterranean with a bucket.

The murderous but fanatical psychopaths of the Red Brigades then assassinated Carlo Casalegno, the editor of Turin's *La Stampa* ("The Press") and blew up the headquarters of the Christian Democrats on the Piazza del Gesù.

A few months later, the *Brigate Rosse* locked horns with the American CIA directly—by blowing up the main gates of the United States Embassy on Via Vittorio Veneto and then, by telephone, warning the embassy officials that if the *"imperialisti americani"* didn't leave Rome within a month, Ambassador Clark Clifford Trentham and his entire family would be "executed." Indirectly, the terrorists sneered in the face of the company by kidnaping Signorina Maria Gondozatti from her modest home in Trastevere section of Rome.

One of the world's greatest mystics and regarded as a living saint, Maria Angelina Gondozatti—a tiny wisp of a woman in her late sixties—had been an enigma to the scientific world for over fifty years. Always a very devout Catholic who went to Mass every day and received holy communion, Maria Gondozatti had startled her family in 1924 by falling into a trance and predicting, with one hundred percent accuracy, the events leading up to World War II. She had been only 13 years old at the time.

Unlike the commercial "psychics" and professional "prophets" who spew out predictions with the regularity of the tides and are always 99 percent wrong, Maria Gondozatti, who had never married, was always right in her prognostications.

Paradoxically, she was almost unknown to the world at large. She lived a very secluded life, spent all her waking hours in prayer (it was said she slept only one hour each night!), and never granted interviews of any kind. Her predictions were never made public; they were too fantastic. They

4

were however, transmitted to the Vatican, which never made comments about them, or her.

The Vatican didn't have to. The CIA had many, many ears, and many of Maria Gondozatti's prophecies reached the inner sanctum of the Agency. As far back as 1969, the mysterious woman had predicted that a man named Carter would become President of the United States. She had accurately predicted an alliance between Red China and the United States and had said that in 1979 there would be a peace treaty between Egypt and Israel.

The Scientific Division of the Central Intelligence Agency became very interested in Maria Gondozatti. How did the woman predict with such uncanny accuracy? The supernatural? Bunk. There isn't any "supernatural," only secrets that are hidden for a time.

The CIA had been toying with ways and means to study Maria Gondozatti—it would have to be through a parapsychology front organization—when the *Brigate Rosse* had kidnaped the living saint, threatening to "execute" the woman unless the Italian government agreed to release all the imprisoned members of the Red Brigades, as well as those on trial. The Italian government had one month in which to decide.

The CIA made its decision in fifteen minutes.

It called in the world's deadliest master of controlled violence—the Death Merchant.

The Deputy Director of Plans gave Camellion one order: *Find Maria Gondozatti, and cut out the heart and the soul of the Red Brigades. How you do it is your business. You'll be in complete charge and have the full cooperation of the Rome station. But remember, if you get caught, we'll never have heard of you.*

Nestled by the side of the wall of grapevines, Camellion stood very quietly, hidden in the black shadows, his built-in warning system telling him that something was very wrong. It was more than an intuition nurtured by years of experience, although a sixth sense perceptivity was part of the whisper of caution. The rest was common sense. Male crickets were no longer calling to prospective mates—not only within the area where he stood, but forty feet ahead as well.

Camellion listened again and analyzed his position. Between the rows of grapes was bright moonlight, but all along each

5

wall of vines was blackness. No one could see him. By like token, he too was "blind."

He was positive. *There's someone up ahead, someone standing in the shadows.* Either he—or they?—was standing at the end of the wall—*But on my side or the other side?*—or at the end of the vines on either side of, and parallel to, the tangled mass beside which Camellion stood. It wasn't likely that the man—or men—was a member of the Red Brigades. If he were, he wouldn't be hidden in the shadows, as if he too did not want to be seen by anyone inside the villa.

Or could they have seen me from inside the villa and have come out to wait in ambush? Possibly. But Camellion didn't didn't like that answer. The members of the Red Brigades were noted for their cleverness. An ambush from inside the house would be the more logical and practical. Either way, Camellion had two choices: he could either go about finding out who it was up ahead, or he could return silently to where McAulay Two was waiting with the car.

It was ridiculous to even think about it. Camellion knew what he was going to do. But he couldn't do it with the Auto Mag. The .44 projectile would bore all the way through the man up front, plow into the villa and warn Vito Camerini and whomever else might be with him. As a backup weapon, Camellion carried a compact Safari Arms .45 Enforcer. But it too had dynamite power. Anyhow, the Enforcer autoloader was not equipped with a noise suppressor.

Camellion grinned like an imp. Ah, all was not lost. He shoved the AMP into the left Jurras-designed shoulder holster, pulled back the suit coat and, with his left hand, pulled a W-4B dart gun from a hip holster. Known by the name of the CIA specialist who had invented it, the Webber[2] resembled an ancient broomhandle Mauser, in that the 26 darts—actually hollow $1\frac{1}{4}''$ long needles—were in a magazine in front of the butt and in front of the trigger guard. Powered by a CO_2 cartridge, each dart was filled with six milligrams of poison from the vicious boomslange[3] and would strike

[2] The 4B is the CIA weapons' classification number and letter.

[3] *Dispholidus typus:* A slender, beautiful green snake native to South Africa. One of the most venomous snakes in the world, the boomslange is one of the few snakes that strikes with its mouth wide open.

with the impact of a .22 bullet. Since the dart would not flatten out like an ordinary bullet, it would bury itself deep within the body of the target, the special needle so constructed that all the poison would be released the instant the dart came to a full stop. Unconsciousness would occur instantly; death, within several minutes.

Camellion pulled the Auto Mag from the shoulder holster and switched off the safety catches of both the AMP and the W-4B "stinger."

Where to place the darts was the next question. The Death Merchant reasoned that if an enemy were at the end but on the other side of the grape arbor, some of the needle-darts would pass through or between the leaves and between the thick vines and find the enemy.

If he's at the end on my side, I can't miss.

Camellion didn't miss. As fast as he could squeeze the trigger, he fired 16 darts, the W-4B making a very slight coughing noise each time the CO_2 sent a dart on its way.

Ten of the darts missed human flesh; four struck the man at the end of the arbor on Camellion's side; two pierced the body of the man at the end and on the opposite side of the arbor. The man on the Death Merchant's side shook half the lattice-type arbor as he sagged against the thick grape vines. The second man cried out in a low voice a split second before he dropped into unconsciousness and fell sideways, his body brushing against the arbor and shaking it slightly for the second time.

Damn! Two of them! Camellion, hoping that no one inside the house had seen the two men, ran forward. He was half-way to the end of the arbor when still a third man stepped out from the end of the row of grapes to Camellion's left, saw the Death Merchant and reacted with all the speed of a pro. Whoever the man was, he tossed himself to his right, swung up the weapon he carried and fired twice as the Death Merchant ducked to the left. There were only soft BZZZZZZ-IITTTTTTSSSS from the man's autoloader which was equipped with a silencer.

One of the bullets tore through the front of Camellion's coat, came within half an inch of his right rib cage, then burned a hole through the rear of the coat. The second bullet breezed by several inches to the left of his head.

While he was diving to the ground, Camellion fired only one round from the Auto Mag, a BZZZITTTTT coming from the noise suppressor screwed to the barrel of the weapon. But a much louder *"UHHhh!"* leaped from the throat of the enemy when the hollow-nosed .44 Jurras projectile hit him in the lower chest, the terrific impact picking him up six inches off the ground and killing him instantly. But the blob of copper-coated lead, boring out his back, had traveled upward at a sharp angle and missed the house.

The Death Merchant got to his feet, an angry scowl on his face.

Who were the men and how many more of them were around?

He sprinted forward. He would soon know. . . .

Chapter Two

Positive that the three men he had just terminated were not members of the *Brigate Rosse,* the Death Merchant glanced around, saw that all was quiet, then raced to the corpse of the last man he had blown away. The first thing he did was pick up the handgun the man had used—a 9-millimeter Beretta, but the silencer was a Russian Dragusnev. By the great god Periwinkle! Could the men be KGB or GRU[1]?

Hurriedly, Camellion searched the body, noticing that the man, in his mid-thirties, wore a light-blue Italian-cut suit—not the cheapest grade, but certainly not the most expensive. Camellion found only a cheap throw-away lighter, a pack of American Viceroys, and a white handkerchief in the left rear pocket of the dead man's pants. No billfold. No identification of any kind.

Many things are fact and unchangeable: ice does not burn. Snow never falls in the South Pacific. And assassination agents of Intelligence Services do not carry identification, or else they carry IDs that are forged. *Lousy KGB "blood wet" boys—stinking pig farmers!* The clincher is that Russian men carry their handkerchiefs in their left rear pockets.

Never one to waste ammo, Camellion shoved the "Stinger" into its holster, picked up the Beretta, crouched beside the

---

[1] The military counterpart of the KGB, the GRU—*Geh Eh Ru* in Russian—is the intelligence arm of the Red Army. Technically, it's the *Glavnoye Razvedyvatelnoye Upravlenie*—hence the GRU—which means Chief Intelligence Directorate of the General Staff.

grapevines and studied the villa which lay twenty yards in front of him.

Resembling a large *pensione,* or boarding house, the kind found in the heart of the anonymous blocks of flats, the kind whose shape hasn't changed since the days of the Caesars, the house could have been a hundred or a thousand years old. It was impossible to tell, for its appearance was that of a patchy, leprous rectangle, punctured with rows of tall windows. In the bright moonlight, Camellion could see that to the right was an unkempt garden with Mediterranean vegetation and a shrine in which the figurine of the Virgin Mary seemed to make an archetypal gesture of compassionate resignation. The only real color about the place was a balcony perched like a nest under the eaves, the red, yellow, and orange flowers, in a long flower box, providing a splash of life and warmth against the drab stucco. A light burned in one room on the second floor, and the tall windows of a downstairs room, toward the center of the house glowed white-yellow. The breeze fluttered frayed drapes through an open French window, but because of Camellion's angle of sight, he couldn't see inside the room.

He jumped over a small hedge, raced across the grass and got down by a hydrangea bush growing by the front edge of the low porch and studied the open window that reached to the floor. Could the window be open as part of a trap? Camellion was positive that it was not. The three men he had just snuffed? The only answer that made sense was that the three had been lookouts for another group that had come on a mission similar to his own, a force that also wanted to grab Vito Camerini, who was a contact man between Red Brigade cells in Rome. As such, he would be an important source of information; he would be able to confess names, locations and other invaluable information.

Lookouts in front also meant lookouts in back. The house was probably crawling with Russian *Mokryye Dela*[2] boys.

Camellion left the shadow cast by the bush, scampered onto the porch, darted to the wall and started moving toward

[2] The "dirty tricks" men—and women, too—of the KGB. The term is an acronym used by both the KGB and the CIA. Technically, these killers belong to the Administration of Special Tasks, and in official reports are referred to as *boyevaya gruppa*—"combat groups."

the open French window. On each side of the open window were two normal-size windows that did not reach to the floor and were closed. The inside glass of the four windows was covered with drapes.

With the Backpacker Auto Mag in his right hand and the Beretta in his left, the Death Merchant moved along the side of the wall. He came to a wooden door and tried the old fashioned iron handle. The door was unlocked. Use the door? No. Better to have a look-see first. He crept to the right, came to the left side of the open window and looked around the edge into the room. It was a living room with a high ceiling, ancient furniture, and wallpaper that was peeling in places.

Camerini must not be a very successful cartoonist!

It was neither the tired looking furniture nor the threadbare red carpet that caught Camellion's eye, but the stone staircase on the far side of the room and the five men on the stairway, one of whom was Vito Camerini, the Death Merchant recognizing the *Brigatista* from a large photograph Robert Ferro had shown him.

There was a man behind Camberini, one in front of him, and a man on each side holding him by the arms and leading him down the stairs. The man in front of Camerini and the one behind him had autoloaders; and from the expression on Camerini's face, he wasn't a willing participant.

The Death Merchant smiled thinly. *If this were a movie or a cop show on the boob-tube, I'd jump in and shout something stupid like 'Hold it!' 'Hands up!' or 'Freeze!' Try that in real life and you increase by fifty percent your chances of getting killed.*

He waited until the man in front of Camerini was almost to the bottom of the stairs. Only then did he step through the open window and begin firing the Auto Mag and the Beretta, the Sionics noise suppressor on the AMP and the Dragusnev silencer on the Beretta spitting like two angry snakes.

Tiny pieces of cloth flew off the left lapel of Rudi Mikovan's suit coat, and Mikovan, the man in front of Camerini, was thrown back violently by the TNT punch of the .44 JHP projectile. The big slug tore all the way through the left side of Mikovan's chest and narrowly missed Gregori Pusnok, the man's to Camerini's left.

Gleb Pavlov, the ruskie to the right of Camerini, caught

the first slug from Camellion's Beretta, the 9-millimeter slug stabbing him high in the stomach and tickling the inner part of his spine. He cried out hoarsely, doubled over and started to nosedive toward the bottom of the steps while the stone-dead Mikovan fell back and Camellion's second .44 JHP projectile ripped into Pusnok's chest and took its exit through his back.

Valeriy Dimitroff, the "blood-wet" agent in back of Camerini, grabbed the Italian and pulled him down when he saw Mikovan fall backward and saw the bearded figure in the window, a pistol in each hand.

Dimitroff didn't know who the man was. He did realize that the intruder was an expert, knew it from the way the man had taken out Mikovan, then Pavlov and Pusnok.

Lying uncomfortably on the stone steps, half on his back and half on his side, Dimitroff was partially protected by a terrified Vito Camerini, who was even more confused than the KGB kill-agent.

Dimitroff realized that he was in a very precarious position. Being trapped on the steps was bad enough, but there wasn't any way he could control Camerini and at the same time fire at the mysterious intruder.

"Lie still," warned Dimitroff in perfect Italian. "Try to escape and I'll kill you."

It was Haydar Tunckanat and Pavl Suslensky who saved Dimitroff's life by coming out of a room to Dimitroff's left.

Within half a minute after opening fire, the Death Merchant found himself faced with a serious problem that he had only seconds to solve. How to blow away the fourth man, who was using Camerini as a shield, and do it without wounding or killing the Red Brigadist?

Camellion found himself confronted with an even more serious problem when two men appeared in an archway to his right, one man carriyng a 9mm Sosso pistol, the second joker lugging a VB Bernardelli submachine gun fitted with a long silencer.

Another man might have made the fatal mistake of trying to blow away the two men in the archway, who were now swinging toward Camellion. If both men had been carrying autoloaders, Camellion would have had a 70/30 chance, his uncanny speed making the extra difference. But with one man carrying a machine gun and with only glass for protection on either side of him, Camellion elected not to take the risk. Instead of wasting time by snapping off a shot, he jumped back, spun and made a dive to the left as the heavyset thug with the sharp chin opened fire with the VB Bernardelli subgun.

A stream of hot 9mm projectiles hissed through the long silencer and exploded the glass of the two windows on one side of the open French window-door. A few inches more and Camellion would have found himself floating around in eternity. Two slugs burned through his flying coattails. Another projectile left a half-inch burn line on the collar of his coat. Several more bullets passed so close to his back that for a microsecond one wouldn't have been able to insert a piece of paper between the rocketing lead and the silken material of his coat. A sharp piece of glass, shaped like a triangle, stabbed the air over his head.

In another mini-moment Camellion was beyond the windows and safe by the side of the wall, almost positive that the two goons wouldn't be stupid enough to dash out through the opening in pursuit. But they might. Even professionals make mistakes.

Camellion came to the door, spun around and looked toward the window. The men were not attempting to follow. He shoved the Beretta into his waistband, gently opened the door, stepped inside, closed the door and repulled the Beretta. There was only a small night-light in the foyer—a door at the end, a door to his left and, just ahead, a small archway to the right. It was a gamble and a dangerous one—and he lost! He was turning into the archway, keeping to one side, when he almost collided with the two hotdogs who had just fired at him. It was obvious that the two goons had correctly deduced that Camellion would try to outflank them and were taking counteraction.

The Death Merchant and the two KGB agents had put on the brakes only feet from each other, the near impact so close that the three men could have reached out and shaken hands. All three made their moves but not to shake hands.

Snarling *"Blyatskaye dyeluh!"*[3] Pavl Suslensky tried to shove the muzzle of the Bernardelli machine gun into Camellion's stomach while Haydar Tunckanat quickly jerked back in confusion, trying to decide whether he might put Suslensky

[3] "Goddamn it!" in Russian.

13

in danger if he fired at the bearded man at such close range. Tunckanat never made the decision. He never had another thought either, not in this world.

Camellion let the Beretta fall to the floor, grabbed the middle of the two foot long silencer with his left hand, snarled *"Idyi k chortoo!"*[4] at Suslensky, and pushed the barrel and silencer of the submachine gun up and away from him. All in the same motion, he kneed Suslensky in the groin and swung the Auto Mag toward Tunckanat. A buzzing sound came from the noise suppressor, then a sort of thudding noise from Tunckanat whose tan tie and the white shirt underneath seemed to explode, as if a tiny grenade had detonated inside the Russian's chest.

His face a grotesque picture of total disbelief, Tunckanat flew backward from the impact, his arms flapping outward, a hole the size of a grapefruit in his chest.

Suslensky, crucified with agony from Camellion's knee-lift, was the next man to die. Made helpless by the pain in his testicles and lower abdomen, Suslensky had a bitter thought about death and knew he was helpless to save himself. With the extra strength always given to the doomed and the damned, he made one last feeble effort to turn the machine gun toward the tall, bearded man, only to feel that weapon wrenched from his grip.

The Death Merchant didn't terminate the Russian with the Auto Mag. Always particular about his clothes, he didn't want to return to Rome with the front of his coat splattered with blobs of the man's flesh and drops of his blood. It would all be so damned messy.

The last thing in life that Suslensky saw were the intense blue eyes of Camellion and his right arm swinging in an arc. Another eye-blink and Suslensky's brain exploded into tar blackness.

Camellion again slammed the side AMP's noise suppressor against Suslensky's skull as the unconscious man sagged to the rug. Camellion was positive that if he hadn't killed the pig farmer, he had at least given him the world's biggest concussion, one that would keep the KGB sonofabitch out of action for months.

After scooping up the Beretta from the rug, Camellion moved to one side of the arch, looked around the edge and

4 "Go to hell!" in Russian.

14

saw that the next room was a small dining area. To his right, toward the front of the dining area, was another archway. Thinking of the distance between the door and the French window, Camellion realized that the arch ahead had to lead into the dining room.

He was almost to the arch when he heard the voice from the living room call out. "Pavl! Haydar! *Polchie vaya nyie rona?*"[5]

The pig farmer with Camerini! Who else?

Gingerly, Camellion looked around one side of the arch and saw that he was right. During that brief moment, he saw that the man who had been toward the bottom of the stairs was now in the center of the room, standing flatfooted on the faded red rug and holding Vito Camerini in front of him, his hand on the man's shirt collar. Camerini stood there with his arms half-raised, a what-will-happen-next look on his face.

Damn it! There was also another Russian in the room. A thickset joker with a Siberian slant to his eyes and a face as creased as sun-dried leather. Like a short, broad bear, he stood to the left of Camerini and the other Russian, a Stechkin machine pistol in his hand.

Well, Good God Girty! I might as well have stayed home!

Camellion's reaction was automatic, based on instinct, a reaction that became reality before logical thought processes could analyze and arrive at a conclusion.[6]

The instant Valeriy Dimitroff and Paul Puzyrev saw the Death Merchant, they too automatically went into action, Dimitroff shoving out his Beretta to the right of Camerini and Puzyrev going into a crouch and tossing down a bead on Camellion with the S.M.P.

But Camellion didn't do what the two Russians had expected him to do. Instead of ducking back around the side of the archway, he threw forward and down, triggering both the Auto Mag and the Beretta while his body was in midair.

Three short coughs from Camellion's Beretta, his AMP,

[5] Did you get him?"

[6] Fact. This is based on the instinct of self-preservation and honed by experience, by numerous fire-fights in which one survives. Often the professional does not stop to "think," he only reacts from pure instinct.

and Dimitroff's Beretta. Puzyrev's Stechkin, not equipped with a silencer, roared on full automatic, the sound of the exploding 9mm cartridges reverberating back and forth across the room.

The Death Merchant scored bull's-eyes. The two Russians hit zero. While their 9mm projectiles passed a foot or so over Camellion, his own slugs went where he wanted them to go.

Three Beretta slugs tore into Paul Puzyrev. One struck the man in the center of his chest and made his tie do a slight flip-flop. The second bullet hit the edge of Puzyrev's belt buckle, deflected slightly, bored into his lower stomach and went upward at an angle to rest against his spleen. The third piece of lead hacked into the hollow of his throat and went out the back of his neck. Puzyrev was a corpse before his body had time to even fall to the floor.

Camellion hated to whack out Vito Camerini, but he didn't have a choice. The .44 JHP bullet first struck Camerini in the chest. It tore all the way through the Italian's body and, like a bolt of lightning, stabbed into Dimitroff's lower chest, coming to rest a tenth of an inch from his spine.

"*OHhhh!*" Dimitroff dropped the Beretta. His eyes went wide, and he released his hold on the collar of Camerini, who was sagging to the rug, and started to double over, realizing that he was dying.

Then he was dead. Camellion, now lying flat on the rug, fired once more with the AMP. This projectile caught the falling Dimitroff high in the right side, ripped through his lungs, tore out his left side and struck a lithograph of St. Joseph on the far wall. Forever, St. Joseph would hang there with a hole in his forehead.

The Death Merchant jumped to his feet, shoved the Beretta into his belt, tore across the room, scooped up the Stechkin M.P., then raced to the rear of the house. The odds were that the dummy with the Stechkin had been one of the guards posted to the rear of the house. Just one guard? *Nyet.* At least one more, probably two. The KGB was practical and methodical. Three in front, three in the back. All nice and tidy.

Running through the dark rooms, he came to the kitchen— *The other pig farmers are sneaking around to the front of the house, trying to come in behind me. They have to be. The noise of the Stechkin was loud enough to wake the dead!*

16

He had no regrets about terminating Vito Camerini. It had been necessary to put him asleep forever in order to ace out the man using him as a shield. Otherwise the mission would have been double-failure.

If I hadn't cowboyed both of them, I would have had to retreat and the KGB would have grabbed Camerini. Better that he die.

Camellion gently opened the kitchen door, went out onto the step, looked around and saw no one. He closed the door very quietly. Either no one had ever been in back—*Damned unlikely!*—or they had skipped around one side of the house and thought they were closing in on him from the front.

Keeping in the shadows, Camellion shoved a fresh magazine into the Auto Mag and crept to the westside of the house and moved quickly south. *And if McAulay says 'I told you so!' I'll ram his German Walther P-38 up his nose and make him whistle Deutschland Uber Alles[7] through the barrel!*

Camellion came to the southwest corner of the old house and looked ahead, his eyes searching the wide and long front yard. Nothing but moon-kissed bushes that needed trimming and a stone bird bath. He looked around the corner. To the east was the half-dark porch, the hedge and the vineyard beyond the hedge, the whole bit cloaked in moonlight and twisted shadows.

A chance? Certainly. But so was crossing the Via della Conciliazione. Or any road in Israel. A real paradox, those Israelis. They have the best intelligence service[8] and the worst drivers in the world.

He scurried around the corner, stepped onto the porch, and, keeping to the shadows by the wall, moved east. He came to the door which was half-open. Good! He hurried past the door and carefully put his feet down on the stones, not wanting the sound of glass, breaking for the second time, to alert his enemies inside. *Like shooting whales in a barrel. Maybe!*

Another ten seconds. He came to the end of the bullet-stabbed drapes, looked into the living room and saw what he had hoped to see. Two men, Sosso pistols in their hands, were in the living room. One man was looking down at the corpse

---

7 "Germany Above All"—the German national anthem.

8 The very efficient Mossad.

of the agent who had tried to scratch out Camellion with the Stechkin. The other man, down on his haunches, was studying the body of the Russian rube who had used Camerini for protection—for all the good it had done him.

Camellion didn't waste time. He stepped to the French window and fired. His first .44 hit the KGB agent bending over, smacked the man in the hip and knocked him over on his left side. His body shuddered several times, then lay still.

The second Russian, seeing the first joker get the big business out of the corner of his eye, was trying to drop to the floor and swing toward the window when Camellion's second .44 projectile popped him in the right side of the forehead and exploded his skull. He flopped backward to the rug and lay sprawled out, chips of bone and tiny pieces of skin and butchered brain floating down after him.

The Death Merchant pulled back from the window, jumped from the porch and ran east. Now, back to the car and back to Rome.

If we're stopped by the police the diplomatic passports had better work, even if they are fakes!

Chapter Three

George McAulay had parked the Fiat station wagon 50 feet off the road, in a grove of holm oaks and in such a position that the car could not be seen. Hearing Camellion's whippoorwill signal, a hundred feet to the northwest, McAulay returned the signal and waited until he saw the Death Merchant approaching, half-outlined in a patchwork of moonlight and shadows, before he stepped out from behind the tree, with an Ingram submachine gun in his hands.

"I heard the chopper," he said when Camellion was closer. "Anyone following?"

"It was a Stechkin, and I'm certain no one is bird dogging me." Camellion touched him on the arm. "Let's get out of here. It's almost eleven-thirty."

"The ruskies!" exclaimed McAulay. "Man, that really ruins the stew." He hurried after Camellion, who stopped at the right front door of the Fiat, turned and looked back at the young CIA case officer. "Don't bother stashing the Ingram in the secret compartment. We might need it if the police or the army has set up one of their ridiculous roadblocks and we can't bluff our way out with the passports."

"Oh boy!" muttered McAulay. "Blowing away a dozen or so I-ties is all we need." He walked around to the driver's side and got into the car. Camellion got in beside him, took the Ingram from the middle of the seat and placed the deadly little chopper on the floor by his feet. The Stechkin and the Beretta went underneath the seat.

"Icepicks in the eyeballs," McAulay said resignedly, starting the station wagon. "I told you so, damn it. I warned that

19

coming out here was like a blind man trying to tie a sackful of rattle snakes."

Without turning on the lights, he expertly backed the car in a half-circle, shifted gears, stepped on the gas and headed the vehicle through the weeds toward the road. Twenty feet from the road, he switched on the headlights.

"George, do you know the words and music to *Deutschland Uber Alles?*" asked Camellion, smiling to himself.

McAulay gave him a quick, puzzled glance, then turned the car onto the brick road. "What's the kraut national anthem got to do with this mess? Or maybe you're trying to tell me something about Riggio and the West Germans?"

"It's nothing," Camellion mused, pulling the Auto Mag from the shoulder holster. "Just a private joke between me, myself, and I. I'll tell you about it someday. Right now I'm more concerned with getting to Ferro's place."

"Shouldn't take over an hour," McAulay said. He speeded up the station wagon. "What happened to Camerini? I suppose the KGB eliminated him to keep him out of your hands."

"It was the other way around," Camellion said. He had pulled the magazine from the AMP, and now shoved in a full clip. He explained to McAulay what had happened at the villa, finishing with, "The ruskies must have used the road to the north. They couldn't have been in the house more than ten minutes before I arrived. Don't ask me how the KGB knew about Camerini. If you can't figure that out, you should get out of this business and drive a beer truck!"

"You're certain they were KGB?"

"I'm positive that they spoke Russian. They were either KGB or GRU on a typical rush-in-and-grab operation. None of them carried ID, at least the ones I blew up in front of the house didn't."

McAulay slowed when the headlights picked up the triangular Dangerous Right Curve sign ahead. "We know that Riggio is a money-hungry double agent. But a triple agent, and working for the KGB to boot? Don't forget, the evidence is only circumstantial. When you get right down to the bottom line, the Russians could have learned about Vito Camerini in any number of ways."

"Yes, we do seem to have a problem, don't we?" Having shoved the AMP into its holster, Camellion straightened his tie and, smoothing out his coat, happened to glance in the

20

rearview mirror. The reflection of a "stranger" stared back at him, a man with a thick, bushy beard, thick, curly black hair, long sideburns and a thick mustache.

Camellion had also disguised McAulay, but without the use of a beard. McAulay did have a thick mustache, a half-bald head and a "face" that didn't even resemble his true features. With plastic putty, greasepaint and other cosmetic materials, the Death Merchant had added twenty years to McAulay Two's life, giving him the appearance of a man in his fifties.

Other than the fact that Camellion liked McAulay—who said exactly what he thought and didn't give a damn to whom he said it—Camellion had chosen "Number Two" for a variety of other reasons. Not only did McAulay speak six languages, but he was also one hundred percent dependable in a fire fight, and in spite of his usually mild manner and appearance, he was one of the deadliest street fighters that Camellion had ever met.

Camellion reached into the dashboard compartment and took out two flat, black booklets. He opened one of the passports, looked at the name, then handed the booklet to McAulay, who accepted it with his right hand and slipped it into his inside coat pocket.

"You're Henry T. Bolden the Third," Camellion said. "Remember that name in case we're stopped."

"I got a funny feeling floating around in my feet," McAulay said. "If the I-ties stop us and these diplomatic passports[1] don't work, We—"

"Think positively!" Camellion cut him short. "Why do you

---

[1] There are three kinds of U.S. passports: the *regular*, i.e., the common silver-green or silver-blue covered document available to all Americans. About three million are issued each year. The *official* passport, which is maroon and issued to Congressmen and government officials. About 75,000 are issued per year. The *diplomatic*, black with gold lettering. Around 6,000 are issued every year, although there are probably never more than 3,000 accredited diplomats at any one time. Most diplomatic passports are "courtesy" passports, issued to non-diplomats at the authorization of the State Department. To get this kind of passport one has to know somebody who knows somebody. The advanage of having a diplomatic passport is that one can obtain a lot of favors, special privileges and some immunities in a foreign country.

think I had you swallow those three tablets before we started?"

"Why, I thought you were trying to knock me off," joked McAulay. "Then I saw you take yours and figured I was safe. I suppose you'll tell me when you get around to it. I figured the pills were an immunization against DA or DM gas. I noticed an unmarked box in the dash."

"Try DC, mixed with disulfiram[2] and you'll be dead on target," Camellion said. "This particular type of DC is odorless and colorless. I'd rather make the cops sick than dead, provided they stop us. The poor guys are only doing their duty."

Camellion removed the small box from the compartment, opened it and took out a dozen of the tiny gray pellets, which could easily be crushed between the fingers. He put six into McAulay's right coat pocket. The other six he dumped into his own pocket.

McAulay speeded up once more. They were no longer out in the country and were now on the highway that would lead into the Via Nomentana. Another mile and they would cross the Grande Raccordo Anulare, the "Ring Road" that completely circled the Eternal City, and be within Rome itself.

The trees had thinned out and instead of secluded villas and small estates, there were houses grouped together, houses made of wood and stone, the trees and flowers used much as if they were materials, to carry out an architectural design. Trees gave way to topiary-work bushes and to potted plants in carefully ordered rows. Some of the facades of the houses were covered, at least in part, by climbing plants which appeared to be something that had happened by accident, the one and only act of rebellion by well-disciplined nature.

Traffic had also increased, yet was comparatively light compared to that in the inner city.

2 The generic name for *Antabuse,* which is a drug used as an alcohol-drinking deterrent. This drug—after one takes a drink of alcohol—interrupts normal liver enzyme activity after the conversion of alcohol to acetaldehyde, this process causing excessive accumulation of acetaldehyde. Symptoms are intense headache, chest pains, shortness of breath, vertigo, confusion, blurred vision and vomiting.

DC gas is *Diphenylcyanoarsine,* a vomit gas, seldom used in riot control because it is highly dangerous. Commercial immunization is not on the market.

McAulay broke the silence. "I wonder why Marsilio Rigianno changed his name to Riggio? Did Ferro tell you or doesn't he know?"

"He told me," Camellion said. "Rigianno, or Riggio—take your choice—is wanted on a manslaughter charge in Milan. That's how the company turned him out—by threatening to tip off the police who he is and where he is."

"Which means we can't trust him any farther than we can see him." McAulay scooted around another car. "Another thing, have you stopped to consider that since the KGB knew about Vito Camerini, the pig farmers might know about us. They have to if Riggio is a triple. If that's the case, then coming to Rome the way we did—all three of us taking separate flights from New York—was a waste of time, including our posing as tourists."

The Death Merchant chuckled. "You sound unhappy, George. You're going to tell me next that you don't like the digs at Ferro's place."

"Huh! You'd better believe it. Not that there's anything wrong with his quarters. Its just that he's a first class screwball. Hell, Richard! He's a damned drunk!"

"But a good street man," countered Camellion. "That makes the difference."

"I don't deny that he's an expert. But I think a lot of this is all cops and robbers crap. I mean, the company's sending us over here as tourists. We should have had a better overcoat,[3] like Pierson. An antique dealer. That's a good cover. And he gets to stay in one of the better class hotels on the Via Veneto."

"Well, smile, George," joked the Death Merchant. "Tomorrow might be worse. Or even tonight if we run into a road block."

"One thing is certain," McAulay said grimly. "We're no closer now to finding Maria Gondozatti than we were before we got here; and when the papers splatter the massacre back at the villa all over the front pages, the Red Brigades will pretty well guess why we—or the Russians—were after Camerini. They might just decide to put a bullet into her and be done with the whole damned business. I don't give a damn what the brain-boys say about the RBs being so clever and intelligent. In my think-department, terrorists are all a bunch

[3] Slang term for cover.

of crazies. Almost always they defeat their own purpose."

Privately, within his own thoughts, the Death Merchant congratulated McAulay. George was correct. Camellion thought of the West German Baader-Meinhof terrorists of the late sixties and early seventies.

Those idiots became isolated and absorbed with the internal dynamics of their own radicalism: they dared themselves to be as terrifying as they could, with each successive attack. After one Baader-Meinhoff bombing, some of the terrorists slipped away from West to East Berlin. The German communists were hardly sympathetic. Indeed not. The East Germans shoved them into a plane and sent them to the Mideast. There they met Palestinian guerrillas, who trained them in terror tactics and sent them back to Europe. *Those young krauts were so stupid that they didn't realize the Arabs were using them—by pitting various Arab factions against one an*other: El Fatah against the Popular Front, Syrians against *Lebanese, Jordanians against Iraquis.*

The first thing the Baader-Meinhoff people did when they got back to Berlin was to attack a Jewish community center. *Ridiculous! Imagine how it affected young people who had been arguing with their parents for years on the very issue of anti-Semitism! The attack was worse than a crime. It was a major blunder of the first order!*

The Red Brigades were just as stupid. All they had accomplished by the brutal murder of Aldo Moro was to cause the Italian nation to close ranks and the government to become stronger and more unified. In municipal elections, soon after Moro's death, the Christian Democrats received a substantial increase in votes and the PCI, the Communist Party of Italy, a decrease from the percentage it had in the nationwide elections of 1976.

The PCI, which had been denounced by the Red Brigades for abandoning its revolutionary principles, led demonstrations against the Brigades, and then formed a coalition with the Catholic Christian Democrats.

Since the murder of Moro had united the nation against the Brigades, it would seem that its leaders might have taken the hint. They hadn't. They had only proceeded to commit an even bigger blunder: they had kidnapped the "Living Saint," Maria Gondozatti—*and in a country that was 95 percent Roman Catholic!*

Like all groups of terrorists, the Red Brigades were very

naive, but highly dangerous—like drunken teenagers with loaded pistols. The formula for mistakes was always the same. First, they would try to tell middle-class people about "imperialism," about right and wrong, foolishly assuming that the middle class would listen and understand. The middle class never did. Then the terrorists would go to the working class, to organize them against the "injustices of the system." Only, the working class didn't give a damn. The final step was always the Third World, but the response was always the same—silence. Finally, in frustration, the terrorists would turn against themselves and everyone around them in an orgy of violence and self-destruction.

The Death Merchant realized some basic facts that were totally incomprehensible to the members of the *Brigate Rosse,* who were convinced that the police enforce repression. What the terrorists could not understand was that if you attack the state, if you attack authority, most people identify with that authority, and they're ready to support measures against radicals and terrorists, no matter how undemocratic and repressive. The *brigatisti* could not realize that in a welfare state, such as Italy, most people were so well off that they feared losing what they already had. The terrorists couldn't protect their revolutionary promises or guarantee an improvement in people's lives, as the guerrillas could do in Cuba or China or Vietnam.

The *brigatisti* were so brutal and stupid that it even denied the pretense of innocence and the option of neutrality. Sympathetic attorneys, impartial jurors, reporters, and anyone who was for law and order became targets, along with police chiefs, plutocrats, and prime ministers. To the Red Brigades, these people were the *soldati piccoli*—the little soldiers—of a system, because they accepted the idea that the state existed, that courts existed, that trials existed. To the Red Brigades there was only total war, and the "little soldiers" were not different from the great generals.

Fanatics of the worst kind! The more of them that die, the better off the world will be. . . .

The Death Merchant saw the flashing blue lights, a fifth of a mile ahead, a half minute or more before McAulay said in a lazy manner, "I guess you know we're coming to a road block?"

"You'd think the *polizia* would have enough common sense

25

to turn off their top lights," Camellion said, a note of calculation in his low voice.

"Maybe they want to warn any potential brigade members," laughed McAulay. He let up on the gas as half a dozen vehicles up ahead slowed because of the checkpoint. "Once they make us get out of the car, we'll have had it—and you with an Ingram at your feet. How do you want to play it?"

"I'll give them credit for having enough know-how where to set up an RB," Camellion said. "It's right on the junction of this road and the Ring Road, and the banks on each side of this road are too steep for a go-around. Yes, sir. We'll have to stop."

"Thanks, old buddy, for the lesson in topography," mocked McAulay. "Now tell me what sort of devilment you've got cooking in that weird mind of yours. I think the passport idea stinks."

"The idea is rather risky. Tell you what—when we're second in line, put the DC capsules in your left hand. If you hear me cough, crush the capsules, then open your hand to the cops on your side. There's a pretty good breeze, so it should take only a few seconds for the gas to reach them. As soon as the gas starts to work, get us out and fast."

"I only hope we don't have to terminate any of the poor bastards," commented McAulay. His mouth became a tight line and his face granite with determination.

By now they were very close to the actual checkpoint, and McAulay had to bring the Fiat station wagon to a complete stop. There were four other vehicles ahead of the Fiat—a Fiat sedan, a two-door Lancia, a Pirelli, and the French Peugeot that was, at the moment, being checked out by the Italian traffic police.

The Death Merchant studied the system the police were using. There were two cops doing the actual inspection, checking the identification papers of the passengers in the cars. Two other cops, in blue uniforms and white crash helmets, were leaning against the police car to the left, both trying to look important. To the right was another copper. He was sitting on the fender of a patrol car, cradling a Beretta 9mm Model 12 submachine gun in his arms.

McAulay, with his quick analytical mind, instantly arrived at the same conclusion as Camellion. "The cop with the chopper," he whispered. "He's the big bug in the soup.

26

He might be able to get off a burst before we're out of range."

"I don't think so," Camellion said in a flat voice.

He used his left hand to pull the W-4B dart gun from his holster. He switched off the safety and, continuing to hold the gun, let it rest in his lap.

"The cop to the left has a flashlight," McAulay said calmly. "The odds are that he will spot the Ingram or the dart gun. He used the flash to rake the inside of the car he just checked out. We can't afford to take time to try the passport angle."

He shifted gears, stepped on the gas and moved the station wagon ahead one space. The Peugeot had headed out, and the Pirelli was now at the checkpoint.

"Yeah, we can't risk the passport bluff," Camellion agreed. "To top it off, we look suspicious as hell in these disguises."

"Now the man tells me!" McAulay growled with mock disgust.

"The instant the cop on your side approaches, let him have the DC. I'll dart the two on my side, then give you the 4B and you can dart the other two. But just in case"—he reached down and pulled the .45 Enforcer from the holster attached to his right ankle—"be prepared to use heavy stuff."

"I'm beginning to feel more and more like Lazarus—the day after!" McAulay said. "We'd better get ready."

When the station wagon was second in line, the Death Merchant switched off the safety of the Enforcer. McAulay reached into his coat pocket and closed his hand around the DC capsules.

The policeman to the left returned the billfold to the driver of the Fiat sedan and, when the sedan moved ahead, motioned to McAulay, who drove ahead, but with effort, having to shift with three fingers of his right hand closed around the capsules of gas.

Ten more seconds and he stopped the station wagon, but left its engine running. He crushed the six capsules and was moving his right arm toward the open window and opening his hand as the cop to the left stepped up to the car and Camellion crushed the gas capsules in his right hand, picked up the dart gun with his left and opened his right hand by the window, smiling at the suspicious-faced officer approaching his side of the Fiat.

The cop to the left was about to rake the front inside of

27

the car with his flashlight when the first of the DC & disulfiram gas struck him in the face. At about the same time, the officer on the Death Merchant's side felt the first effects of the gas, both men acting as if they had been struck by invisible bolts of lightning. They began to gasp. They staggered back, eyes and mouths open, while violent waves of nausea rolled through their stomachs.

"Ohhhhhhhh!" The victim to McAulay's left dropped his flashlight and started to vomit. The cop on Camellion's side, realizing that something was very wrong, raised a hand and motioned to his partner, who, with the Beretta submachine gun, had slid from the fender of the patrol car and was staring at him in astonishment. Surprise and helplessness was still on his face when Camellion's dart struck him in the chest. He blinked, looked down at his chest, dropped the sub-gun and toppled forward.

The last two cops to the left were moving toward the man who had sunk to his knees and was vomiting all over himself —one man glancing angrily toward the Fiat and pulling a Beretta from a flap holster. He was too slow and too late.

Camellion had handed the dart gun to McAulay, who placed a dart in each man. The two cops fell without making a sound, and by the time they were dead, McAulay had started the car and it was moving down the road at ever-increasing speed.

"George, pull off the road the first chance you get," Camellion said. He turned in the seat and stared out the rear window. No one was following. "Any place where we can switch plates."

The three Italian policemen who had been darted crossed his mind.

A shame, but necessary. There was far far more than three lives. He hoped that McAulay wouldn't ask about the three cops. Even if he didn't—*I still have to tell him. He'll read about it in the papers. What a dirty business this is. . . .*

Every now and then McAulay glanced at a car going in the opposite direction. None were police cars.

"It will be a while before anyone back there can radio our descriptions and the description of the car," he said curtly. "We'll be safe once we change plates. There must be ten thousand Fiat station wagons in Rome. Lordy, I'll be glad when I get my own face back."

"I'll get the 'bald' off as soon as you park," Camellion said.

He reached underneath the seat and took out a small box of cotton pads and a bottle of acetone mixed with alcohol and senferin. He uncapped the bottle and saturated one of the pads with the liquid.

Camellion had removed his beard and mustache by the time McAulay pulled off the road and parked among some chestnut trees, fifty feet to the east of a long billboard—and 3.7 miles later.

McAulay reached underneath the seat and pulled out a license plate around which was tied a pair of pliers and a screwdriver. He got out of the car and went to the rear. Camellion got out on the other side.

It took McAulay less than a minute to remove the imitation license plate and slap the genuine one in the center of the bumper. He was tightening the second bolt when Camellion cleared his throat and said, "McAulay, there is something I must tell you."

McAulay glanced up in slight puzzlement.

"Shoot."

"I did and you did—the three Italian policemen back there," Camellion said stiffly, shifting from his left foot to his right.

McAulay finished tightening the bolt and stood up. For a moment he looked at Camellion, having the vague impression that the Death Merchant was trying to be delicate. "All right. We put them to sleep for a while. What about them?"

"Not for a while, George. Forever!"

Short anger and long surprise flickered on McAulay's face, while his eyes impatiently demanded an explanation.

"I didn't have any tranquilizing darts," Camellion said, without any preliminaries. "I had to use the poisoned variety. I didn't tell you because I didn't want the knowledge of it to interfere with your efficiency. Back there, a single second could have meant the difference between success and failure."

McAulay took the imitation plate and sailed it up and out into space. Then his eyes caught Camellion.

"I suppose in a war the innocent have to die with the guilty," he said, his voice tight and hard. "But I'm glad you didn't tell me—back at the intersection. I might have hesitated."

"Let's get your 'bald' piece off," Camellion said. He turned and got back into the car. Once McAulay was inside, Camellion went to work with the cotton and solvent.

In another ten minutes the Fiat was on the Via Nomentana, each second bringing Camellion and McAulay closer to the heart of Rome.

The citizens of Rome have their own customs. The *pranzo*, the midday meal, is a hasty affair. Not so the evening meal, the dinner hour beginning as late as nine or ten o'clock. This is the *cena*, which is meant for relaxation and is conducted at a leisurely pace. This is the period during which the Roman adjusts to a relaxed tempo if he is dining alone. In every restaurant there are solitary diners, each islanded at an individual table, pensively nibbling bread to keep the pangs of hunger at bay, contemplating the affairs of the day, or just sitting there waiting for the first course.

It is not difficult to spot the foreigner—and this includes the Milanese and the Florentine as well as the Englishman and the American—in a Roman restaurant: the restlessness, the waving of menus, the gradually mounting irritation that leaves the waiter completely unmoved. Service is very slow. Native Romans are used to it. And they retire late. For this latter reason there were crowds of people on the streets and relaxing in the open air *ristoranti* (restaurants) of the piazzas.

McAulay stopped the car for a red light at the four-way intersection of the Via Nomentana and the Via delle Quattro Fontane.

"What gets me about this damned town is that every fourth or fifth person seems to be speaking Chinese," George said, hunched over the wheel. "I guess you know why?"

"Unless my memory fails me, the language for Rome is a *'lingua toscana in bocca romana,'*" Camellion said, his eyes on several girls wearing shorts. "Anyhow, that's what the language is supposed to be. Actually, no one understands anyone else because the city is flooded with immigrants from the south. They've been pouring into Rome since the turn of the century and insist on clinging to the dialects of their birthplace."

"I'm just happy that I'm not stationed here," McAulay said. "I'm not like you, Richard. I'm at home only in the U.S., with just a sprinkling of Canada. Man, do I feel sorry for Bob Ferro!" He glanced up at the red light again. "Damn thing! It takes forever to change."

"Rome is a paradox in more ways than one," Camellion

offered. "At the present time, ninety-eight percent of the population consists of baptized Catholics. But the mayor is a Communist. In the U.S., church and state are separate, but religion and society are intertwined. The reverse is true in Italy. Church and state are woven together."

The light turned to green, and McAulay stepped on the gas. "Well, their legal system isn't worth a damn, either. I don't think much of a country that doesn't have municipal courts or bail or make use of a habeas corpus. No wonder there are terrorists and that most of the people are anticlerical."

McAulay drove another two blocks, went past the Via Leonina and continued in a southwestern direction. Camellion glanced curiously at the young CI-nick, knowing that he had not forgotten the turn.

"Why didn't you make a left on the Via Leonina?" he asked. "Personally, I'm not interested in the sights."

"I wanted to miss all those damn cats on the Via Leonina,"[4] McAulay said. "There's so many of them on that street that they actually interfere with traffic. We're safe enough. We've passed half a dozen police cars and they didn't even give us a second glance."

The Death Merchant guffawed. "That's rich, coming from a cat-lover like yourself," Camellion chided, with a grin. "The way you've raved about your Cerridwen, I'd think you'd be wanting to take a couple of hundred of Rome's cats back to the States with you."

McAulay gave Camellion a dirty look and jutted out his jaw.

"My Cerridwen is not a common, dirty alley cat," he said fiercely. "Why, I even keep her fur perfumed."

"Sorry, old buddy. I didn't know." Camellion couldn't have been more amused. As far as McAulay was concerned, insult-

---

4 Tribes of cats haunt many areas of Rome. They are the descendents of a flourishing feline population that was commented on by writers as early as the fifth century B.C. Imported to Rome from cat-worshipping Egypt, they have survived from age to age, proceeding in haughty detachment from the affairs of human beings. They are fed by people who make it their business to offer them a regular tribute of food. Completely disdainful, the cats act as though Rome belongs to them, and in a sense the city does.

ing his precious Cerridwen was the same as screaming "Down with the Pope!" in St. Peter's—during Christmas midnight mass!

The flow of traffic had increased. The great, green buses of Rome, at least half as wide as the road, hurtled by at top speed, pushing a mass of air before them and sucking up dust and refuse in their wake. Private cars shot by like bullets, along with careening trucks.

Just ahead was the King Victor Emmanuel II monument, at the Piazza Venezia. This was the heart of Rome, dominated by the massive monstrosity of the monument that had been built by Mussolini, a monument so grandiose, so laden with white marble and statuary that the Romans called it the "Wedding Cake."

"Man, look at it," McAulay said. "It would embarrass a Las Vegas architect!"

He turned left and quickly drove into the Via dei Fori Imperiali, the road that would take him and Camellion directly to the ancient, but quintessentially Roman Suburra, which was just a few hundred yards north of the Colosseum.

The Suburra was something of an anomaly. It was the most ancient inhabited area of Rome; yet few maps bothered to identify it, and only the more dedicated guidebooks even referred to it. In essence, the Suburra had been cut adrift from the rest of the Eternal City. Once the long, narrow street that today goes under the names of the Via Leonina—at the eastern end—and Via Madonna dei Monti—near the western end—ran straight to the great Forum, the square that was the hub of Ancient Rome. But in the first century A.D. the emperor Nerva severed the link by building his own forum squarely across the course of the road, a separation that was made permanent when Mussolini carved his massive Via dei Fori Imperiali along the side of the ancient Forum. Now the Suburra's western boundary was sealed by lethal streams of traffic, and although the eastern boundary had become indeterminate, the other two were almost as clear-cut and modern as Mussolini's monument to Fascism: to the south, the Via Cavour, fussy, pompous and depressing; to the north, the Via Nazionale, cheerful and well-mannered.

During the day the little Via Leonina that ran parallel with the Via degli Zingari was often filled with clerkly figures, disgorged by the *Metro* at the bottom of the street and taking short cuts to the shops and offices of the Via Nazionale.

At high noon the rhythm of life in the Suburra begins to slow down as the city enters the trance—the coma of the three midday hours known—with a touch of irony—as the lunch "hour." In this respect, Rome is more akin to Athens or Algiers than to Florence or Milan.

But once the sun has gone to bed and darkness settles, the Suburra is left to its own devices . . . to earn a living in its own fashion, as it has done for the past 2,000 years.

"We're almost home," McAulay muttered wearily. He made a right turn and entered the Via degli Zingari, where there were nearly forty businesses, many of them side by side: an antique shop, several garages or cycle repair shops; a cobbler's; a maker of handbags and umbrellas; and food shops—bakers, pizza, wine and oil. But, ominously, there were almost as many shops closed as open, for the Suburra was suffering from a drastic decline in population. There was something else missing: the sight and sound of children at play. Day by day, the Suburra was becoming an area of the elderly, of those who cling to the locality where they were born, but who would not be replaced after they had died.

Now that the station wagon had entered the Via degli Zingari, it was as if Camellion and McAulay had entered another world. The working-class shabbiness of the dun-colored buildings, the clusters of small shops and the black-paved road gave the impression not only of age and great tiredness but of homogeneity. Buildings crowded the street without any fringe of trees or flowers to provide color. The Via degli Zingari, as well as the rest of the Suburra, was a secretive, inward looking, working-man's world. The area was also a staunch Communist stronghold, but of the typical Italian kind: flexible, sophisticated and complex, owing as much to Machiavelli as to Marx, yet with a veneer all its own.

Like the proprietor of the *trattoria*[5] next door to the building that Ferro had converted into a home. A burly, sardonic man, he was an active member of the Communist Party. Nevertheless, he wore a necklace with a crucifix. One day, he had told Camellion, "Christ I love, but the priest and the rich people I hate. They are all worms." His sentiments had had the authentic ring of the true Roman, for whom anti-clericalism is often the reverse side of a passionate faith.

McAulay, coming to the center of the block, turned right

5 Tavern.

into the mouth of a dark alley. He drove sixty feet, then made a left and guided the Fiat into the parallel alley. Robert Ferro's garage was only half a block away.

Four hours earlier, Camellion and McAulay had begun the dangerous mission. They had returned safely—yet neither man was happy. The strike had failed. Vito Camerini was dead. Worse, they had been forced to terminate three Italian policemen. Worst of all, they did not have the least idea where the Red Brigades were holding Maria Gondozatti, the living saint of Rome.

Chapter Four

The midmorning sun was hot and already beginning to bake the stones and concrete of the pavements, but the three leaders of the *Brigate Rosse,* inside the small basement room hidden behind a fake wall, were not concerned with the temperature. Their immediate problem was a possible leak in security, a grave matter that involved why Vito Camerini had been murdered. Equally as important was WHO had murdered him. Once they knew the "who," the "why" would automatically fall into place.

Luigi de Santis, the Chairman of the Revolutionary Council, poured a glass of Bordolino for himself and pondered Marcello's theory. Joseph was usually right. There was something very odd about the shooting at the villa. The police hadn't killed Camerini, and neither had the *autonomisti.* The stupid members of the *Autonomia Operaia* beat up a lot of people and caused the police trouble in any number of ways, but murder was out of their league. All the other men who had died with Camerini! Who were they? There were possibilities. But *porca puttana!* A battle between two opposing intelligence units of foreign nations? Ridiculous! Or was it?

De Santis picked up the glass of wine, stared at it for a moment, then looked thoughtfully at Giuseppe Marcello, who sat to his right at the plain wooden table covered with a checkered oilcloth. Of medium height and weight and only 27 years old, de Santis' appearance was very deceptive to those who didn't know him, his small features giving the impression of weakness. He was not a muscular man and didn't appear to be very strong. Yet if one looked very carefully, one could see that his eyes were cold, devouring and possessive. He didn't even look Italian. With his light hair, almost blond and carefully trimmed, he could have been Nordic.

His butternut jeans and light brown cotton shirt were as neat as his physical appearance.

"*Il Tempo* and several other papers didn't even hint that the other dead men might be foreigners," he said in a careful voice. "*Il Tempo* did say that the police think the murders were 'terrorist inspired'—whatever that's supposed to mean. On that basis, we can assume that the police suspect us."

Joe Marcello, his elbows propped up on the table, his chin supported on his locked hands, didn't move a muscle, didn't look at de Santis. "*L'Osservatore Romano* carried the villa shoot-out on page one and linked the murders with the killings of the three policemen at the roadblock. That damned rag said that both incidents were either the work of the Brigade or inspired by us."

Francesco Alongi removed the pipe from his mouth and snorted.

"Who bothers to read *L'Osservatore*? No one believes anything the Vatican prints, except priests and nuns. *L'Osservatore* is always calling us communists, and even the police know that's a lie."

Ignoring Alongi, who was in charge of all *Brigate Rosse* communications throughout Italy, de Santis looked searchingly at Marcello, who was blessed with a logical, orderly mind.

"Giuseppe, tell us why you feel that maybe it was American agents and Russian agents who shot it out at the villa. We know we can't believe what the papers print. The police often withhold information from the media."

Marcello straightened up and reached for the bottle of Bordolino and a glass. Large, heavily built, and a year older than de Santis and Alongi who were the same age, Marcello was a blunt-looking man whose good manners and speech seemed not quite to belong to him. His thick black beard was clipped short and tidy, his shoulder-length hair neatly combed. He always exhibited a warm courtesy through which gazed a pair of highly intelligent eyes. Like de Santis and Alongi, he too had quit his university studies to devote his full time and efforts to reforming society and smashing what he *Brigate Rosse* called "the false ethical values of a decadent society."

"There is no other answer that is logical," Marcello said, pushing the cork into the neck of the green wine bottle. "We didn't kill Vito and those men. The police didn't do it, and none of the smaller reactionary pulled it off. It had to be foreigners."

"You are only guessing," Francesco Alongi said, emphasizing his words by pointing the stem of his pipe at Marcello. "The fact that identification was not found on the corpses is not significant. We never carry papers when we go out to carry off a project."

"The police—*falsità e cortesia!*"[1], de Santis said. "They could have lied to the press. Those men might very well have carried papers, drivers licenses and the like."

"I think the police told the truth," Marcello said patiently, then took a long sip of wine. "They wouldn't have anything to gain by concealing the truth. I think that a unit from one foreign intelligence outfit got to the villa and grabbed Vito. The second foreign group arrived when the first was leaving. The result was a gun battle in which Vito was killed, either deliberately or by a stray bullet. I also feel that the two men who killed the policemen at the checkpoint were part of one of the forces. They were either Americans or Russians."

"I'd say the American Central Intelligence Agency was involved," de Santis said, his troubled voice reflecting his uncertainty of how to handle the situation that had arisen. "It's rather obvious why. We gave the Americans an ultimatum— one month to leave our country. The CIA is retaliating."

"As well as trying to find that silly old woman we have hidden," sneered Alongi. "They will never find her. No one would ever think of looking there."

"Brothers, the government will never agree to our demand," Joseph Marcello said as a pronouncement. "The government will never release Curcio and the fourteen other *capi storici*.[2] We tried to force them to release Curcio and the others when we kidnapped Moro. All we accomplished was to unite the Comunisti with the Christian Democrats." He put down his

[1] "I wouldn't trust them an inch."

[2] "Historic chiefs."

glass of wine, leaned back, folded his arms and looked down at the table. "We might as well release Maria Gondozatti or execute her. We will have to do one or the other at the end of the next three weeks."

"We can't release her," Alongi said fiercely, "or we'd look like fools. The people would say our threats were hollow and made of straw. If the government does not give into our demands, the woman will have to die. We know what the vote will be." He blew out smoke in agitation and again jammed the air with the stem of his pipe. "We should go through with our plan to destroy the American Embassy. We have the rocket and the launcher. What is to stop us?"

Luigi de Santis pushed back his chair and, deep in thought, stared at Giuseppe Marcello, disturbed at the tone of finality in his friend's words. Deeply worried, de Santis looked around the tiny room, which was bleak, to say the least. Other than the table and four chairs, there was an old blue sofa and a card table on which rested a West German Neiderlund police scanner. Against one wall were stacked crates of machine guns and fragmentation grenades stolen from police armories. The ceiling was so low that the men almost had to stoop when they stood erect. It too was white-washed like the walls, walls already old when the United States was still thirteen colonies, for the house had been in the de Santis family for almost 400 years. As the eldest son, Luigi de Santis had inherited the house when his father had died.

Strangely enough, there was one ornament in the room, on a small shelf on a wall. A wooden sculpture by Anri of Italy, the two hand-carved, hand-painted figures revolving when the music box played a tune.

De Santis' eyes finally came to rest on Alongi. "We have three weeks to decide about Signorina Gondozatti, and we don't know what the vote will be, not until one is taken. Remember that, Francesco."

Alongi's thick eyebrows knitted in a frown. "The members voted to execute Moro, and they will vote 'yes' to execute that crazy woman who thinks she talks to God! You will see."

"There may not even be a vote," de Santis said evenly, one part of his mind vaguely wondering why the members of the other cells throughout Italy had voted Alongi to the Council. Francesco was a good man; he was dedicated to the cause, and would give his life if necessary. But he was too rash, too impatient, too prone to violence. "We can be certain that the

Vatican is pressuring the government to release Curcio and the others. The Vatican doesn't want to see Maria Gondozatti executed by us. How would it look to the people? Why, it would be as if God favored our side." His eyes swung to Joseph Marcello. "Right now our problem is overall security, provided your theory about what happened at the villa is correct, Giuseppe. We can't afford to assume that it isn't."

"Perhaps in the long run, it would be better if we killed the foolish old woman," Alongi said between clenched teeth. "Religion is a slow poison that is destroying all Europe. Gondozatti's death would be a severe blow to the people and certainly shake their faith in heaven.

"Her death could also backfire and unite the people against us," Luigi de Santis said roughly, with a wave of his hand. "At the present time, the people have a sense of secret respect for violence against the symbols of state power, even though they condemn the acts of violence. The average citizen doesn't like us, but he doesn't hate us either, and he does have a secret respect for our methods."

"That's true enough," Marcello said. "Only the other day, I was talking to a professor at the university. He said that the *rapimento* was the most brilliantly planned and executed campaign any Italian has made since Caesar conquered Gaul."

Alongi put his pipe in an ashtray, pushed back his chair, stood up, put his hands on his hips and looked down at de Santis and Marcello.

"I refuse to believe that there's an informer within our ranks!" he snapped. With that, he turned, walked over to the sofa, stretched out on his back and put his hands under his head. "Another thing," he said, looking up at the ceiling, "we don't know that whoever went after Vito knew he was a brigatisti contact-man. That's more supposition."

"Do you have a better answer?" Joe Marcello flung back. "Why else would anyone try to kidnap Vito Camerini? He wasn't a man of means. He barely made a living as a freelance cartoonist. I doubt if he made a hundred thousand lire[3] a month."

"Yes, you're right, Giuseppe," de Santis intoned firmly. "Whoever the men represented, whether CIA or KGB, they

---

[3] Under normal economic conditions there are 625 lire to the American dollar; during inflationary periods it can fluctuate up to 900 lire.

went after Vito because they knew he was a courier and could supply valuable information. I said knew! Only one of our people could have supplied that information. One of our people is a traitor, an informer."

"Vito Camerini had contact with only seven cells, excluding Leo-4, the cell to which he belonged," Marcello said.

"Of course. Therefore one of the eighty is the traitor," de Santis said.

"One in seventy-nine," Marcello corrected de Santis. "You also counted Camerini."

De Santis showed his teeth in an evil grin. "Very well. One in seventy-nine. The trouble is, we have no way of knowing who, among the seventy-nine, the traitor is. We could seal off those eight cells until we decide on a plan to expose the traitor, but if we did that, we'd take a third of our Rome force out of action.

"We would also warn the traitor," Marcello said. He blinked at de Santis, then finished the glass of wine and once again reached for the bottle.

"For the time being, there is only one course of action we can take." De Santis paused to mop his brow with a handkerchief. The basement room was cool, but de Santis always perspired when nervous. "The only thing we can do is not let any of the eight cells know our real plans regarding the American Embassy and Signorina Gondozatti."

"What I'd like to know is—are we going to blow up the American Embassy, or aren't we?" Alongi called from the sofa.

Joseph Marcello glanced suspiciously at Alongi, who was well-built, had a beetle-brow handsomeness and dark hair that, in waves over his ears and with just a dash of premature gray, lent him distinction. His manner was always brisk and massively forceful. But when he wanted to, he could disguise his sharpness with an air of worldly urbanity.

Privately, Marcello considered Alongi a dangerous fool and often compared him to those idiots who felt it their personal responsibility to carry on the noble traditions of Casanova.

"As I said earlier, we have three weeks," de Santis replied while looking at Marcello. "If the Americans are still in Rome, we shall have a total vote. I don't have to tell you the rules, Francesco."

"Rules!" sneered Alongi, with an ugly little laugh. "We

know that everyone will vote in our favor, once they know what we have decided."

Joseph Marcello took a swallow of wine, put down the glass and locked eyes with de Santis, a silent understanding passing between the two men. Alongi had spoken the truth, but he shouldn't have phrased it so bluntly. There must always be that pretense of "Democracy." Marcello and de Santis also knew that if the Americans did not close the United States Embassy in Rome, the *Brigate Rosse* would make an attempt to blow up the main building.

There wasn't any question about the fate of Maria Gondozatti. Should the Italian government decline to release Renato Curcio and the rest of the historic chiefs, the woman would be executed and her corpse dumped in St. Peter's square.

Both men had made up their minds. There would be no compromise.

Either Curcio and the others would gain their freedom or Maria Gondozatti would die.

Not even God would be able to prevent her execution!

Chapter Five

"In my opinion, Signor Giordano is an alcoholic, very sot in his ways—and I mean sot," Pierson said to Camellion who was walking next to him on the sidewalk. "He's lucky his *mamma mia* is such a good cook. Those egg noodles were some of the best I've ever eaten. *Fettuccine*. Isn't that the term for egg noodles?"

"Affirmative," Camellion said. "*Fettuccine* is the word."

"What was the name of the dish you ordered? The meat looked like veal cutlets. I suppose that's why you and McAulay eat there, because the food is so good."

"I had *osso buco*," Camellion said. "It's a veal specialty for which Milan is more famous." He glanced up at the sky, where the sun was polishing a few scattered clouds, then paused and waited for Pierson who had stopped to light a cigarette. "Angelo's lucky too, that his *osteria*[1] is in a good location. There, in the Piazza Madonna dei Monti, he catches a lot of tourists who wander into the Suburra."

Camellion and Pierson resumed their walk, their destination the home of Robert Ferro, only three blocks away.

"Is he always half-juiced?" This assignment was Pierson's first trip to Italy, and he was as curious as a child at Disneyland.

"Now and then I'll have morning coffee and a bit of brandy at the *trattoria* next door to Ferro's dump," Camellion explained. "At lunch time, McAulay and I usually go to Gior-

---

[1] A kind of informal restaurant where home-cooked meals are served.

dano's. He would have come with me today, but he's helping Ferro repair the transmitter. The damned thing went out last night." Camellion, his cold blue eyes behind the dark sunglasses alert to every passerby, laughed lightly. "Yeah, Angelo's always pickled with *vino*. But he's in great shape! His arteries are as hard as his liver."

"At least he could provide menus for his customers!" Pierson said drily.

"There's no written menu, for it's assumed that you know what's available," Camellion said with a laugh. "If you ask him, Angelo will rattle off the names of the dishes that his wife has prepared; but since he speaks dialect in a slurred monotone, and with his own abbreviations to boot, the average tourist is left no wiser. I like the old guy because he's honest. He makes no attempt to exploit foreign visitors. They are charged and treated exactly the same as the locals."

By now, Camellion and Pierson were only several blocks from Ferro's house, and as they turned into the narrow Via degli Zingari, cloaked with shadows, Pierson commented on the increasing number of men and women who were in the fall or icy years of life.

"The young people have all left," Camellion said. "You saw all the children, those who remain, in what is the real heart of Suburra: back at the small Madonna dei Monti plaza we just left. The children are there because of the fountain."

At a leisurely pace, they walked down the Via degli Zingari, Pierson exhibiting a lot of interest in the old buildings, some of which dated back to the Renaissance. Here on the Via degli Zingari one could buy soap in great yellow wedges or cheeses in great yellow wedges; or cheap wines and liquors. There was a small *farmacia* (pharmacy), a tiny clothing store and other hole-in-the-wall businesses.

Soon, Camellion and Pierson came to Robert Ferro's house, which was not a house at all, but part of a larger building that contained two other businesses, a *trattoria* to the north of Ferro and a sausage shop next door to the south.

In 1977, Ferro had acquired an eight year lease on the section of the building that, on the ground floor, had been a toy shop, and, on the second floor, a three room apartment for the proprietor, his wife and bambinos. The only things that appeared to be halfway modern about the front of the place were the bricks filling up the places where the display windows had been. The rest of the bricks, showing through unpatched stucco, looked as ancient as the huge, ornate marble doorframe that had come from the remains of the nearby Portico of Octavia, which Augustus had dedicated to his sister Octavia in 23 B.C. On the second floor were two shuttered windows, a ceramic reproduction of a Renaissance relief between the two windows, in this case a relief of the Holy Family.

But the large wooden door was very modern, and so was the shiny lock. Across the door, someone had printed in chalk, *Attenti! Al Cane Edmondo*.

"The writing in chalk, what does it say?" Pierson asked while the Death Merchant pulled a key on a chain from his pocket and inserted it into the lock.

"It means 'Beware the dog Edmondo'," Camellion said. "We don't know who wrote it. The owner of the trattoria next door has a dog, but the mutt's name is not Edmondo. Somebody got mixed up somewhere along the line."

Pierson removed the dark glasses from his boyish face and sighed.

"Ferro's place isn't exactly the *Cavalieri Hilton*," he said slowly.

"It's not supposed to be." Camellion pushed open the door. "Ferro's cover is that of a black sheep of an old American family. He's established himself as an American expatriate living on money his family sends him, on condition that he never returns to the United States."

Once they were inside, Camellion closed the door and relocked the deadbolt-type lock. Pierson noticed that there were two other deadbolt locks on the inside, one at the top of the door and one at the bottom. He assumed that these two other locks were used at night.

Looking around, Pierson saw that he and Camellion were in a narrow hallway that was the length of the entire front, and that in the center of the inner wall was another door that Camellion was unlocking.

In another few moments, they were inside the first room, the Death Merchant was relocking the door, and George McAulay and Robert Dominic Ferro were looking up at them.

After Camellion introduced Pierson to McAulay and Ferro, he and Pierson took off their coats and sat down—Camellion choosing a rocking chair; Pierson, a Crewel wing chair.

44

"You should have come with me to Angelo's to meet Tom," Camellion said to McAulay. He slipped off his shoes and stretched out his legs. "You missed a very good meal."

"Italian food is too fattening." George patted his stomach. "I'm about five pounds overweight."

"No problem. Angelo serves skinny spaghetti," Camellion said, then swung his gaze to Ferro, who was in his late-thirties and looked like a Mafia hit-man, the kind of man a first class casting director would choose for a first class motion picture.

Ferro was one tough-looking customer. Glacial eyes peered fiercely beneath thick black brows. A nose as questing as a hawk's beak. Shiny black hair—a bit thin on the crown—that needed cutting. A two days' growth of beard. A slit of a mouth that some would describe as cruel. Barefooted and dressed in an open madras shirt and shorts, also made of denim, he was very hairy, especially his chest that was carpeted in a tangled mass of black.

"What about the short wave?" Camellion inquired. "Did you get it fixed?" He reached over to his coat, draped over a chair, and pulled a flat box of candied orange slices from the left pocket.

Ferro nodded. "It wasn't the set. The trouble was in the Black Box.[2] A wire was loose in the continuity-transfer contact." Noticing that Pierson was watching him stir the ice in the glass with a swizzle stick, he grinned, showing big white teeth, and added, "I always start drinking around noon in case it gets dark early."

Pierson smiled. "That's as good a reason as any." He laughed.

And so did McAulay when Camellion, about to pop an orange slice into his mouth, said, "Tom, you have to get used to Bob. It's his nature to see a glass half-empty rather than half-full."

Not the least bit insulted—he knew Camellion was joking— Ferro took a drink of scotch, licked his lips and grinned. "I couldn't sing or dance, so I joined the company. I was going

[2] A nickname for a device that picks up radio messages—or transmits them—in a signal that is known as a "squeeze." In the parlance of the trade, the message is "squirted" into the atmosphere within a microsecond, this fantastic speed making it impossible for an enemy to pick up the message and/or to lock in on the source of transmission with tracking equipment.

to resign when they sent me to Italy, then found out the booze would be on the expense account. Pierson, what is your exact function in this project?"

Somewhat taken back by the abruptness of Ferro's question, Pierson instantly deduced that Ferro was one of those individuals who jumped from one subject to another without pausing to take a breath. As a trained psychologist, Pierson knew that this trait—highly annoying to many people—was indicative of a high order of intelligence, of a rapidly thinking mind that was constantly analyzing and always acutely sensitive to its environment, but not necessarily a mind that was disciplined.

"I'm a psychologist with the F.I.D.,[3]" Pierson said casually. "My function in Italy is to evaluate the moves of the Red Brigades and try to formulate the line of logic and reasoning behind those undertakings. It's part of a company study regarding the mentality processes of terrorists. In turn, that's part of another research of anticipating crisis in terms of sensing system disequilibriums."

"The hell with the blockbuster words. Condense it to a bottom line," Ferro said. He raked a glance across Pierson, got up from the four-legged stool and walked over to the liquor "cabinet," a small refrigerator in one corner of the room.

Pierson thought for a moment. "I suppose you could call it the pooling of prophecy, as opposed to random happenstance."

Grinning, Ferro dropped ice cubes into his glass. "Ha! All you F.I.D. guys need is Maria Gondozatti. I understand that her record of predictions is one hundred percent accurate. But I hope she's wrong on her last prediction."

George McAulay was suddenly very interested. "Uh-huh! Such as?" He looked from Ferro to Camellion, the latter of whom he considered a walking encyclopedia on such matters.

"The end of the world," Camellion said, "before the end of this century. According to Gondozatti there will be only two more popes after this present pope, John Paul II. She referred to John Paul II as *De Medietate Lunae,* or 'Concerning the Half-Moon.'"

"Interesting, but what does it mean?" asked Pierson.

3 Foreign Intelligence Division.

The Death Merchant finished chewing an orange slice before answering. " 'Half-Moon' suggests a connection with events in the Mohammedan world, or even the moon itself, during a space probe. After, John Paul will be the pope Gondozatti calls *De Gloria Olivae*. This could be interpreted as a papal reign of peace, but it could have another meaning. I think it has, because Christianity is on its last legs the world over."

"And the last pope?" McAulay asked, very seriously.

"She predicted that the last pope will be *Peter the Roman*. During his reign the papacy will be totally destroyed, as well as Rome and Europe. The *'Third Temple'* will be annihilated. And—"

"Modern-day Israel—the Third Temple!" Pierson said.

"Exactly. It will all be part of the last big bang. World War Three will explode over humanity. Civilization will end and man will go the way of the dodo bird—if Maria Gondozatti is correct in her predictions."

"Yeah, 'If!' " McAulay said gloomily. "If our reports are accurate and our man in the Vatican didn't get his wires crossed, she's never been wrong. I'm going to have a can of beer on that!"

He got up and started for the refrigerator.

"I for one don't believe in the supernatural," Tom Pierson commented. "So the obvious question is, how does Maria Gondozatti do it? I'm told that she doesn't have any conscious control over the mechanism involved in her psychic predictions. She goes into a trance and speaks in Latin. She doesn't know what she has said until she regains consciousness and others tell her."

"You mean, like Edgar Cayce, the 'Sleeping Prophet' back in Conus,"[4] said Ferro, who had returned to the foot stool with his drink.

"Exactly. But with a difference. Cayce's predictions have not come to pass yet. California and Japan haven't slid into the Pacific Ocean. The waters of the Great Lakes are not flowing into the Gulf of Mexico."

Ferro's expression became very serious and his gaze skipped to Camellion. "You know, she has made some predictions that intrigue me, assuming they're not just rumors. She said

[4] A trade term. It means the Continental United States.

47

that historical records would be found in a secret room under the pyramid of Giza, near Cairo in Egypt. But she didn't say when."

"It had better be damn soon," McAulay said, pulling the tab off the can of beer. "We've only got another ten years of civilization left."

"Bunk and bull!" Pierson said. "I heard that prediction and some others she's supposed to have made. She said also that some of the descendants of the original Atlanteans have a highly technical underwater civilization, one far superior to our own. I ask you—who can believe such nonsense? It's as unscientific as a 'flat earth!' "

Ferro was lightning quick to defend himself. "Scientists aren't goldplated gods," he snapped, then belched loudly. "Less than two hundred years ago, the scientific community was convinced that 'stones cannot fall from the sky.' No one today in his right mind will deny the existence of meteors. Scientists laughed too at the story of the Flood. It was only a quaint parable they said. Now we know that there was a worldwide flood. I thought your cover was a dealer in antiques! What's this psychology business?"

"I am a qualified psychologist!" Pierson said stiffly, almost angrily. "Antiques are a hobby of mine. For that reason I was given the cover of being an agent for a company in Conus dealing in antiques. Getting back to science. The various disciplines demand—"

"Men, we're getting off the road," the Death Merchant interrupted. "You're both right and you're both wrong. What actually is, is that some people are dissatisfied with the criteria used by science to determine truth. The result is that they are ready to believe the other alternatives.

"On the other hand, science itself has become a church, a church with its own dogmas, hierarchies, 'truths' and 'heresies.' It has its popes and bishops and cardinals and the power to excommunicate any scientist who challenge prevailing scientific orthodoxy."

"Damn right," growled Ferro, scratching his chest. "Look what happened to some scientists who suggested that Velikovsky's theories be tested. Well, by God! The surface of Mars is cut up and beneath all the clouds of Venus it is hot enough to melt lead! But whether Velikovsky is right or wrong

48

is not the issue. What I'm talking about is the nasty retribution dished out to the few who wanted to be openminded and explore Velikovsky's theories."

"You're absolutely correct," Pierson admitted, looking at Ferro, then turning to Camellion. "So are you, Camellion. Both of you have to concede that civilization has advanced not because of crackpot theories but in spite of them, and that it's been science that has brought about that advance."

"I agree with you, Tom." Camellion flattened the empty box of orange slices and expertly flipped the crushed wad of cardboard into a wastepaper basket across the room. "Yet what you seemingly fail to realize is that reality is far more complex than we can imagine. It's very possible that there are dimensions of 'real experience' that the scientific method cannot illuminate. Think for a moment. Suppose our present conceptions of time make it impossible for us to understand certain kinds of fundamental processes? What if certain physical laws do not apply equally throughout the universe. Suppose certain sections of the universe do not touch the minor suburb we call 'reality.' Today, I feel that many scientists are too dogmatic about the past and too restrictive in what they regard as 'worth' studying—and none of this has a damn thing to do with this mission. Let's get down to business, shall we?"

"Another failure like we had the night before last, and we might as well return to the States," McAulay said forlornly. "Even if the fault wasn't ours."

A deep frown crossing his forehead, Bob Ferro snorted. "I'm telling you again"—he glanced at McAulay, then dug his gaze into the Death Merchant—"the leak wasn't Marsilio Riggio. We've set up all kinds of tests, any number of traps, for the spaghetti-bender, and he's breezed through every one."

"Hold on!" Pierson sat up straighter and made a motion with his right hand. "I want to get everything straight in my mind. Riggio is the agent working for the West German BND. Correct?"

"Camellion and I think he's a triple." McAulay, toying with the can of beer in his hand, looked straight at Pierson. "Ferro is convinced otherwise."

"A triple!" An expression of urgency flickered over Pearson's even featured face.

"The Agency has a 'mole'[5] in the BND,"[6] Camellion spoke rapidly and mechanically. "It was the M who discovered Riggio here in Rome. What was so important about Riggio is that he's a member of the *Brigate Rosse*, in Sagittarius-2. Each Red Brigades cell is named after one of the signs of the zodiac. Since there are only twelve signs in the zodiac and scores of terrorist cells, there are duplications of signs. For example, Vito Camerini was in Leo-4. Do you understand?"

Pierson nodded, and Ferro said, "It was a CI-nick street man who blackmailed Riggio into working for us. No, it wasn't me. I'm in DC,[7] and this place is an ultra-safe house. I make contact with the street men through a system of deaddrops and once a month a certain CI-nick comes here to report orally."

Camellion turned an irascible scowl on Ferro, who either didn't notice or didn't care, and said quietly to Pierson, "The KGB got to Vito Camerini's house a short time before George and I did. Riggio had to have tipped off the Ruskies, which means he's not only working for the BND and the company, but for the KGB. What went wrong was the bad timing of the Russian 'blood-wet' boys. But"—he sighed—"the fault really wasn't theirs."

Added McAulay, "Only Riggio and Ferro knew that we were going to black bag Camerini. What would you deduce, Tom? As if I didn't know."

"The same as the two of you—that Riggio tipped the KGB." Pierson smiled crookedly and turned his head toward Ferro. "Or that Ferro did."

"You can't be stupid enough to be serious!" Ferro's black eyes flashed angry fire, but his voice was as soft as a drifting feather. He stared in warning at Pierson, who was mild mannered and had an evanescent personality, the kind of man most people felt comfortable with and liked instantly.

"I'm too smart to be brave and not dumb enough to be

5 An intelligence agent who has succeeded in becoming a member of another nation's intelligence system, either a friendly or an enemy nation.

6 The *Bundesnachrichtendienst* is the Federal Intelligence Service of the Federal German Government, established, with the help of the CIA, in 1956.

7 Deep-cover.

serious," Pierson said firmly, "and logical enough to know that if Riggio and you knew about the strike—and only Riggio and you—either Riggio or you talked to the Russians. Or do you have a better answer?"

Pierson's answer had surprised Ferro and McAulay, but not the Death Merchant, who, on first meeting Pierson, a few hours earlier, had assessed him as having not only a quick analytical mind, but a backbone filled with tempered steel.

"Ask Camellion," growled Ferro.

Pierson looked from Ferro to Camellion, then back again to Ferro, whose eyes had narrowed to slits and whose left hand had knotted into a fist.

"Ask him what?"

"Tom, you've made a wrong turn on the road of logic." The Death Merchant was amused. Pierson wondered why. He soon found out.

"As a security measure, we let Riggio believe that McAulay and I were going to make the strike against Camerini on Tuesday, which was last night. Instead, we shoved the deal up a night, and tried to grab him Monday night. Ferro knew the truth. If he were a double and had tipped the KGB, they would hardly have arrived about the same time I had. *Capisci?*"

Yes . . . Pierson understood, and felt uncomfortable, realizing that he should have guessed that Camellion, with all his caution and professionalism, would never have placed his life in the hands of a foreign agent, particularly one who was a double agent, and quite possibly a triple.

At the same time, Pierson reasoned that he had had a right to suspect Robert Ferro. Good Lord! Anyone with common sense could see that Ferro was a first class screwball. Most experts in-the-field had to be; normal men could take the pressure of minute-to-minute uncertainty. But Ferro was a double ding-a-ling. Years before, he had suggested to company officials that the Agency use mind-control experiments in which hypnotized subjects would have uncontrollable impulses to commit nuisance acts on Groundhog Day!

And just look at how he had furnished this room! Nothing matched. The long blue couch was completely out of place with the bright green carpet. There was only one end table at the end of the couch, and it was a walnut two drawer filing cabinet. The solid cherry chest of drawers belonged in a bedroom! There were some antiques in the room, all shoved against one wall, side by side as in a warehouse.

"You're saying that it was sheer coincidence that the KGB chose the same time—roughly—as you and George," Pierson said.

"That's it," Camellion said. "Coincidence that loused up the whole show in more ways than one. The chiefs of the Red Brigades have to be wondering how we knew about Vito Camerini."

"A severe setback," Pierson said. "I'm beginning to get the picture."

"Give the man a teddy bear for a prize!" McAulay glanced at Pierson, his bitter laugh a jangled dissonance without mirth.

Pierson, taking cigarettes and lighter from his shirt pocket, turned his attention to Ferro. "I owe you an apology."

A sinister, mocking smile creased Ferro's hard face.

"No, you don't. I would have considered you a fool if you hadn't suspected me. I don't like to work with a fool."

"It was a test then!" Pierson felt tiny worms of anger crawl within him. Coconsciously he took a Camel from the pack of cigarettes.

"And you passed it," drawled the Death Merchant.

"Okay. He made a straight A," McAulay said impatiently to the Death Merchant. "So what are we going to do about Riggio? He doesn't know about Bob and his safe-house, and we were in disguise when we talked to him. I still don't like the way the situation has developed. No doubt the KGB is looking all over Rome for us. Thank God they're looking for two men who don't exist."

"The KGB isn't stupid, George," Camellion said. "They'll suspect disguises. Even the Italian police suspect that the two 'assassins' in the car were in disguise—and the Rome police are so dumb they have to have written instructions how to find their rear ends when they go to the john."

Pierson said, "According to the papers and the newscasts, the police suspect the *brigatisti* of the killings at the villa."

The Death Merchant stifled a yawn and began to rock slowly back and forth in the rocking chair. "Actually, the police are running around in circles. The *Autonomia Operaia* are also suspect, as well as the *Spontis*."

By way of totally explaining the various factions at work in Italian society, Camellion added that the *Brigate Rosse* and the *Autonomia Operaia* were not friends, the *Autonomia Operaia* convinced that the *brigatisti*'s strategy of terror and violence only reinforced all the oppressive measures utilized by the police.

The slogan of the *Autonomisti* was *Nè con le Brigate Rosse, nè con lo stato*—"Neither with the Red Brigades nor with the State."

Naturally the *Autonomisti* were split and constantly arguing with each other.

"If there are four Italians in a political group," Camellion said, "there will soon be four different views, each differing violently with the others."

A small but dangerous wing of the *Autonomisti* was made up of crackpots who liked to brandish automatic pistols, especially German Walther P-38s—and they were named after this weapon. It was the habit of the P-38s to show up at demonstrations and provoke confrontations by shooting off their guns while others "were shooting off their mouths." The gun-toting hoodlums also trashed banks, office buildings, and automobile showrooms.

"The *Autonomia Operaia*. What does the name mean?" Pierson inquired slowly. "My Italian is pretty rusty, but I can't make any sense from the name."

"Don't feel bad about it," Camellion said. "*'Autonomia Operaia'* is an untranslatable title. The literal meaning doesn't make any sense, and the closest one can translate to English is 'Working Class Autonomy.' There isn't any difficulty with *Spontis,* which is derived from spontaneous and means the 'Spontaneous Ones.'"

"They're the counterpart of the *Autonomisti,* right?" asked Pierson, who noticed that Ferro had returned to the refrigerator and was filling his glass with scotch—and be damned if he didn't appear to be cold sober!

"Yeah, that's it. The *Spontis* trash offices and wreck coin machines at bus and train stations. Oh yes, something else. They indulge in shoplifting, to which they give the ideological appellation of 'proletarian expropriation.'"

"You gotta understand something else, too," Ferro said, returning from the refrigerator and sitting down heavily on the couch. "The spaghetti fuzz tar the *Autonomisti* and the *Spontis* with the Red Brigade brush. The differences between the three groups are not always clear, except to the cops who consider violence and terrorism as one and the same. If the authorities had any brains, they'd do what the krauts do when things get too rough—have the imprisoned terrorists conveniently commit suicide."

Pierson wasn't amused. "What else can you expect of a nation that turned millions of people into ashes?"

Ferro, whose secret hero was Adolf Hitler, merely shrugged and sipped at his cold scotch.

"Violence and terrorism are two different things," McAulay said. "People who suffer because of poverty or lack of education or unemployment have a lot of violence boiling in them, and not infrequently they express it in revolutionary situations. What happens is that pure, planned terrorism expropriates the natural violence of such people and places it smack into the hands of the self-appointed 'saviors' of society. That's what's happening in Rome."

"And in other parts of Italy," Camellion said quickly. "Milan, Turin, and other cities. But not in Sicily. The Mafia still is in firm control, and the old Dons won't tolerate a disorderly society."

"Naturally there's violence in Turin," Pierson said. "After all, Turin is the birthplace of the Italian Socialist Party and the 1968 student revolt."

"As well as the headquarters of Fiat," added McAulay, "the largest private business in Europe."

Ferro laughed loudly, then said, "I thought we were supposed to be figuring how to blow up Riggio?"

"First we trap him, then we terminate the dirt-bag," McAulay corrected Ferro.

The Death Merchant rectified McAulay's mistake. "You're slipping, George. We first trap Riggio. We will then use him to our own advantage. He's not worth a damn to us dead. Even after this is all over, he'll still be of use as a switch-around. We'll be able to feed the KGB all sorts of false information, or rather you diligent Case officers of the CIA will. When the KGB gets wise that Riggio's nothing but a great big source of disinformation, they'll blow him away."

McAulay made a face and waggled a foot. "So who's perfect?"

"We'll use the patsy plan we discussed yesterday afternoon," Camellion said. In response to the questioning expression on Tom Pierson's face, he explained that when Marsilio Riggio had revealed the function of Vito Camerini, he had also mentioned one Alfredo Bertini, who was supposed to be the paymaster for all the *Brigate Rosse* cells in Rome.

Riggio had carefully explained that he had obtained the information about Bertini from a member of Sagittarius-2, the cell to which Riggio himself belonged. The member who had told him—John Boncalli—had obtained the information from his brother, who was a member of Virgo-9, the same cell of which Alfredo Bertini was a member.

"Can you believe Riggio?" Pierson asked with curious interest. At the same time he wondered what the other rooms of the safe-house looked like.

Camellion's voice was calm. "Who knows? He did tell the truth about Camerini. At least we are assuming he did. We'll never know, not with Camerini a corpse."

"Yes, but if Riggio is a triple, he has to be having second thoughts about his own personal survival," Pierson pointed out. "I take it he's a natural-born survivor. Since the fiasco at Camerini's house, Riggio must suspect that you suspect him of being a triple."

"Again, give the man a teddy bear," McAulay said, keeping his voice low to disguise his uncertainty. "What worries us is that Riggio might skip. We'll know tonight."

"We haven't seen Riggio since Monday afternoon." The Death Merchant smiled philosophically. "He's scheduled to meet a CI-nick at eight tonight, near the Spanish Steps of the church of the Trinità dei Monti in the Piazza di Spagna. I think Riggio will show. He's not only a survivor, he's also a very cool customer."

"When you get right down to it, he doesn't have much choice." McAulay sounded slightly optimistic. "If he tried to run, he'll have more than the company's Q-boys after him. He'll be the target of the KGB and the BND. Hell, he wouldn't be safe at the South Pole."

"It's the KGB who might force him to go underground," Ferro cut in. "Riggio knows that the Russians have to be having second thoughts about him because you showed up at the villa. The poor bastard's trapped between a tornado and volcano!"

Pierson lighted another cigarette and his gaze darted to the Death Merchant "This patsy plan. I take it you're going to set somebody up, but for what?"

"The plan is contingent on Riggio's showing up tonight,"

Camellion said. "The contact is going to ask him if he has any information about a clerk named Paul Campanella. Campanella works in a paint store and is an insignificant *Autonomista*. The contact is going to tell Riggio that Campanella has valuable information on where the Red Brigades are holding Maria Gondozatti.

"Then all we have to do is sit back, wait, and see what happens to Campanella, whether Riggio gives the information to the KGB or the Red Brigades?" Pierson, his face intense, began tapping his fingers on the left arm of the chair.

Camellion stopped his rocking. "Right on, but first—"

"Listen," butted in Ferro, holding up his almost empty glass. "If we're going through with this deal, I'd better get on the radio and squirt off a message to the station at the embassy. Now make up your mind."

"Do it," Camellion said. "You know the details. Just make sure you tell the station that the sooner the street boys bug Campanella's appartment, the better off we'll be on this end. And remind them that they have three days at maximum to do the job."

"Got it." Ferro finished his drink and got up.

"Three days?" protested Pierson, watching Robert Ferro disappear into the next room.

"It isn't likely that whoever grabs Campanella will do it where he works," Camellion said. "He works in a paint store. If he is grabbed, it will be at his apartment. We're hoping that the bugs will give us a clue as to who does the job."

McAulay joined in. "The contact is going to let Riggio know that we're going to kidnap Campanella either this Friday or Saturday. Such a time schedule will give the KGB or the Red Brigades plenty of time to get there ahead of us. McAulay paused for a moment before saying in a crisp, brittle voice, "I guess you know the punchline to all this scheming? If you don't, the wheels in your head need oiling."

Pierson tried to decide whether he liked McAulay. He concluded that maybe he did.

"I think so. While Riggio and the opposition are concentrating on Campanella, you'll go after Alfredo Bertini, the paymaster—you and Camellion."

"You've just won another teddy!"

"But you were off slightly," Camellion said, smiling slightly. *"We'll* be going after Bertini—tonight, as soon as the sun sets."

Camellion's announcement made Pierson's heart beat faster. He had always wanted to experience action in the field. Now he wasn't so sure. At close range, violence and possible death were not the least bit attractive. . . .

Chapter Six

The world fears only time, and time fears only the pyramids.

Richard Camellion had only the fear of failure. And so far, even this had been one big flop. Alfredo Bertini was a mechanic, and it had not been feasible to grab him at the garage where he worked. It had been even less practical to kidnap him at his home. He lived with a married sister and her husband and the couple's six children, in the poor Cassarina section of the city, a twelve block area even more crowded than the rest of Rome.[1] Here in the Cassarina area there was only one toilet for every ten people and five people for every room. Yet, peculiarly enough, most Italians, like the Japanese, didn't mind being packed together.

The Death Merchant minded. The crowded sidewalks made kidnapping Bertini all the more difficult. It was Bertini's custom to come home, eat a light meal, and then go to the *trattoria* half a block east of the old building where his sister and her husband had a cramped, dingy apartment on the third floor. On the corner of the Via Testina and Via Pta Paolo, the *trattoria* was not only a popular neighborhood meeting place, but also a stop for people passing through the district, such as tourists out slumming. Strangers, even tourists, were ignored and never bothered. Romans pay the foreigner the compliment of presuming that he has his own affairs and that what he does is none of their business. Because of this attitude on the

---

[1] The correct name of Rome is *Comune di Roma,* and S.P.Q.R. —Senate and People of Rome—is still a symbol.

part of Romans, the stranger is able to melt into the background and to come and go unnoticed.

Alfredo Bertini had not come to the *trattoria* on schedule. By 8:30, he was an hour and a half overdue, and Camellion began to formulate a new scheme for putting a sack over the *brigatista* paymaster's head, at the same time wondering if Marsilio Riggio was making-the-meet with the CI-nick and if McAulay and Ferro's patience had been stretched to the breaking point.

An hour and forty-five minute earlier, McAulay had posted himself at one of the sidewalk tables of the *ristorante* directly across the street from Bertini's apartment house.

Half-slumped in the front seat of a Fiat with Lola Presswood, Robert Ferro was parked in the Via Testina, a hundred feet west of the apartment house. Since 80 percent of the automobiles in Rome are "500" Fiats, no one paid any attention to the couple. They were just another pair of lovers escaping an overcrowded apartment.

Lola Presswood was one of those tenth wonders of the world: a woman member of the Counterintelligence Division of the CIA—and a "street man" to boot. Although fairly attractive, she was not the least bit glamorous. A formidable woman, she wore her hair cut short, little makeup, was an expert in karate and spoke three of the various Italian dialects, especially *bocca romana,* the language of the educated, and *romanesco,* an argot heard mostly in Trastevere, the district on the west bank of the Tiber which houses the oldest and most firmly implanted of Roman communities. The Cassarina section was in the Trastevere district.

She didn't wear a "Little Willie," a special communicator disguised as a hearing aid. She didn't need one. Ferro had a plug in his ear, a thin wire from the plug running to a flat case in his shirt pocket. The device was very simple. Once the button on Little Willie was pushed to ON, all one had to do was push his chin down and speak just above a whisper, and the mike, in the case, would transmit the words to any other person wearing a similar "hearing aid," the message coming in over the ear plugs

Dressed in working man's clothes, including a coat, and sitting at a table not far from the sidewalk, Camellion sipped a white wine. All around him was Roman society at its worst —but not any worse than any other society.

The sidewalks, up and down the Via Testina and the Vie

Pta Paolo were as crowded as New Orleans during the Mardi Gras, not only with people strolling, but with vendors selling ice cream or hot dogs and hamburgers.

The Death Merchant made up his mind. If the mountain wouldn't come to Mohammed, Mohammed would run to the damned mountain. He finished his glass of wine, left the table, went to the sidewalk and started walking west, stumbling a bit as though drunk. He pushed Little Willie's plug more firmly in his ear, removed the transmission case from the breast pocket of his coat and tapped it, as though checking to see if it was working. Anyone who might notice would think he was only checking his hearing aid, or listening to an ordinary pocket radio.

"We can't wait any longer for Bertini," he whispered into the set. We're going in and get him. George, Bob, you two follow me when you see me go into the building. Doll, start the car and keep the motor running. We might have to pull out in a hurry. Confirm."

"Confirmed," McAulay and Ferro said in unison.

The Death Merchant pushed his way through the mass of people on the sidewalk. He passed the narrow mouth of an alley and saw a drunk curled up by some trash cans, sound asleep. Close to the drunk sat three cats, staring disdainfully at the world around them. Why not? Rome was their city, too.

Camellion chuckled mentally, thinking of the twenty buck bet he had lost to McAulay. "I'll bet a sawbuck you don't know the origin of my cat's name?" McAulay had challenged him.

"A Basque name?"

"Wrong! Cerridwen is from a Welsh and Celtic legend. The name means 'Lady of the White Witches.' You owe me twenty bucks."

The Death Merchant moved down the block at a slow pace, staggering every now and then and occasionally bumping into a passerby, mumbling, *"Mi scusi"* ("Pardon me"). Or *"Mi dispiace"* ("I'm sorry").

When he was only fifty feet east of the dingy apartment house where Alfredo Bertini lived, he saw McAulay get up from the sidewalk table of the *ristorante,* saunter to the curb and wait to cross the road that, in the words of Angelo Giordano, was a "ribbon of tin." From the corner of his eyes, as he reached the walk and turned in to the apartment house, he saw Robert Ferro, carrying an old faded leather briefcase, come around the rear of the Fiat parked up ahead.

The front of the apartment house was a mess. Camellion had seen better on Salvation Army stores. The entire building needed a coat of paint. For that matter, so did all Rome, but like Angelo Giordano had once said, if the city were painted, it no longer would be Rome.

Drunken philosopher that he was, Giordano, who was a Sicilian from Palermo, disliked mainland Italians in general and Romans in particular. "You can always tell a Roman," was his advice "He is always ignorant and arrogant."

Giordano also had what he called the perfect solution to the traffic problem—"Wait until the whole damned city is locked in one big traffic jam, then cover it with asphalt and start all over again. Then he would mumble what he wanted on his tombstone, *"Fui un Pedone!"* ("I was a Pedestrian"', because he felt that not to have owned a car was his principal distinction.

The front of the apartment house was a faded yellow, the huge stone pediments above each window chipped and with numerous stones missing. The windows were so dirty one could not see through them. At the bottom of faded yellow walls were azaleas and rhododendrons, fighting with all their might in a sea of weeds.

The Death Merchant staggered up the three stone steps and through the street door which was wide open, as was the metal grille behind it. Once inside, Camellion felt he was a thousand miles and a hundred years from civilization. The various aromas of cooking drifted to his nostrils as did the fragrance of wood smoke.

Ahead, to Camellion's left, was a long dirty hall and half a dozen trashcans over which crawled cockroaches. At the end of the hall was a door that opened to the rear. In front of Camellion was the stairway to the second floor. He started up the steps, on his way up unbuckling the straps that held the two 9mm Brownings snug in their shoulder holsters.

The front hall of the second floor was as dirty as the one downstairs, and just as he had started across the threadbare carpet he saw, to his far right, two men come down from the end of the stairs that led to the third floor. Camellion could not see the full length of the stairs. From his position, the stairs were hidden by the side and the rear wall of the first room to the right of the hall just ahead of him. But he knew there were more than two men. He couldn't see them, but he could hear their feet pounding on the stairs.

Staggering slightly from side to side, a silly grin on his face, Camellion lurched in the direction of the two men, both of whom were in their late twenties and dressed in cheap suits He could tell from the way they sneered at him in contempt that they considered him just another harmless drunk, a worker doomed to toil in some factory, his only release from misery the illusionary solace of cheap wine.

"*Buona sera! Come stanno? Hanno delle sigarette o tabacco?*"[2] he said in a loud voice, slurring his words.

One of the men pushed at him and said roughly, "*Sparisci! Cretino!*"[3]

By then three more men were at the bottom of the stairs, two of them holding the arms of the man in the center.

DAMN! There was no mistaking the short, stocky man, with the smooth glossy cheeks, black hair and heavy spectacles. The Death Merchant had seen a blown-up photograph of him made a day earlier by CI-nicks.

The man in the center was Alfredo Bertini!

Behind Bertini and the two men holding him came three more men.

God Almighty! Seven of them—and from the look on Bertini's face, he'd rather be some place else. KGB? No way. These jokers are Latins—either fuzz or brigatisti.

During those few seconds, the Death Merchant knew that he wasn't the only one caught in a highly precarious predicament. McAulay and Ferro were in the same leaky lifeboat. He could not open fire until he had the protection of the rear wall by the flight of steps to the third floor. McAulay and Ferro would have practically no protection on the steps—*Unless I open fire first and can warn them.*

Camellion reached the steps to the third floor, got on the second step and, crouched by the wall, pulled out the twin Brownings, thumbed off the safety catches, spun around and pulled the triggers, just as the first two men reached the mouth of the stairs that led down to the first floor.

Camellion did not have noise suppressors attached to the Brownings. With silencers, the two automatics would have

2 "Good evening. How are you? Do you have any cigarettes or tobacco?"

3 "Beat it! Idiot!"

62

bulged too much under his coat. The two Hi-Power auto-loaders roared, filling the area with crashing noise. Two of the three men in the rear cried out and were flung forward from the impact of the 9mm projectiles hitting them between the shoulder blades

Lag time was against the remaining five terrorists. The first two men, on the first steps of the stairs to the first floor, spun around, their hands going underneath their coats. The two men holding Bertini attempted to reach for their weapons and at the same time drop to the floor and pull Bertini down with them. The last man in the rear froze in alarm and looked toward the left, at the body of the man falling to the floor.

A micro-moment later, the Death Merchant shot him in the back of the head and exploded his skull. His hat hit the floor before he did. The bullet from Camellion's left Browning stabbed into Stefano Orlando, the crazy to the left of Alfredo Bertini, who had dropped to the floor and was lying on his stomach.

Synonymous with the barking of Camellion's Brownings, there was a lower but much rapid chattering from the bottom of the steps. Robert Ferro had pulled the vicious little Ingram submachine gun from the briefcase and was using it with deadly efficiency against the first two men at the top of the stairs, a dozen 9mm full metal jacketed slugs raking across the left side of Enrico Lambassi and the small of the back of Davide Aldobertese. Lambassi fell and started tumbling down the stairs, while David Aldobertese first did a dying man's two step, then started to fall sideways.

Beniamino Fintacco, the last *Brigate Rosse* man alive, almost got off a shot. To the right of Bertini, Benjamin had managed to turn around and pull a 7.65mm French Le Francias automatic from his belt. That's as far as he got! The Death Merchant fired both Brownings and Benjamin Fintacco, two slugs in his chest, took several steps backward, tripped over his own feet and went down, the darkness of the dying swirling around in his brain.

It was Camellion's sixth sense, plus the redhot anger of Alberto Cristiana that saved the Death Merchant's life. At the same instant that Camellion spun around and looked up toward the top of the stairs.

Alberto Cristiana, the husband of Alfredo Bertini's sister, came to the end of the hall. A short, fat man with a head as bald as a stone, Albert yelled, *"Alto! Non si muova!"* and started to swing a double-barrelled shotgun toward Camellion.

"Stop!" and "Don't move!" Fat man, your request is impossible! The Death Merchant also believed in the truism that only fools argue with an enraged man carrying a shotgun.

He fired both Brownings at the same time he threw himself flat on the steps. One bullet crashed into Cristiana's fat belly. The second hot projectile stabbed him high in the stomach, an inch below his breastbone. Unconscious almost instantly, Albert never knew when his finger contracted against one of the triggers and the left barrel boomed like a cannon, filling the air with a cloud of leaden pellets that pinged like hail as they fell beyond Camellion, who managed to jump up and jerk back in time to avoid the dead body of Cristiana as the corpse tumbled past him and landed on the floor, one foot resting on the last step. Cristiana lay there on his back, his eyes open, a trickle of blood running from the left side of his mouth.

Worried that Alfredo Bertini might try to escape down the hall of the second floor, Camellion turned and looked toward the area between the first flight of stairs and the hall. He needn't have worried. Bertini was still flat on the floor. And here come the Marines! Ferro was racing up the first flight of steps, the Ingram in his right hand. McAulay, a .45 Enforcer in each hand, was right behind him.

Camellion moved over to Bertini and pushed his left foot against the man's hip. "Get up, stupid! You're going with us." Then, to Ferro, who looked happier than a hog knee-deep in slop—"Check the stairs to the third floor. Humpty-Dumpty over there tried to blow me away with a shotgun. There may be more of them coming down."

"He's my brother-in-law," Bertini said in a sad voice, getting to his feet.

"He was your brother-in-law," Camellion snapped, shoving the muzzle of a Browning under Bertini's face "Now he's not even a member of the universe, and if you give us any trouble, you'll go to hell just as fast."

McAulay, standing to one side of the end of the second floor hall, triggered off three rounds from one of the .45 Enforcers when he saw several doors open and heads pop out, but he was shooting only to frighten, unlike Ferro, who, seeing three men appear at the top of the stairs to the third floor, shot to kill. The three men didn't have any weapons in their hands, but that didn't make any difference to Ferro. His philosophy was simple and practical—Kill 'em and blame their murders on the Red Brigades. Besides, one of the men wore metal-rimmed eyeglasses, and Ferro never did trust an individual who wore metal-rimmed glasses.

The three men—one at least sixty, the other two in their early forties—tried to jump back out of the line of fire when they saw the Ingram submachine gun, which was only eleven and a half inches long with the stock retracted. Expert that he was, Ferro triggered off a long sweeping burst that caught the three men in the lower legs. And he yelled, *"Complimenti delle Brigate Rosse"*—"Compliments of the Red Brigades!"

- From down the second floor hall a man began to yell, *"Chiami la polizia!"* A woman began to cry out hysterically, *"Aiuto! Aiuto!"*

"Let's get out of here," Camellion yelled in Italian to Ferro and McAulay, adding in Russian which neither man understood, *"Yanvarronezha v yakh za titiisy dnoye!"* ("We're going to have to put wheels on our feet").

He spun the terrified Bertini around, grabbed him by the back of his shirt collar, jammed the Browning into the small of his back and warned in a cold voice, "Try to run and I'll blow your spine apart."

With Bertini in front of him, Camellion started for the steps. Again someone had gotten to the target ahead of him —*But this time we grabbed the target!*

McAulay tossed a final shot down the hallway and moved quickly toward the Death Merchant. Ferro shoved a full magazine into the Ingram, dropped the empty magazine into the briefcase, and took a fragmentation grenade from the case. He pulled the pin and tossed the grenade up the steps, making sure it hit the carpet a dozen feet back from the top step. Then he turned and ran toward McAulay, Camellion, and Bertini, all three of whom were hurrying down the stairs.

The grenade exploded with a crashing roar that shook the whole building and sent parts of the rug and floorboards flying in all directions. Part of the ceiling of the first floor hall collapsed, plaster falling downward and sending up a shower of gray dust.

Reaching the bottom of the steps, Camellion shoved Bertini against the wall and jerked his eyes to McAulay. "Cover the rear when we leave. Anyone with a gun—kill 'em!"

"I'm sure not going to kiss 'em!" McAulay snapped back, looking up toward the top of the steps.

"Ferro, check the outside," Camellion ordered.

Ferro trotted to the side of the door, stuck his head out and looked around. Groups of people had gathered in front of the apartment house and across the Via Testina. Traffic was moving, although drivers slowed to look around when they saw everyone staring toward the north. Ferro looked to the right and saw that Lola Preswood had started the motor of the Fiat. No problem there. The thing to do now was to create more confusion.

The drivers speeded up and the rubberneckers on both sides of the street began to scatter when Ferro shouted, "We're the Red Brigade and we'll kill anyone who tries to stop us. Down with the government! Up with the common man!" then sprayed the air with a short burst of Ingram fire, firing the small machine gun as one would use a pistol, while holding the briefcase in his other hand. He motioned with the briefcase to Camellion and McAulay.

"There's no opposition, but we'll have to run for it," he said.

Ferro then moved through the door to the outside. The Death Merchant, prodding Bertini with a Browning Hi-Power, and McAulay headed out behind him, Camellion snarling at his captive, "We're going to run to a car parked down the street. Try to get away and I'll blow your head off." And to McAulay, "Watch the front of the buildings on this side. Who knows who might have guns?"

Down the walk, then west they ran, no one opposing them, people ahead diving to the grass or underneath cars. Even people on the other side of the street almost trampled each other in their haste to put distance between themselves and the four men they believed to be members of the dreaded and fanatical *Brigate Rosse* They were only one-fourth right!

Twice the sharp-eyed McAulay spotted men about to fire either rifles or pistols from apartment house windows, but each time he changed their minds by throwing .45 slugs crashing into the windows.

Laboring for breath, Camellion and the three men reached the Fiat. Presswood scooted over in the front seat as Ferro ran around the back of the car and got in behind the wheel. On the other side, McAulay jerked open the rear door and climbed in. Camellion shoved Bertini in behind McAulay, then crawled in himself. The instant he closed the door, Ferro stepped on the gas and began to turn the Fiat into traffic. Not only was he a very good driver, but he also knew the Cassarina section with the same thoroughness that the Death Merchant knew the Big Thicket region of Texas.

"W-Who are you people?" Alfredo Bertini found the courage to ask, his voice off-key and resembling a croak.

"Silenzio!" Camellion jammed Bertini in the side with a Browning.

Ferro was now in traffic, and as he speeded up the car, Lola Presswood turned around in the front seat, bracing herself against the momentum of the swaying vehicle, and looked at Camellion. "How many are dead back there?" She spoke Italian, her voice as calm as the surface of a pond.

"We didn't have time to count," Camellion answered. "What we did, we did it to get the job done."

"Don't let it worry you, honey," McAulay said in a light voice. "In another three blocks—or is it four?"

"It's four," said Ferro.

"So, in four blocks we'll be safe, just as soon as we switch cars," McAulay said.

"I'm not your 'honey,' and I'm not worried," the young woman said severely." She glared at Camellion "And I don't like being referred to as a 'doll.' Nor do I like working with a professional mercenary. I understand that's what you are, Mr. Camellion."

If this doesn't tear the feathers from an ostrich's butt! Miss Stupid's a moral philosopher! "Sister, in one way or another we're all bastards," Camellion said mockingly. "But God loves us all. Just remember that while I may be rancid butter in your eyes, I'm still on your side of the bread."

"Hallelujah!" shouted Ferro. "Praise the Lord and pass the righteousness!"

"Yeah, and don't forget," McAulay said. "He owns the cow and the bakery too. He should! He gets a hundred grand a mission."

Lola Presswood drew back, her eyes wide with astonishment. No man was worth that kind of money!

"Hang on!" Ferro called out. Seeing his opportunity to cut across traffic headed in the opposite direction, he made a sharp left turn, causing some drivers ahead to slam on the brakes, and curse him loudly. The Fiat shot into an alley like a rocket, cats screeching and jumping out of the way.

Half a block away, the siren of a police car began to scream.

"Oh-me, oh-my! We've been tagged," McAulay said.

"Earn your pay, Miss Presswood," Camellion said, emphasizing the Miss. "You're not just along for the ride"

The young woman gave Camellion and McAulay a final dirty look, turned around in the seat and opened the dash compartment, taking out four silver balls that could have been Christmas tree ornaments. Known as a "Skid-All," each glass ball was filled with a colorless oil that had been chemically treated to make it more slick, as slick as newly formed ice. Once a car's tires were coated with Skid-All, that car would be unable to negotiate a curve at more than ten miles per hour. Presswood tossed out the silver balls, one by one, and they fell to the pavement and broke. God help any car that roared through the Skid-All.

God didn't! By the time Ferro had driven the Fiat down the alley and had turned to the right and was headed toward another alley, a police car roared into the south end of the first alley, its tires going through the Skid-All. The car reached the other end of the alley and, at thirty-five miles an hour, the driver atempted to turn. No sooner had he started than the back end of the vehicle began to skid. A few seconds later, momentum took over and the entire car began to skid sideways, the driver desperately fighting the wheel, the other three cops in the car all yelling and shouting three different sets of instructions at the same time.

But it had happened too fast. The driver might as well have tried to climb a mountain wearing roller skates. The right rear fender of the police car slammed against the left front fender of a small Pirelli whose driver was breaking the car frantically. An instant later, the left front fender of a small Pirelli crashed into the right front fender of the police car. With a shrieking of brakes that could be heard a block away, all three cars finally came to a stop, while vehicles, coming from both directions, skidded to a stop.

In the meantime, Robert Ferro had driven down another alley and had parked the Fiat at its other end.

"Derstine had better be there," McAulay said and opened the door.

"If he isn't, another man will be," Lola Presswood said evenly.

"Move," Camellion ordered Alfredo Bertini. "From now on we ride in style"

Ferro and Presswood went first, then Camellion and Bertini, McAulay bringing up the rear. They walked out onto the Via Donatelli, which was alive with people, and saw that the sleek black Alfa Romeo was parked in the middle of the block. In a very short time, they were in the expensive car and headed west.

"The Vatican passports are in the dash," Conrad Derstine told Lola Presswood, who was in the front seat. "Pass them out."

The Death Merchant felt halfway satisfied. This time the strike had succeeded and they had black bagged the target. Alfredo Bertini was their prisoner. . . .

Chapter Seven

Humming a tune from the classics, Lola Presswood handed out the Vatican passports,[1] first checking the photographs on the inside cover of each red book.

"First rate forgeries," Ferro commented, staring down at his photograph and seeing that his name was Paul DiComa. Sitting between Derstine and Presswood, he shoved the passport into his left inner coat pocket. "If I didn't know better, I'd say they were genuine." He turned his head to the left and directed his question at Conrad Derstine, who was a long-faced man in his late forties. "Who did the job? Some of the boys at the E-Station?"[2]

"I suggest you ask me when members of the opposition aren't present," Derstine said mildly.

For a second, Ferro looked in disdain at Derstine, who was dressed in the uniform of a chauffeur "Tell you what. You worry about the driving and let us worry about our friend back there. He's not going anywhere. If and when he leaves us, he'll be a corpse."

The tone of Ferro's voice indicated that to him the matter was settled and that he considered Derstine a security-conscious boob.

---

[1] Since the Lateran Treaty of 1929 ceded the Vatican to the Pope, the Vatican, as distinct from the Holy See, has issued "laissez-passers"—letters of passage—to cardinals, and passports to individual citizens.

[2] Embassy-Station.

In the back seat, the Death Merchant smiled ever so faintly.

"I say, Robert, I think you're frightening our guest. We don't want Signor Bertini to think we're barbarians."

Camellion poked Bertini in the ribs with the muzzle of the Hi-Power Browning in his right hand. "I'm sure you don't think we're savages, do you, *amico mio?*"

Bertini, sitting as rigid as a bronze statue, stared straight ahead. "You know my name, but obviously you would. You're wasting your time. I don't know where Maria Gondozatti is hidden. Furthermore, I would not tell you if I did know."

Camellion sucked in his lower lip. George McAulay seemed mildly surprised. "You're supposed to say that you're only a poor working man," George said calculatingly, "and that we have the wrong man. And then when we say that you're the paymaster for all the Red Brigade cells in Rome, you're supposed to deny it. Hell, don't you ever watch programs *americani* on television?"

Bertini did not make a reply, and in the dimness within the car, McAulay and the Death Merchant could see his Adam's apple moving rapidly up and down, and silver beads of sweat crawling slowly down his cheeks and forehead. The man was brave, yet frightened. He continued to stare straight ahead, as if his backbone had been welded together and he was unable to move his head.

"I'm inclined to think our friend here is a practical man," Camellion said to McAulay. "The *Brigate Rosse* has a reputation for recruiting only highly intelligent men and women. That's why a Brigadist is so difficult to spot. He is very careful to stay current with all auto-related taxes and payments, and wtih his rent. He obeys traffic laws. He avoids arguments in public places. He is well dressed, keeps his beard neatly trimmed and his hair properly cut. He assumes a reassuring, polite demeanor with his neighbors, and never comes home after midnight. He has a car of modest size and power which he keeps clean and in perfect mechanical condition. But he changes autos frequently, always acquiring a different model and color from the previous one—right, Bertini?"

The trapped terrorist remained mute.

"Ah, but now and then people more clever manage to trap a Red Brigade member," McAulay taunted. "And when it's our group that does the trapping, the Brigade member can either cooperate and live or go the other route. That's the choice you now have, Bertini."

"I'm not fooled by your lies," Bertini said calmly. "I've heard you call each other by name. I think you're Americans. Whatever your nationality, you don't dare let me go. You have to kill me. Go ahead and shoot. I'm not afraid to die."

"Tch, tch, tch," mocked Camellion. "You should be concerned about the fate of your immortal soul!"

"Death is only the end of life," Bertini said mechanically. "Man's own fears created a god, and hell is only a reflection of man's own bigotry."

The Death Merchant thought of what a quick check had revealed about Bertini, that the man was a good son who loved his family. He especially loved his mother.

"It doesn't matter," Camellion drawled. "We don't intend to kill you, even if you don't come up with the right answers." Then came the Big Lie. "But . . . if you don't cooperate, we'll kill your father and mother. We'll kill your brothers and sisters and their husbands and children As for you—"

"You've already made one sister a widow," McAulay said. "How would you like to read in the papers about her kids being burned to death in an apartment house fire? We can be mean bastards when we have to be. Fact is, we consider you Red Brigade goofs a bunch of fumbling fools. You create a lot of excitement, but you haven't accomplished a single thing."

"As for you," Camellion said, "we wouldn't kill you. How can a man suffer when he's dead? We'd inject you with a substance that kills certain centers in the brain. You'd spend the rest of your life deaf, dumb, blind, and paralyzed from the neck down." Seeing the fear and horror reflected on Bertini's face, Camellion was confident that he and McAulay had stormed the last trench of the terrorist's resistance.

"It's your choice," McAulay said.

"It would also seem that the higher-ups in the Red Brigades consider you a threat," Camellion said. "Those men weren't taking you to a picnic. You poor fool! We could let you out of the car right now, and the Brigatisti would gun you down within a week. Quit kidding yourself."

An indecisive expression drifted over Bertini's face. Nervously he adjusted his heavy eyeglasses and turned toward the Death Merchant.

"What will happen to me if I do cooperate?"

"You'll be taken to the United States and given a new identity, a new start in life," Camellion lied, noticing that Lola Presswood was watching him in the rearview mirror.

"You're all CIA?"

"We're asking the questions," Camellion snapped. "The answers come from you."

Ferro called from the front seat, "Why did you stay home tonight, Bertini? Why didn't you go to the *trattoria* on the corner?"

Bertini hesitated for a moment, obviously unsure of himself. Finally, assuming that the Death Merchant was the leader of the group, he turned to Camellion. "Whatever your source of information was, it was not entirely accurate. I'm not the payman for all the cells in Roma, only fifteen of them. Whoever—"

"The man asked you a question," Camellion said. "Answer him."

Bertini cleared his throat. "I received a phone call at work," he explained. "It was from a woman who belongs to my cell. She said I should wait at home, that a special messenger would pick me up, and that we'd be going to a special meeting. You know the rest. Seven of them showed up. They told my sister and her husband that if they called the police, they'd kill me."

"We saved your bacon for you, dummy," Ferro said roughly.

Lola Presswood said in Italian, "You can name all the members of the fifteen cells, or don't you know them all?"

"I can name only the chiefs." Bertini reached for a handkerchief in his back pocket. "I had contact with only the chief of each cell. I would give him the money and he would distribute it to the members of the cell. I have never kept any of the funds. I have always been honest and have fought for the revolution, for the destruction of the global system of exploitation of the proletariat. Why should they want to execute me?"

McAulay guffawed. "Man, the only thing you've ever been is a damn fool, a rebel without a cause. Like all Marxist-Leninists, you can't see the trees for the forest. Next you'll be rattling about 'alternative social organization and structure.' The trouble with all you nutty revolutionaries is that when you're pinned down, you prefer generalities to specifics."

"The *Brigate Rosse* despises Marxism," Bertini said proudly. "We're as antagonistic to Communism as we are to Democracy. We are not fighting for a change in government, but for its total annihilation."

A phantasmagoria of color, from neon lights on both sides of the street, reflected eerily from Bertini's smooth, round face. The Alfa Romeo was traveling through the Via Morani, a middle class shopping center filled with clothing and appliance stores.

"Look, dummy. Forget this 'we' stuff," Robert Ferro said with a snicker. "You're out of it. The Red Brigades don't want your help. The Brigadists would like to see you stretched out on your back in the morgue. They consider you too dangerous to live, too dangerous because you know something that could lead to the people at the top."

Alfredo Bertini drew back in sudden realization and inhaled with a shudder. His eyes grew more round and the expression of shock locked on his face.

"It was you people! You who killed Vito Camerini!"

"The KGB arrived at the wrong time," the Death Merchant said. "Camerini died in the gun battle." His voice became more firm and determnied. "Do you know any of the people in the Brigade leadership? Do you know any of the people at the top?"

McAulay jumped in with more clarification. "Camerini was a courier, which is why we went after him. You're a paymaster, which is why you're our prisoner. Whoever the bosses are, they've figured out our strategy. You were slated to die before we could get to you."

The Death Merchant said emphatically, "Whether you realize it or not, you have information that is extremely dangerous to people at the top of the pyramid."

"May I smoke?" Bertini asked, moving his head slowly from side to side. He appeared to be more confused than ever, as if he were having a terrible nightmare and was making a supreme effort to wake up.

"You can burn, for all we care—as long as you tell us what we want to know," McAulay said, taking out his pack of cigarettes. "Here, have one of mine."

He and Camellion waited patiently while Bertini lit the cigarette, inhaled and blew out smoke. The Death Merchant then said, "Make no mistake about it, Bertini. The leadership of the *Brigate Rosse* wants you turned into cold meat."

74

"But the true leadership of the *Brigate Rosse* rests with Renato Curcio, Alberto Franceschini, and the other *capi storici,* and they're all in prison. All of Italy, the whole world, knows that Curcio was the founder of the Brigades. Why should he and the others want me dead? To keep me from telling what? It's ridiculous!"

In more ways than one! Camellion reflected. Although the Red Brigades was charged with scores of murders, bombings, and numerous bank robberies, Curcio and the other "historic chiefs" were arrested in 1976 and were safely in prison during the worst onslaught of violence, culminating in the kidnaping of former Prime Minister Aldo Moro in March of 1978 and his murder in May. Thus the charges against the first-generation *Brigatisti* were relatively minor: membership in an armed band, assaults and conspiracy. The bulk of the evidence against them was supplied by a proclaimed former priest who had been a revolutionist in South America—"Brother Machine Gun"[3] who had infiltrated the organization and had succeeded in making tapes and notes of conspiratorial conversations. The priest was now safely hidden and refused to testify in person. Another reason why the trials of Curcio, Franceschini, and the rest of the historic chiefs was being dragged out was that the men and women defendants refused to let attorneys, appointed by the Italian Constitutional Court, defend them. During the years, nineteen different attorneys had been appointed. Red Brigade members on the outside had assassinated twelve of them!

The Death Merchant, turning sideways, studied Bertini and slowly moved the Hi-Power Browning from side to side. "Let's start with the person who gives you the money, the money you give to the individual chiefs. What's his name?"

Alfredo Bertini faltered, his inner struggle, the battle to live pitted against his not wanting to be a traitor, telegraphing itself to his face.

"This is your last chance," McAulay warned.

"And I had better warn you," Camellion said softly. "The first time we catch you in a lie, that single false statement will be the death warrant for every single member of your family."

[3] The nickname of a revolutionary priest who at one time operated in Brazil.

"I will go to the United States? You will keep your word?" Bertini stared at Camellion and nervously took another drag on the cigarette.

"You will go to the United States," Camellion replied sincerely.

"A woman." Bertini's voice was barely above a whisper. "Angelina Moretti gave me the money. She and her husband share the leadership of Leo-2 cell in Campagna."

"These Morettis. Are they Regulars or Irregulars?" asked Camellion.

"What's the difference?" For the first time, Conrad Derstine had interjected a question.

"By God! He can talk!" mumbled McAulay with a tiny laugh.

"The Regulars are the underground," explained the Death Merchant. "They are wanted by the police, so they have to hide out and keep on the run. Respectable men and women—like Bertini here—compose the Irregular force. They lead normal lives and are unknown to the police."

"The Irregulars are organized into cells," thrust in Bob Ferro. "Both the Regulars and Irregulars are grouped into 'Columns.' Both groups are thought to number about three thousand men and women, all over Italy."

Ferro had taken a pint of brandy from his inner coat pocket, had taken a drink and now was capping the bottle. As Derstine made a right turn, Ferro leaned heavily against Lola Presswood, who grimaced from the heavy odor of brandy on his breath.

"Do you have to drink that damned stuff while I'm in the car?" she said angrily. "It's disgusting!"

"Yes it is," Ferro said sweetly. "I think I'll run out before we reach the safe-house."

McAulay, smiling, said, "There are reputed to be another ten thousand sympathizers of the *Brigate Rosse*. From time to time, this 'Third Circle' lends support and gives some kind of aid. You know, transportation and apartments for hide-outs."

The Death Merchant tapped Bertini on the knee with the underside of the Browning. "Get with it!"

"The Morettis are Irregulars," admitted Bertini. "Their cell is very important to the Roma columns because it's responsible for arms and explosives. Signor Bernardo Moretti

76

is an explosives expert. I was told that he makes bombs for the *Brigate Rosse*."

McAulay asked, "What cell do you belong to, Bertini?" He knew that the terrorist was a member of Virgo-9, but he wanted to ascertain the man's truthfulness.

"Virgo-9," came Bertini's prompt reply.

"What do you mean, you were 'told' about Mr. and Mrs. Moretti?" demanded the Death Merchant. "I thought one cell wasn't supposed to know what another cell was doing?"

Bertini looked down at the floor, and his voice shook. "I am not sure that I'm right about Signor and Signora Moretti. I am only going on what I was told by the chief of another cell, Sagittarius-2. His name is Giovanni Boncalli. He told me—it's been more than a month ago—that he had learned about the information, about the Morettis, from his brother Carlo Boncalli. Carlo belongs to my cell, Virgo-9. When I asked Carlo about what his brother had said, Carlo explained that he had heard about the Morettis from a man named Ernesto Borgo. Carlo told me that Borgo was a member of Scorpio-3. This is the cell that is controlled by Bernardo and Angelina Moretti."

"Have you ever discussed any of this with Bernard or Angelina Moretti?" asked Ferro. "And you had better not be lying!"

"No, I never did," answered Bertini quickly, "and I have no way of knowing if Carlo was telling the truth."

George McAulay leaned forward and looked around Bertini at the Death Merchant. "Are you thinking what I think you're thinking?"

Camellion smiled. He didn't have any doubts about John[4] and Charles[5] Boncalli: the two were a couple of gossips. And so was Ernest[6] Borgo. A damned good thing too that they were. Camellion considered these talebearing traits the worse flaw of the Red Brigades.

The Death Merchant liked the Italian people because, as inheritors of all the beauty that surrounds them in such pro-

---

[4] Giovanni in Italian.

[5] Carlo in Italian.

[6] Ernesto in Italian.

fusion, they had that old, conservative respect for technical competence, which had come to them from a long background in which artisans were very careful of their work.

There was the basic honesty of the Italian people. You always knew where you stood with them, their reactions, vocal and often violent, as direct as a child's. They never bottled up their resentment; they just exploded. Yet their approach was always refreshingly direct, in a simple friendly way. Less closed, more accessible and far more sentimental than the French or the one-track-minded Germans, they will proudly show you their *bambini* and ask to see photographs of yours; and they will put themselves out for you in any number of ways.

"*Babuino!*" said Alfredo Bertini. "They call Bernardo Moretti 'baboon' because he is so ugly!"

"What they call him is not important," the Death Merchant said. "I'm interested only in what you tell us. What's his line of work? What does Bernard Moretti do?"

"He's a dentist," Bertini said stiffly, tugging at his collar. "He has his office in his house." He looked around as if he had lost something.

McAulay thrust a half-full pack of cigarettes into Bertini's hands.

"Take mine. I have another pack."

"Let's get on with it, Mr. C.," growled Ferro from the front seat. "Let's hear your conclusions."

"Tell me yours," Camellion said, leaning back.

"It's the same as yours. The Morettis supply the big bucks for Bertini. I think the head boys of the Red Brigades wanted him scratched so he couldn't lead us or anyone else to the Morettis. I think the head boys have deduced what we're doing and are cutting off all possible leads that could point a finger in their direction—killing any messengers or couriers who might be a danger to them. Bertini knows Mr. and Mrs. Moretti. The Morettis can name the leaders. Therefore, Bertini was slated to go bye-bye—permanently."

"All we have to do now is decide when we're going after Mr. Dentist and Mrs. Dentist," McAulay said hotly, "and how we're going to do it. And we won't be able to drag our feet about it either."

Bertini dragged deep on his cigarette and stared in disbelief at McAulay, who met his gaze with cold eyes and a grim scowl. "Don't worry. You won't be going with us—

and stop your fidgeting. If you've lied about the Morettis, we'll turn you inside out!"

"Campagna is less than fifteen miles to the south," the Death Merchant said, his full lips forming a reserved smile. "It won't be difficult for us to get there . . . say, about ten o'clock tomorrow morning."

"Not in this car you don't!" Conrad Derstine ground out. "This automobile belongs to the embassy. It's Ambassador Trentham's personal car."

"My God! Does Ambassador Trentham know we're using it?" Lola Presswood sounded as though she might be in the very first stages of shock.

"No, he doesn't." Derstine was nervous and agitated. "I don't mind telling you—all of you—that I'm taking an enormous chance by hauling your butts in this vehicle. But you're not going to use it to go to Campagna—no way!"

"What a lousy way to run an intelligence agency!" grunted McAulay. He reached for the side strap and swayed with the motion of the car as Derstine made a left-hand curve and headed into the Via della Conciliazione. Several blocks to the west was the world famous Piazza di S. Pietro and Vatican City. Ahead, across the Tiber River, was the gigantic Castel Sant'Angelo.

The Death Merchant looked into the rearview mirror and saw a sharp calculating expression on Derstine's putty-colored face.

"I suppose you've seen the numerous police cars that have passed us?" Derstine went on. "You know why they haven't stopped us? They haven't because we're in an Alfa Romeo. They assume we're important people and would raise a rumpus with the Italian government."

"Well, now," mused Camellion. "We are important. This life is all we have."

Derstine was not amused. "I'll tell you something else. You'd better not let Bertini get away from you. If he does, we'll all have had it."

Robert Ferro laughed, but the laugh was forced and shaky. "What about the Chief of Station? Does he know you're using this car?"

"I am the Chief of Station!" flared Derstine bitterly. "I came myself because I didn't want to burden any officer with the responsibility—should something go wrong. The shortage of trained people, especially in Covert Action is unbelievable.

Ever since the liberals back home began tearing the Agency apart with 'exposés,' we've had one budget cut after another. I'm even my own Operations Assistant![7] Imagine! In a city as important as Rome!"

"I agree with you," Camellion said sympathetically to Derstine, "and we do appreciate the risk you're taking. But rest easy. We're not going to use this machine to drive to Campagna. Not only is the hour too late, but even in the daytime a limo like this would attract too much attention."

Relieved, Derstine relaxed. "What are your plans, or do you prefer to wait until we get to the safe-house?"

The Death Merchant patted Bertini's right knee with the Browning autoloader. The man's eyes widened with fear. "Don't worry, Derstine. Our captive is not going to tell anyone about anything."

"And your immediate plans?"

"We'll stay overnight at the safe-house. About eight in the morning, when the streets are full of people going to work, we'll take Ferro's Fiat and drive back to his place in the Suburra. We'll proceed from there to Campagna."

"Yeah, we'll need silencers and gas grenades," Ferro said. "We can work out the details after we have a longer talk with our spaghetti boy back there."

"That's reasonable," Derstine said affably.

"Derstine, I think it's high time you told us the real reason why you showed up this evening," Camellion said calmly.

"You're convinced there is a special reason?" Derstine's voice was strained and off-key.

"Chiefs of Stations don't do what you're doing unless something very vital comes up. Let's have it."

"About Maria Gondozatti. If and when you find her, she's not to be released in Italy."

McAulay and Presswood perked up. The Death Merchant didn't bat an eye. Ferro turned squarely to Derstine. "What the hell are we supposed to do with her? Don't tell me Eagle-1[8] wants her terminated?"

[7] Usually, a "Girl Friday," who types all cables and dispatches and reads all incoming traffic from divisional command headquarters. She keeps careful accounts of the station's finances, and replenishes each case officer's revolving fund. Needless to say, such women are chosen with great care.

[8] The headquarters Center at Langley, Virginia.

Lola Presswood snapped at him, "Is that all you ever think about—killing someone?"

"Most of the time!" Ferro responded, not looking at her.

"She's to be taken to Conus," Derstine said. "A sub will do the job of hauling her back to the States. I'll tell you when and where after you find her and she's stashed in a safe-house."

McAulay turned to Camellion in disgust. "This is the living end! We haven't the least idea where she is, and already we've gotten orders to get her to an S-house."

"No one said the job would be easy," Lola Presswood said.

"We never thought it would be, Mother Superior!" McAulay enjoyed watching anger flash over Lola's face. "But we're not supposed to be able to work miracles either. That's in Maria what's-her-name's department."

Alberto Bertini spoke up. "Giovanni Boncalli told me that there are any number of men and women at Bernardo and Angelina Moretti's house. Many of them are Regular brigade members, hiding out at the Moretti's place. I want you to know about them, or you'll think I've lied."

"How big of a house do the Moretti's have?" asked Ferro. "How many Brigade people are there?"

"A large house. I think the place used to be a nursing home. I'm not sure. I don't know how many people are there. The house is on the west edge of Campagna. I can show you on a map."

"You will," Camellion said, "as soon as we get to the safe-house."

"I think we'll have to take Pierson with us on this strike," McAulay said absently. He turned and looked at the Death Merchant. "But what about the radio?"

"Presswood can take over the radio watch," Camellion said, looking out the window at the Baroque angels that lined the bridge leading over the Tiber to the Castel Sant'Angelo. Built as a tomb for the Emperor Hadrian, the castle had been a papal fort in medieval times. Now the gigantic circular structure was a tourist attraction.

Ferro finished his bottle of brandy, recapped the empty bottle and said to no one in particular, "If you ask me, this entire deal is turning out to be like a friend-in-need—a pain in the butt!"

Camellion smiled tolerantly. "This new development only

proves the validity of Murphy's Fourth Law—'Left to themselves, things tend to go from bad to worse.' "

"Ditto to the fourth law. It's the fifth that bothers me," Ferro said and belched. "If there is a possibility of several things going wrong, the one that will cause the most damage will be the one."

"This Signor Murphy," inquired Bertini in a small voice. "He is an American scientist?"

"He's a thirty year old nonperson," Camellion said. "Half-Russian and all nonsense."

"Don't let him kid you," McAulay said. "The real truth is that Murphy was a woman. What happened is that one day she raised the lid from her pot of chowder and discovered a pair of socks. Her first words were, 'Whatever can go wrong will go wrong.' "

Chapter Eight

Planning the invasion of Dr. Bernard Moretti's large house had not been easy, the strategy having consumed the better part of the early morning hours. At first, the task—based solely on what Alfredo Bertini knew of the area—seemed to be an impossible one.

Bertini was not sure, but he "thought" the house was several hundred feet from the road. There were trees around the house; yet all around the house and trees there were wide open fields. An approach from any direction was not possible, not without being seen by someone inside the house.

Drive up to the house and pose as new patients of Dr. Moretti?

Not very likely. Four men in a car would arouse instant suspicion.

"It wouldn't work, George. We'd have machine guns pointing at us before we could even leave the car," Camellion said.

"Have you thought about a night attack?" suggested Wynn Rockford, one of the CI-nick "street men" who lived at the safe house to which Conrad Derstine had driven Camellion and his party.

"We'd still have to drive up to the house," Camellion said. "And at night there's a good chance that the Morettis might not be there. It's they we're after. Even as things are now, we might still be too late. The morning papers will be full of news about the shootout in the apartment house on the Via Testina. The chiefs of the *Brigate Rosse* already know we have Bertini. They might have told him to flee."

"There's another possibility," suggested Ferro. "We have

Bertini. The chiefs could anticipate we'll make him talk. They might be preparing a warm welcome for us at the Morettis' place. . . ."

The Death Merchant nodded. "I'm counting on it, amico. That's still another reason why our approach must be," he laughed sinisterly, "above reproach."

Camellion did some hard but practical reasoning. It isn't generally known, but in spite of Hitler's insane and monstrous attempt to eliminate "inferior peoples," there are still quite a few Gypsies in Europe. This is especially true in Italy where Gypsies sustain their lives largely through spontaneous Italian generosity.

Gypsy street singers and fortune tellers are not uncommon in Rome. Tourists flock to watch them at their dancing and singing. Gypsy women's brightly colored dresses writhe to the sound of flamenco guitars and harsh songs; they clap hands and tap their feet in a frenzy of wild rhythm. The Gypsies are brash, in their inimitable nomadic way taking advantage of their audience.

At 03.19 hours the Death Merchant announced, "We'll go as Gypsies. We'll drive right up to the back door and try to sell the creeps something!"

Wynn Rockford—hard, keen-eyed and well-muscled—gave Camellion an odd look.

Ferro's reaction was instantaneous and exhilarating. "I've heard of some nutty stunts in my time, but going in as Gypsies would take the cake. In fact, it would take the whole goddamn bakery!"

McAulay's laugh was an unpleasant, sarcastic cackle, although he knew Camellion well enough to know that the Death Merchant was serious.

"Pray tell, dear boy, where are we going to get Gypsy clothes, a Gypsy car and Gypsy junk to sell?" Abruptly, McAulay's face erupted with inspiration, and he proceeded to answer his own question. "Come to think of it, there are Gypsies around the Colosseum, a whole band of them."

"They're there to catch the tourist trade," Ferro said and took another sip of coffee laced with wine.

"Yeah, and they'll sell anything for a price, except pus—!" Wynn Rockford caught himself, remembering that Lola Presswood was present. "Except their women," he finished.

Tom Pierson said, "I read somewhere that the Gypsies are more protective of their women than the old school Italians."

"You're right," Rockford said. "The Italians are tolerant of a lot of new habits and customs. I remember the first time I was in Rome. As part of my cover, I was out on the town. I went to a gambling joint and made the mistake of saying *casino* the way it's pronounced in English!"

"Right," Camellion said, smiling. "You were asking for a house of ill repute. When you use the word casino in reference to a gambling establishment, you pronounce casino with the accent on the last syllable." He looked over at Rockford. "How much cash does the station here have on hand?"

Rockford thought for a moment. "Maybe five grand American and a grand in lire. How much do you think you'll need?"

"I'm not sure. But I want to have at least ten Gs. Better radio the Embassy station and have Derstine send four thousand in lire—no! Tell him to send the equivalent of ten thousand American in lire. By special messenger, no later than eight o'clock in the morning."

"Derstine will sure appreciate being awakened at this hour in the morning!" Rockford snubbed out his cigar, got up from the easy chair and left the room.

Pierson said thoughtfully to Camellion. "I can't see all of us trotting down to the Colosseum and buying all that stuff!"

"I can't either," Camellion said. "But I can see Presswood and me, posing as middle-aged tourists, doing the job. So the Gypies will think we're a couple of crazies! Who cares? We'll buy a car, clothes and junk to sell, then drive back here. From here we'll leave for Campagna."

"Middleaged tourists!" Lola Presswood sat up straight and stared at the Death Merchant.

"Your makeup kit is at my place," Ferro reminded Camellion.

"I know," Camellion nodded. "Lola and I will drive over to your place after the messenger brings the money. It's the time loss that bothers me. By the time I get make up on Lola and myself, get over to the Colosseum, wheel and deal with the Gypsies—you know what I'm getting at."

"Sure we do," Pierson said uneasily. "By the time we get to Campagna, it will be four in the afternoon."

"Or later," tacked on McAulay.

Fifteen-thirty hours. The 1968 Dodge, painted bright blue and decorated with expertly painted sunflowers, moved along the wide Via delle Termi di Caracalla, its engine working perfectly. No matter the age or make of a Gypsy automobile, the engine was always in tip-top shape. A car to a Gypsy was like a camel to an Arab living in the middle of the desert: whether car or camel, it was his transportation.

Robert Ferro, familiar with the route to Campagna, was driving. Next to him sat Lola Presswood. A woman in the car was necessary, to make the entire party seem less suspicious.

In the rear seat sat the Death Merchant. On the left side was McAulay. Pierson sat in the middle. Camellion and the other three men were decked out in gaudily colored shirts, dark trousers and Pyrenees-peaked hats. Presswood wore a blood-red skirt, a bright green blouse and a red, green and black scarf tied around her head. Her arms were loaded with brass bracelets of various kinds. But she didn't feel half as conspicuous as the men, who too wore clamp-on earrings. As for the rest of the disguise: Camellion had had time only to darken his own face and the faces of the other four, and to attach beards, mustaches, and wigs.

Under their wide Bolero-type shirts, they wore shoulder holsters filled with Hi-Power Browning autoloaders; spare magazines in their pockets. On top of the Dodge there were various sized baskets woven of straw, as well as crudely made brooms, cheap pots and pans made of tin, and long, low wooden chests, gaily painted and decorated with ornate carving. In one chest there were three High Standard 12-gauge pump shotguns, an Ingram submachine gun, and a bag of spare magazines for the Ingram. In the second chest was a bag of MK3A2 offensive hand grenades and a canvas bag of TH3 incendiary grenades. The whole business was well secured with ropes.

Several blocks behind the Dodge were Wynn Rockford and Larry Kolswith, two CI-nicks from the safe-house on the Via De Medicis.

Sixteen hundred hours. At four in the afternoon, the streets were crowded, the air heavy with exhaust fumes, and the city gasping. Nor did the traffic thin out when Ferro turned onto the Via Cristoforo Colombo.[1] They were now close to the southern edge of the city and soon were passing the Janiculum

---

[1] Our very own Christopher Columbus.

Hill, whose tree-clad lower slopes were largely a rubbish dump.

"I'd like to know what we're going to do if some cop stops us and says, *'Signori, per favore, le vostre carte d'identità!'?"*[2] McAulay said gloomily, hunching down in the seat.

"There's very little danger," Camellion reassured him. "The police almost never ask Gypsies to ID themselves. Trying to make Gypsies carry identity cards or pay taxes would be as futile as trying to blow away the Alps."

"Hey, what road is this?" asked Pierson as Ferro swung the Dodge onto a long stretch of four-lane highway.

"We're on the Banca di Santo Spirito—'the Bank of the Holy Spirit,'" Ferro said. "This highway will take us straight to the town of Campagna."

"Where Moretti's place is out in the country, several miles to the west of the town," added Camellion, looking at the sky in the distance. There wasn't a single cloud. "Unless Bertini lied about Moretti's place not being very ritzy and sitting out in the middle of a big field, we can't miss it. He said there's a sign out by the main road."

"We'll find it," McAulay said grimly. "Bertini knows what would happen to him if he lied." He laughed sardonically. "He believes that crap about our making him go blind and paralyzing him."

"He's lucky he doesn't know the real truth," Ferro said between clenched teeth. His foot pressed down on the gas pedal and slowly the needle of the speedometer began to climb.

Gradually buildings became more and more scarce and farther and farther apart. Southern Rome does not crawl into the suburbs, like Paris or Chicago, but cuts off short. Very quickly, Camellion and party were in open country where fields bloomed with red poppies and the tall grass rippled with the hot wind.

Yet every now and then the Dodge zipped past young women dressed in shorts, wearing high-heeled shoes, sun glasses, and carrying shoulder bags. They were prostitutes who hailed cars, particularly trucks, passing by, and offered their "special services" to the drivers.

* * *

[2] "Gentlemen, your identification, please."

Very quickly the Dodge closed in on Campagna, and in the distance the five people in the car could see the hazy outlines of buildings, none of which was over eight stories tall.

"I hope you're sure of the cutoff road?" Presswood said, looking at Ferro. In the back seat, the Death Merchant turned and looked out the rear window.

"I know where the road is," growled Ferro. "The last thing I need is a front seat driver next to me."

"The Pirelli is half a mile behind us," Camellion said. "Rockford and Kolswith are hanging right in there." He turned around and faced the front. "Once we spot Moretti's place, we'll go by and let them catch up with us. Ferro, you're sure there isn't any other place?"

"Not unless you want to drive for six or seven miles," Ferro said resignedly. "The monastery of the Camaldolese[3] is about two miles south of the Moretti's joint. Our best bet is to pull into one of their fields and turn around to go back to Moretti's place."

"I don't like it," Tom Pierson said gruffly. "Look how we're going to do it! We pull in, turn around and head back. Then Rockford and Kolswith pull in and wait. Those monks are going to think that something mighty odd is going on."

George McAulay frowned at Pierson in consternation. "Rockford and Kolswith have to signal the helicopter and pull us out of the house if this buggy is riddled."

"The monks won't think anything to our detriment." The Death Merchant's tone was impatient. "They've had their heads in the mists of mysticism for so long that they'd trust Satan himself. You're forgetting, Tom, that Rockford and Kolswith are going to fake engine trouble. By the time the monks do realize what's going on and the police from Campagna get underway, we'll be in the chopper and lifting off."

"All on the assumption that the chopper will show up," Pierson countered humorlessly. "And that's Murphy's first law—'If anything can go wrong it will!'"

"If the chopper doesn't show, we'll all end up dead," Camellion said. "Everything out here is open highway. There's no way we could get past the road blocks and back to Rome. So I suggest you think positive!"

[3] A barefooted order of Benedictines founded in 1012 by St. Romuald.

Lola Presswood turned in the front seat and addressed Camellion. "I think I should go in with the rest of you instead of waiting by the car!"

"Like hell you will!" exploded Ferro before Camellion could reply. "Women have a habit of gumming up the clock works. You're not going into the house with us. Forget it!"

"I probably have better reflexes than you!" flared Lola, her eyes flashing fierce anger. "And for your information, I happen to be a crack shot."

"How much farther, Bob?" interjected Camellion, effectively squelching what could have developed into a shouting match between Ferro and Presswood.

"Another half mile and we'll turn into the Festa di Noi Altri,"[4] Bob growled. "That road will take us around the west side of Campagna and goes right by Moretti's house."

The Death Merchant leaned back, the intensity of his thoughts clouding his face. The messenger from Derstine had brought more than money. He had also brought a coded message: Marsilio Riggio had met the CI-nick contact near the Spanish Steps of the Trinità dei Monti. I was right about Riggio. He does have nerve! Lots of it! Furthermore, the CI-nicks had worked very fast. They had succeeded in placing six bugs in Paul Campanella's house. The helicopter? The flight from Leonardo da Vinci Airport, where the L-14 Lorsinni was parked, would require less than ten minutes. The chopper was registered under an alias. The Pirelli had phony plates. It and the Dodge would be destroyed after the chopper set down east of the Campo Veranc Cemetery in eastern Rome. But no matter what happens—yeah!

The Dodge swayed. Ferro was turning into the Festa di Noi Altri.

[4] Feast of us others."

Chapter Nine

As the Dodge ate up the asphalt, it became increasingly evident that Alfredo Bertini had told the truth. The countryside was as flat as a pane of glass and as tired looking as an eighty year old man dozing on a park bench. The trees, old oaks and tall elms, were scattered about in a random pattern.

Tension increased. No one spoke, each member of the strike force mentally keeping track of the distance. Finally they saw the house that had to belong to Bernardo and Angelina Moretti. The house had to be the target. No other house was in sight.

A lane of crushed white rock led to the structure that sat 150 feet back from the left side of the road. Built of stone blocks and painted a deep green, the two story house had a red tile gambrel roof and windows that were horseshoe shaped at the top, except where there were small wrought-iron balconies on both floors. The outlet to these balconies were double-window doors. The house rested close to the ground and there was no front porch, only vines crawling up the front wall. There were flowerbeds of African daisies in the yard.

The only features that seemed out of place was the large picture window in the southeast corner of the first floor, and the very modern concrete block garage to the east of the house, large enough to hold four cars. Several cars were parked in front of the house, a pickup truck in front of the garage.

"It looks sort of idyllic, doesn't it?" said Presswood.

"It certainly doesn't look like a bomb factory, or a place

90

that would harbor a nest of Red Brigadists!" McAulay commented, uncertainty in his voice.

The Dodge roared past the sign to the left of the road—*B.N. Moretti, Dentista.*

"I wonder what the 'N' stands for?" murmured Lola.

Ferro reduced speed to let Wynn Rockford and Larry Kolswith, in the Pirelli, catch sight of them.

"I don't like it," Pierson said in a quiet voice. "I don't like the layout of the place."

McAulay flashed a mean, uncertain look at Pierson. "Is that the only damn record you know?"

"Tom's right," Camellion said stoutly. He glanced at another sign, this one to the right—ATTENZIONE! PONTE STRETTO ("Careful! Narrow Bridge"). "If the Brigadists have anticipated our move and are expecting us, that big garage could be full of the lice. The house is big, at least twenty rooms. There could be a dozen more upstairs."

While McAulay glanced at the Death Merchant in surprise, Ferro said, "Get to the bottom of the barrel, Mr. C."

"Driving around to the back and putting on our Gypsy selling act is out," Camellion said. "We'll turn around in the monks' field as planned, but before we head back this way, we'll stop, get the shotguns and other stuff out of the chests and get rid of all the junk on top."

McAulay squirmed. "Suppose the monks see us taking out shotguns and grenades?"

"The hell with the monks," Camellion said carelessly. "Don't you see the telephone line strung out below the electric lines on the roadside poles. We'll cut it. Even if the monks got wise and drove to town to call the police, it would take them fifteen minutes. By then we'll be out of the house and headed back to the field."

"So how do we go in?" Pierson said.

"Through the picture window in the corner," Camellion said. "Ferro, there's no porch and the house is low. All you have to do is drive across the flower bed and smash the glass with the front of this junk heap. It won't damage the car a bit."

"No problem," Ferro said.

"What about me?" asked Lola Presswood.

"You'll be safer with us than staying in the car," Camellion told her. "And no arguments out of you, Ferro."

Ferro slowed the car to twenty miles per hour and headed

the car onto the one lane steel bridge spanning the wide but shallow creek that twisted like a long, muddy worm across the countryside.

Ferro shrugged philosophically. "It's your show and her funeral."

Four minutes later, they passed the monastery of the Camaldolese Order—a grouping of low buildings, each one painted white and as neat as bows on a little girl's braids. The field was a quarter of a mile east of the monastery buildings, a long row of hornbeam trees, between monastery grounds and the wheat field, serving as a windbreak, the smooth gray bark of the trees encased in bougainvillea. Along the side of the road was Mediterranean *maquis* or scrub dotted with dandelions.

Spotting an opening in the wire fence, Ferro turned to the left and drove the car into the large clearing that was used for trucks during the harvest. Everyone saw the sign, neatly painted on a board nailed to a fence post—*AVVISO. NON ENTRARE. VIETATO POSTEGGIO* ("Warning. Do not enter. No Parking").

"We are obviously not welcome!" remarked McAulay.

No one answered him.

Ferro turned the car around in the large open space and parked to the right, with the front of the Dodge pointed toward the road.

"Don't slam the doors," warned Camellion, his hand pushing down on the handle.

Once Camellion and his party had left the car, they quickly went to work. McAulay crawled on top of the car, opened the chests and began handing weapons to Ferro and Presswood while Pierson began cutting guy ropes with an Argonaut knife he carried underneath his shirt—a pink shirt with horizontal blue stripes. All this time a deep fear had been eating at him—suppose the Gypsy who had worn the shirt—and the pants too—had had lice?

The Death Merchant didn't bother to check the two Backpacker Auto Mags in their shoulder holsters. He knew they were fully loaded and in perfect working condition. He looked around. The breeze rippled the wheat into brown waves. Birds sang in the distance. As far as he could detect, no one was around.

The deadly calm before the tornado! He bent over, pulled up his right pants leg and unsnapped the .380 Walther PP pistol from its ankle holster. He stood erect, took a five-inch-long noise suppressor from a hip pocket and began attaching it to the muzzle of the German-made autoloader.

He was finishing the operation and McAulay was pushing baskets and brooms from the top of the Dodge when the black Pirelli pulled into the clearing. Wynn Rockford turned the car around; then he and Larry Kolswith got out and stared at Camellion and the other four who were checking shotguns, pistols and the deadly little Ingram submachine gun.

Larry Kolswith, a short, wiry man with a pointy chin, took off his sun glasses and put his hands on his hips. "What gives, a change in plans?"

"Life is fired at us point-blank," Camellion said. "That's how we're going to tackle this job—head-on. Have you brought our regular clothes?"

"In several suitcases in the trunk," the thickset Rockford said in a tired voice. "We got plenty of other stuff—walkie-talkies, smoke grenades, and two Beretta subs. Oh yeah, about a dozen grenades. When do we call the helicopter?"

Rockford and Kolswith stared around curiously at Ferro, Pierson, and McAulay, who were strapping shoulder holsters on the outside of their shirts; and at Lola Presswood, who had already strapped a holstered Browning around her waist and now was checking the Ingram.

Kolswith laughed mockingly. "Jesus! You all look like you're going to a masquerade!"

The Death Merchant spoke rapidly, "The second we pull out in the Dodge, get on the radio and tell the chopper to come in. What kind of call are you going to use?"

"The forty-one meter band," said Rockford. "That's seven-point-one-dash-seven-point-three MHz. We'll converse via the old 'hot weather' code. Larry will figure out the coordinates. He used to be a navigator in the Navy."

"Good enough. The pilot can land in the wheat field," said Camellion. Just make damn sure you give him the right instructions."

Kolswith blinked at Camellion. "When do we come in?"

"Wait until you hear shooting. Then one of you take the car and park at the end of the lane. If we lose the Dodge, you can haul our tails back here." Camellion turned to his people who were watching him with bold expectation.

"Let's not forget the telephone line," Ferro said, eyeing the Walther in the Death Merchant's hand.

"I haven't." Camellion raised the Walther, resting the middle of the silencer on his left wrist, and carefully aimed at the slender wire stretched between two sagging electric line poles. He squeezed the trigger. The silencer went ZZZII-TTTTTTT, and the line parted, the two ends falling to the maquis by the side of the road.

Rockford and Kolswith exchanged glances and walked back to their car. The Death Merchant and his crew piled into the Dodge, Camellion taking Lola Presswood's place in the front seat. Before Ferro started the motor, he reached underneath the seat, pulled out a pint of peppermint schnapp, uncapped the bottle and tilted it to his lips.

"My God!" burst out Lola, listening to the liquid gurgle from the bottle. "You've got to drink at a time like this? Camellion, why do you permit such behavior."

"He knows what he's doing," Camellion said unconcernedly.

When the bottle was half empty, Ferro lowered and capped it. He wiped his mouth on his sleeve, shoved the bottle under the seat and turned the key in the ignition. "I just hope you know how to use that machine gun and don't shoot yourself, baby. In the meanwhile, mind your own damn business."

"You go to hell!" snarled Presswood, "straight to hell!"

Ferro snickered loudly and started to move the Dodge forward.

"Honey, I think we're all on our way to hell."

Chapter Ten

Unaware that their immediate environment would soon be turned into a nightmare of death and destruction, the three patients—a man and two women—thumbed through magazines in the waiting room while, in the work area, Dr. Moretti, assisted by his wife, filled one of the bicuspids of a patient.

Of medium height, but with broad shoulders and a slim waist, Dr. Bernardo Nicola Moretti did have features that were unsightly, the face pushed in, the mouth big, the nose long, the eyes small, the eyebrows thick, long and wide. The appellation "baboon" was not exactly a misnomer.

Angelina Moretti—thirty-four years old and thirteen years her husband's junior—was a plain-faced woman who, eleven years previously, had been introduced to her future husband by Giuseppe Marcello, one of her brothers.

Neither Dr. Moretti nor his wife showed the strain they were under, the worry that plagued their minds. Both hoped that Giuseppe was wrong, that the mysterious group wrecking the plans of the *Brigate Rosse* would not attack the house. Not that the house was defenseless. Giuseppe and eight men waited in the garage. Seven more *Brigadisti* were upstairs. There were more men and women *Brigadisti* in the subterranean ruins of the ancient Roman temple northwest of the house.

It wasn't fear of getting killed that worried Dr. and Signora Moretti. But how would they explain such an attack and dead bodies to the police? *Dottore* and *Signora* Moretti were highly respected. They had always kept a very low profile and there was not a particle of connection between them and the murderous *Brigate Rosse*. If the house was attacked, the *polizia* might have second thoughts. And what would their patients think? Any publicity of an adverse nature would destroy the wealthy clientele from Campagna.

Since Dr. Moretti was standing to the right of the patient, with his back to the picture window, he did not see the brightly painted Dodge when it turned into the lane and started toward the house, its speed increasing. Nor did Angelina Moretti, who was to the left of the patient—not until she happened to look up, in the process of adjusting the flow of water into the spit-basin, and her gaze wandered out the window. By then, the Dodge was halfway up the lane and Ferro was turning off the lane onto the grass and lining up the car with the picture window.

"Oh, my God! The window! Look Alfredo!" she gasped.

Moretti switched off the drill, turned around, and saw the bright blue car decorated with sunflowers—headed straight for the window. During those brief moments, Moretti caught sight of tall hats, bright shirts and two grim faces peering at him through the windshield. Instinctively he knew this was it, the beginning of the expected attack. But like this? Ramming the house with an automobile and disguised as Gypsies?

"Let's get out of here!" Moretti yelled. "They're going to crash into the house!" He stumbled from the side of the chair and pushed his terrified wife toward the doorway. Behind them, Dominic Bruni, the awe-stricken patient, tore the white cloth from underneath his chin, jumped up from the chair and scrambled after the Morettis. All three had just reached the hall when Robert Ferro slammed on the brakes and tires shrieked on grass and the rock edging around a flowerbed of pink and white peonies. The grille work of the Dodge smashed into the glass with the force of a twenty-five pound sledge and the glass shattered and fell to the ground, and to the floor inside the office, with a loud crash. The vibration of the big slam had cracked the other window in the southeast corner, and it too fell apart, large jagged chunks of plate glass breaking as they hit the ground.

Minus their hats, the Death Merchant and his force of four vacated the Dodge with amazing rapidity, Camellion holding a Backpacker Auto Mag in each hand. He and Ferro had seen the white coated Bernardo Moretti only momentarily, but they had seen enough of his face to know that he was the target, the prize they were after, and they were anxious to get their hands on the man—preferably on his thick throat.

"McAulay, take the left on the outside," Camellion ordered. "Link up with us from the rear. Pierson, go with him. Ferro. Presswood. Keep an eye on that garage."

Shotguns in their hands, McAulay and Pierson ran to the west. And while Ferro and Lola Presswood watched the concrete block garage from the corner of the house, Camellion climbed through the window into the office. One eye on the doorway, Camellion darted around a cabinet of instruments and looked through the broken window on the east side.

Men were running from a side door in the garage!

In the meantime, Dominic Bruni and the other patients had thrown themselves flat on the rug in the waiting room, the women sobbing and imploring the Virgin Mary to help them.

Mr. and Mrs. Moretti had reached the kitchen where the seven *Brigatisti*, who had been upstairs, had been enjoying a meal of ravioli, but were now grabbing Bernadelli and Beretta submachine guns.

"They rammed the office window with a car," Bernardo said to Arnaldo Binetelli, who was the leader of the group and was called *"Piccolo* Mussolini" because he resembled the dead Italian dictator.

"They're disguised as Gypsies!" cried Angelina, almost panting from nervous tension. "Kill them! Kill every one of them!"

"We'll butcher those pigs, whoever they are!" Binetelli said fiercely, his black eyes looking around the large kitchen at his force.

"We're going to the cellar and through the tunnel," Doctor Moretti said. He grabbed his wife's hand and motioned to the elderly cook and her helper, both of whom were standing like statues by the sink.

The Morettis and the two cooks hurried to the back door, Bernardo having pulled a Spanish Astra pistol from a holster underneath his smock.

Little Mussolini wiped his bald head and spit out orders to his men, one of whom was a woman. "Three of you make your approach through the music room. The rest of us will move down the hall and go through the dining and living rooms."

"Suppose the police arrive before we kill whoever it is?"

The woman, Elisabetta Sarto, was a stout round-faced Red Brigade fanatic whose only claim to beauty was her waist length luxuriant black hair. She had a large mole on her right cheek and breasts as big as small watermelons.

"They'll all be dead by then," sneered Binetelli, throwing off the safety of a Beretta sub-gun. "Even so, if the going gets rough, we can always take the tunnel and hide below in the ruins." He pointed a finger at three of the terrorists. "You three come with me."

The group split up, Binetalli and three of the men creeping to the left, Elisabetta Sarto and two men going down the narrow hall to the right. All seven paused when they heard the roar of a submachine gun to the east side of the house, followed by the thunderous explosion of two grenades that sounded almost like one detonation.

Standing to the side of the window, the Death Merchant watched the eight men rush from the side door of the garage, some armed with pistols, others with machine guns. He shoved one Auto Mag into a holster, dipped into the bag on his hip and took out an MK3 offensive grenade. He saw another man dart from the rear of the garage and race toward the back of the house. Camellion wasn't concerned. He only hoped that Ferro and Presswood wouldn't get overanxious and open fire before the brigadists were halfway to the house. With the grenade tight in his right hand, he hooked his left thumb through the ring, pulled it and waited.

One of the terrorists must have spotted Ferro or Presswood—or both—looking around the corner. The man jerked up the Beretta in his hands and got off a short burst of 9mm slugs that cut into the stone blocks at the east corner and showered Ferro and Presswood—standing at the corner on the south side—with dust and chips.

The eight *Brigatisti* were two-thirds of the way across the open space when Camellion tossed the grenade out the window, and Ferro, a microsecond after him, flipped a second one around the corner. One thousand and one! The double blast shook loose glass from the already shattered picture windows, cracked all the rest of the windows on the east side of the house and made the ground tremble.

The two grenades—20 ounces of TNT—ripped the eight men apart. Not only did the terrific blasts rip off arms and legs and toss bodies up into the air, but the fragments produced from the serrated wire coil, fitted to the inside of the sheet metal grenade body, ripped like high velocity bullets into the bodies of the men, pinged against the stone side of the house and broke six windows. A few of the metal fragments even shot through the broken picture window on the east side and broke the glass door on a cabinet whose trays were full of dental instruments.

The Death Merchant jerked out the other AMP, looked for a moment at the dismembered corpses on the blood soaked ground, then turned and saw that Ferro and Presswood were crawling through the south window.

Ferro chuckled. "These MK3s are great little noise makers!"

"I gave you half of what we had," Camellion said. "Don't use them unless you have to."

Ready to put a .44 JHP projectile into the first terrorist he saw, Camellion moved across the office to the side of the doorway facing the T-shaped hall. Ferro took a position on the other side. Presswood got to the wall behind Camellion, her eyes going from window to window.

Meantime, McAulay and Pierson had moved a third of the way up the west side of the house, McAulay watching the windows and the balconies on the second floor, Pierson keeping an eye on the windows of the first floor. Pierson was staring toward the northwest corner of the house when he saw a man, running horizontally several hundred feet ahead, stop and swing toward him and McAulay with the Beretta submachine gun. Pierson reacted by throwing himself heavily against McAulay, who was on the outside. While a stream of 9-millimeter slugs hissed by, both men fell heavily against the thick hedge, then fell flat to the grass. They looked up in time to see the man race past a row of empty chicken coops, run to a green and white storage shed, move inside and close the two sliding doors.

"He picked a poor place to hide," whispered Pierson. "That shed is only thin sheet steel. Even pistols could riddle it!"

"I know. It doesn't make sense." McAulay picked himself up and glanced admiringly at Pierson. "Your quick action saved our lives. Thanks, old buddy."

Camellion, Ferro, and Presswood, feeling their hearts pounding, stood and listened. The Death Merchant was the first to hear floor boards creaking, in the room to the north of the hallway. He looked over at Ferro and whispered, "I'm going to surprise 'em. You and Lola come in behind me."

The Death Merchant didn't wait for a reply. He eased out the door, glanced down the long hall, and saw that there was a wide archway that opened to the rooms on the east side of the house. A door to the left opened to the waiting room. Another entrance arch to the right, to the rooms to the west. An alcove in the center of the hall, to the right. Here were the stairs to the second floor.

The Death Merchant moved along the carpeted hall toward the first arch. When Ferro and Presswood slipped out the door of the office, Camellion motioned to the waiting room door and to the alcove and the other archway, but indicated he wanted them to wait until he was inside the first room east of the first arch.

Camellion crept forward along the side of the wall, took a deep breath, then moved through the arch into the living room. He saw at once that he had stuck his head in the lion's den. Four men had just entered the opposite end of the room and were spreading out—*Be damned if one doesn't remind me of Mussolini.*

Used to staring Death in the face, eyeball to eyeball, Camellion was not unduly surprised to find the enemy only twenty feet away. In contrast, Arnaldo Binetelli and the three men with him pulled up short and stared at the Death Merchant, giving Camellion a "two thousand and two" lag time. Four-point-seven seconds was all he needed. He snapped up both Auto Mags, mentally aimed and pulled both triggers simultaneously.

A bullet smacked Antonio Scuba in the center of the chest, tore a hole in him the size of an orange and knocked him back as though he had been hit with a cannonball. The .44 magnum projectile from the left Auto Mag stabbed into Anthony Romero's midriff and threw him against Arrigo Centifisla, who was trying to raise a .38 Llama Martial revolver at Camellion. During the next few seconds, the Death Merchant was diving behind a leather recliner-type chair, and "Little Mussolini" was triggering the Beretta in an effort to stitch him with slugs.

Little Mussolini had been a second too slow. The hot line of 9mm slugs chased Camellion all the way to the back of the chair, several bullets biting at him. One bullet missed the back of his head by less than half an inch; another actually burned the hairs on the back of his neck and tore through the right side of his collar in its passage. But before Little Mussolini could rectify the trajectory, the Death Merchant was down behind the big chair.

Little Mussolini Binetelli, realizing that he was exposed, backed off, ducked behind a heavy armchair and continued to fire short bursts. To his right, Arrigo Centifisla sought the closest protection available: the end of a couch that was against the west wall.

To avoid the projectiles he knew would come, Camellion stretched out flat on his stomach, angry over the loss of time and waiting until the terrorist emptied the mazagine and tried to reload.

The actual blast lasted less than a fourth of a minute, but during those thirteen seconds, full metal jacketed projectiles ripped the leather to shreds, the impact of the slugs creating a small cloud of leather and, eventually, wads of cotton padding. There were subdued ricochets as slugs struck steel springs, and long, low vibratory sounds when springs popped through shredded covering.

The firing stopped. Binetelli yelled at Arrigo Centifisla, "Keep the sonofabitch pinned down while I reload."

As anxious as Little Mussolini to end the standoff, Centifisla tossed several .38 slugs into the half-blown-apart chair. The echo of the second shot was still tumbling around in the air when Camellion did what he had to do, knowing he didn't have time to get to his feet.

He rolled to the right, away from the chair, onto his back, then again to his stomach, and saw Centifisla, who was leaning out from the end of the couch, about to get off another round from the Llama revolver. All in the same moment, Camellion heard the Red Brigadist behind the heavy armchair pull back the cocking knob of the Beretta.

The Death Merchant fired both Backpackers, confident that the .44 projectiles—the most powerful in the world—were capable of getting the job done. They were, even if he had "Dutch loaded"[1] each magazine of each AMP.

A .44 projectile from the left Backpacker struck the bearded Centifisla high in the right chest and spun the doomed terrorist, a turn that would have been a full circle if the dying

---

[1] The cartridges are alternately a hollow nosed bullet, then a metal piercing deal, that is, solid nosed bullet. Or these can be alternated with hollow base wadcutters loaded backward with gas checks.

man's body hadn't been stopped by the couch. Centifisla's face slammed into the end of the arm and that stopped the turn. He fell to his back, unconsciousness dropping over him . . . a deep blackness before the final oblivion.

Little Mussolini was getting ready to lean around the side of the chair and fire the Beretta when the first .44 AMP projectile ripped through the back of the chair and ripped off his right hand, the forefinger of which was inside the trigger guard and resting lightly on the trigger. The severed hand jumped, the finger pulled against the trigger, and the Beretta chattered, five 9mm slugs plowing at an angle into the high ceiling. Little Mussolini never heard the roaring. The Death Merchant's second .44 bored through the chair, hit the half-unconscious terrorist in the chest and, because the projectile was hollow nosed, tore a hole in him as big as a man's fist. The next .44—a solid nosed bullet[2]—hit him in the forehead and exploded his head into a mess of butchered bone, brain, and blood that splattered the floor, the back of the chair and parts of the rear wall. The impact of the projectile was so great that a shard of the parietal section of the skull stabbed into the flowered wallpaper behind the corpse of Binetelli.

Positive that he had sent the two terrorists into infinity, Camellion looked around his playground of death, rolled back behind the shattered recliner and quickly reloaded the two Auto Mags. What were Ferro and Presswood doing? There hadn't been a sound from the other side of the house.

Camellion sniffed the air. The fumes of burnt powder hung in the air as heavily as anvils. Too bad the terrorists couldn't have been trash from Mother Russia! He got to his feet, ran across the room, jumping lightly over two corpses on his way, and moved cautiously into the dining room.

---

[2] A high-speed hollow point bullet provides the best results when it strikes soft tissue. On the other hand, if the bullet strikes bone, a heavier missile is superior, even if it is somewhat slower. This is because a bullet hitting bone breaks off fragments of bone.
These secondary missiles go off in various separate directions, each producing its own separate wound channel and enhancing the destruction. The energy imparted to these bone fragments depends on the momentum—mass times velocity—of the original bullet rather than its kinetic energy which is equal to half the product of its mass and the square of its velocity.

Ferro and Presswood had not been able to move across the archway until the now dead Arnaldo Binetelli had stopped firing the Beretta machine gun. Little Mussolini's first stream of slugs, directed at Camellion, had zipped through the archway and had riddled the door to the waiting room, killing Signora Agnese Zappare and Dominic Bruni, who, trying to escape, were fleeing through the front door behind the other two patients.

When Binetelli stopped firing and dropped down to reload, Ferro and Presswood raced across the archway and the alcove to the right side of the wide opening to the music room. While Lola watched the east end of the hall, Ferro stuck his head around the molding and looked into the music room. He almost got his head blown off!

There were three terrorists in the big room. A burly built garlic-snapper was moving along one side of the baby grand piano, a Spanish Parinco 3R chatter box in his hands. With his long hair and full beard, the freak looked like an angry Jesus Christ dressed up in twentieth century clothing.

The second Red Brigade revolutionary, a clean shaven beefy crud wearing a beret, was six feet to the left of the first man. He held a Heckler and Koch 9mm P9 autoloader in each hand.

The third Brigadist was a dumpy, fat-faced broad with long hair. An Argentine "MEMS" submachine gun in her pudgy hands, she looked as surprised as the other two when she saw Ferro's head pop out from around the side of the arch.

Seeing Ferro, Cristoforo Madda cried *"Porca puttana"*[3] in hate, swung up the Parinco and cut loose, the sound of the exploding cartridges reverberating throughout the large room. The 9mm solid nosed projectiles chopped into the molding on the east side of the archway and caused splinters to splatter in all direction. But not a single bullet came close to Ferro, who had jerked back, belched, and arrived at the grim conclusion that if he didn't act half as fast as a bolt of lightning, the three Brigadists would race forward and blast him and Lola Presswood to that zero point where everything existed in the uncreated. He and Lola might get two of them, maybe terminate all three; yet at such close range, it was a sure bet that the terrorists would also get in killing shots.

[3] "Goddamn it."

"Va a fare in culo"[4] muttered Ferro, then did the only thing feasible under the circumstances. The instant the last slug of the burst slammed into the side of the archway, he threw himself widely to the left. He caught a blur of faces and forms and pulled the trigger of the shotgun as he jerked forward, on his way down to the rug.

The shotgun roared, the 27 pellets of the number 4 buckshot[5] dissolving Madda's chest in a shower of blood, flesh and cloth, and pitching him back with such a violent force that he crashed against a frightened Elisabetta Sarto, causing her to half-fall to the floor. She had gotten only a momentary glimpse of the attacker and deduced that, with her machine gun, she would have a better chance of killing Ferro from the side of the doorway between the rear hall and the music room. Hurriedly she backed off into the doorway.

His own confidence shattered, Ermanno Stefano desperately tried to get off shots with his Heckler and Koch autoloaders. He couldn't react fast enough. While he was trying to line up the pistols with the lone invader, Ferro, half-flat on the floor, pumped the shotgun, pulled the trigger, and belched again. A loud roar, the big slam-bang blast of pellets tearing out Stefano's stomach, picking him up off the floor and pitching him almost to the doorway to where Elizabeth Sarto was raising her MEMS. She was so engrossed in seeing Ferro riddled that she didn't hear George McAulay and Tom Pierson, both of whom had crept up the west side of the house, had sneaked into the kitchen and now were coming in at the other end of the back hall.

"Aw jeepers," said McAulay in a whisper, looking at the back of Elisabeth Sarto. "You're dead, bitch!"

He dropped the barrel of the shotgun and pulled the trigger. The big blast blew Elizabeth Sarto's legs out from under her, and while chunks of bone and flesh and blood slapped the walls and carpet, she flopped sideways, dropped the MEMS, and fell heavily to her back.

---

4 "Screw you!"

5 At close ranges of up to twenty-five yards, number 4 buckshot is a very good combat load. Its twenty-seven pellets increase the hit potential over most other buckshot loads, which have one-third fewer pellets and not much of a pattern at the same distance.

Never in his life had Thomas Pierson seen such fear and astonishment on the face of a human being. The woman's mouth opened and closed, as if her jaws were fastened to rusty hinges. She looked up at the two men and tried to speak, her eyes swimming in shock.

"Arrivederci, puttana,"[6] McAulay said with a smile. Once more the shotgun roared, and the woman's head vanished in an explosion of bloody flesh and numerous pieces of skull bone. Part of her scalp with its long black hair sailed eight feet and fell on top of the dead Ermanno Stefano.

"Having fun, McAulay Two?" The Death Merchant had moved through the east side of the house into the kitchen and had come up behind them.

Camellion and Pierson, their eyes watching the back yard through the windows, waited in the kitchen with Lola Presswood, who kept her Ingram trained on the hallway and the east side kitchen door.

The cook had been preparing spaghetti, and the scent of garlic, parsley and strong peppers, fried in oil, was heavy in the air.

"Moretti and his woman could be hiding in the root cellar," Pierson said. "The cellar doors are just off the back steps."

The wheels of reasoning spun rapidly in Camellion's sly mind.

"You're positive that you and McAulay saw a man run into the shed?"

Pierson's expression of easy amiability faded and his face grew serious. "We're not given to hallucinations," he said, trying to conceal his irritation at what he considered an insult to his mental faculties. "A man went into the shed—period. End of message!"

He turned and looked at McAulay and Ferro who were running into the kitchen.

"They're not upstairs," Ferro said in a half-snarl. "And no place where Moretti and his bitch could be hiding . . ."

"They're not in the house," McAulay said, looking expectantly at the Death Merchant. "Something's going on we should know about."

"Let's have a look at the root cellar," Camellion said. He turned and hurried to the kitchen door.

6   "I'll be seeing you, bitch."

Chapter Eleven

The backyard was as ill-kept as the front lawn was neatly mowed. Other than the empty chicken coops and the seven-by-nine metal storage shed, there was only a lot of weeds, several small elm trees, a pile of red stone used for edging around flower beds, and a rusty wire fence. At one end of the low porch hung a bunch of red peppers. To one side of the cellar doors, tomatoes had been cut in half and spread on a table to dry in the sun.

An Auto Mag in his right hand, the Death Merchant stood to the side of one door, his back to the stone of the house, while McAulay, on the other side, prepared to open the other door. In front of McAulay was Pierson, his shotgun pointed at the slanted doors. Ferro stood next to Camellion. Off to one side, Lola Presswood watched the metal shed and the rear windows of the house. None of them was concerned about the front of the house or the road. Wynn Rockford had backed the Pirelli into the mouth of the lane and was waiting.

McAulay jerked open the door on his side, then jumped back and picked up his shotgun. Camellion reached out, grabbed the top edge of the other door and pulled it open. Wooden steps led down to the dark cellar.

"I wish I had a hot fudge sundae," muttered McAulay. He watched Camellion take an offensive grenade, from which he had removed the delay train and pyrotechnic igniter, and flip it into the dark cellar.

Silence. No wild scrambling. No gunfire. Nothing. The cellar had to be empty. Only the sphinx could have remained passive and quiet in the face of a grenade.

106

The Death Merchant nodded at Ferro and together the two men crept down the steps into the darkened opening. To the heavy frame of the entrance, on Camellion's left, was an old style flip switch. He pushed the switch, and a light, hanging from a twisted cord in the middle of the low ceiling, came on.

The sight was depressing. There were wooden shelves filled with fruit jars full of home-canned food—jelly and preserves of various kinds. Pickles, jars of tomato paste. Tall green bottles full of wine. An old tool chest, lots of spider webs and dank cool air. A large cardboard box rested in one corner.

"It's a cinch the Morettis aren't hiding in the jelly jars," Ferro said in disgust.

Camellion looked at the large box in the corner. "Notice that box? It's not a new box. Yet there aren't any spiderwebs on it. Don't you find that odd?"

Ferro cocked his head curiously at Camellion. "What's the punch line?"

Camellion moved over to the box and gingerly pulled it from the corner. Beneath the box, a metal trapdoor was set in an inset in the stone floor.

There's your whole nine yards," Camellion said triumphantly.

We have them," Ferro said coldly. "We have them trapped down there. Getting them out alive is another matter."

He laid his shotgun on the floor, pulled a pint bottle from his hip pocket, uncapped it, and took three long swallows of brandy.

"Not necessarily," Camellion said, staring at the ring in the top of the trapdoor. He turned to Ferro who was shoving the bottle into his pocket. "Tell you what. Go back upstairs, take Lola's Ingram and riddle that metal shed from top to bottom. Then see if you can find a trapdoor inside the damn thing. Take George or Tom with you."

Ferro's eyes lit up with comprehension. "Ah, so that's it! Okay. I'll be back in a flash—minus the cash."

"Hold it. How's Presswood reacting to this mess?"

"Scared stiff, but doing her job as a backup. I've no complaints."

Ferro turned and went up the steps. The Death Merchant reached down, took hold of the ring and attempted to open the trapdoor. Locked. From the way the side edges moved, there was a single slide bolt holding the door in place.

Presently he heard the Ingram chattering out a full magazine. Camellion watched the trapdoor and waited.

When Ferro returned to the cellar, his sweaty face was glowing with triumph. "You were right," he whispered. "The shed is sitting right down on the ground and there's a trapdoor under an empty wooden box. It's locked. I've posted Pierson inside with the Ingram and gave him a grenade, just in case. Whoever's in that tunnel—no doubt the Morettis—we've got them trapped between here and the escape hatch in the shed."

Camellion reached into the bag on his hip and took out a grenade.

"We can't be sure. There could be another escape route. Personally, I think the whole kit and caboodle is some kind of underground ruins. What went wrong is that McAulay and Pierson weren't supposed to see the man who ducked into the shed. Here, take the grenade."

"Whoever he was, he wasn't the doc," Ferro said, taking the grenade. "It's probably the same coward you saw deserting the others at the garage. Some brave revolutionary!" He looked down at the grenade in his hand. "What do you want me to do?"

"I'm going to blow off the bolt holding the trapdoor. When I raise it, I want you to throw in the grenade and run like hell. I'll be right behind you."

"Wait until I put the shotgun on the steps."

Camellion nodded and took the "Dutch load" clip from the AMP and shoved in a magazine containing only solid nosed bullets. When Ferro returned, stood back six feet from the trapdoor, aimed at the vicinity of the bolt on the other side of the square piece of metal, and fired the first round. There was a roar, a loud PINGGG and a half-inch-diameter hole appeared in the edge of the trapdoor.

He fired three more rounds, each roar deafening, after which he bent over the trapdoor, approaching it from the side opposite to the pull-ring. He grasped the ring, tugged at it, and felt the door raise a few inches. The bolt was free. He glanced at Ferro, who nodded that he was ready and who had kept a distance of five feet between himself and the trapdoor.

Camellion pulled the trapdoor all the way back, jumped to one side and let the square lid clang loudly to the stone floor. Neither he nor Ferro were unduly surprised. when an automatic weapon roared from below and slugs burned upward through the entrance at an angle that forced them to bury themselves in the low ceiling.

All business, Ferro tossed the pineapple into the square hole. He and Camellion could hear the grenade plunk-plunk-plunking down the steps as they darted for the outside entrance. Ferro was picking up the shotgun on the steps and Camellion was in the doorway when the grenade exploded and the doorway to the cellar became filled with smoke and dust. Camellion and Ferro were beyond the steps when they heard a large section of the stone floor cave in and seal the trapdoor entrance.

Camellion took out another grenade, pulled the pin and tossed the ten ounces of TNT down the steps through the cellar door. There was a tremendous roar and a flash of flame and smoke. This time part of the kitchen floor and most of the floor of the back porch caved in, filling the cellar with smoking rubble.

"They won't be coming out that entrance," Lola Presswood said nervously. She held a Hi-Power Browning in one hand, and a pleased Camellion noticed that the muzzle of the weapon was pointed toward the ground.

"Bob, lob an incendiary into the house," Camellion said. "I want to make sure that the *Brigate Rosse* will never use this place again."

He and McAulay and Presswood watched Ferro take a TH3 incendiary grenade from his bag, pull the pin and expertly toss it through one of the open kitchen windows. The grenade exploded with a loud whoosh, the bright blaze of light flaring up like an exploding flash bulb. There wasn't any doubt in anyone's mind that the house would burn to the ground. The thermate filter of an AN-M14 grenade burns for forty seconds at 4,000° F.—a fire so hot that it will burn through a one-half inch homogenous steel plate. The thermate produces its own oxygen and will burn under water.

Camellion took the slim walkie-talkie from his belt, switched it on and held the set close to his mouth. "Rockford, how is everything out front?"

"I haven't seen any police cars, if that's what you mean?" Rockford's voice came back over the set. "But I suggest you get your butts in gear and hurry it up. The chopper landed and is waiting. It came in high, circled and landed from the east, in case you didn't hear it. Anything else?"

"Out," the Death Merchant said. He shut off the walkie-talkie, shoved it into its case and cleared his throat. "Let's get over to the shed."

"They'll never surrender," said Ferro, who was hurrying next to Camellion. "We all know that."

"I'd like to know how we're going to get to the Morettis without killing them?" chimed in McAulay. "If we blow up the trapdoor entrance, they won't be able to get out but we won't be able to get in."

"It's too bad we didn't take some smoke grenades from Rockford and Kolswith," Camellion said reprovingly when they reached the shed that, full of bullet holes, looked like a giant cube of white and green Swiss cheese.

"But we do!" Ferro swung to Camellion. "I picked up three smoke grenades at the safe house. I thought at the time we might be able to use them."

Camellion's smile was from ear to ear. "I knew you were a smart cookie and a piece of good luck. We can use all three."

Ferro swallowed the compliment with another broad grin. "We'll still need a diversion of some kind, and it will have to be a damn good one."

"Opening that trapdoor and dropping straight in would be suicide," warned Pierson. He stood in the doorway, the Ingram in his hands pointed at the trapdoor in the center of the floor.

The Death Merchant motioned for the others to stand back, including Pierson, who picked up his shotgun and handed the Ingram to Lola Presswood.

The Death Merchant carefully put three .44 solid nosed projectiles into the center edge of the trapdoor on the side opposite the hinges. He reloaded the AMP, then motioned for the others to come forward and cover the top of the entrance with their weapons.

Placing a foot on each side of the trapdoor, he reached down, took hold of the ring and, as he moved back, lifted the metal square until the trapdoor was perpendicular to its hinges.

Several submachine guns, or automatic rifles, roared from below, the lines of high powered missiles shooting up through the opening and zinging out through the slanted metal roof. Stepping back, Camellion tugged at the trapdoor and let it fall back to the floor. There weren't any more shots from below. Evidently fearing grenades, the terrorists below had moved back from the entrance.

The Death Merchant got down on his knees and leaned close to the square opening. "We're giving you one chance to surrender, you unfortunate halfwits," he yelled in Italian. "Either you come up right now or we'll bury you down there. What's it going to be?"

"Va a l'inferno!" a man's angry voice floated up from below.

"No, moron brain! It will be all of you who are blown to hell! You have ten minutes in which to say your Hail Marys and ask God's pardon."

Camellion picked up a large stone, about a fourth of the size of a building brick, and flung it through the opening. A few moments later, he and the others heard the stone hit bottom.

"I'd say not more than ten feet," whispered Ferro. "I'd bet my life on it—I probably am!"

"What do we do now?" whispered Presswood, her voice shaking with a fear she was trying to control.

"We create a diversion," replied Camellion with a gratifying sense of achievement. "Tell you what we're going to do. . . ."

The Death Merchant and Ferro, who was carrying the Ingram, left the shed. Ferro went to the northwest corner of the small steel sided building and watched the Death Merchant pace off a hundred feet to the south.

Ferro felt a chill crawl along his spine. A man who feared death but pretended he didn't, he glanced up at the late afternoon sky. The sun seemed enveloped in thin yellowish gauze. Shreds of grayish clouds skimmed across the sky. There would be rain before midnight.

He watched Camellion take out five grenades and place them in a row on the ground, then turn and hurry back toward the storage shed.

To the south, the entire north side of the house was blazing, wood cracking from heat, smoke and flames leaping and racing to the sky. Ferro waited.

Camellion went back inside the storage shed, his eyes going immediately to McAulay and Pierson. McAulay carried the last two grenades in the sack, Pierson the bag of incendiaries.

"A second after those grenades explode, you two get out there," Camellion said. "If you can see below through the crater, drop in a grenade and an incendiary. You got that?"

McAulay frowned in resentment. "We heard you the first time, Richard. We've been through deals like this before together—remember?"

The Death Merchant's gaze softened and so did his voice. "Yeah, you're right, McAulay."

He turned, placed both Auto Mags close to the trapdoor, then picked up an M18 smoke grenade and heard Ferro call out in English, "How about it, Mr. C?"

"Let her rip," yelled Camellion.

"We shall now sing, 'Shall We Gather At The River?'" McAulay whispered solemnly.

Ferro raised the Ingram, looked down the sight painted white, measured the distance, aimed carefully at the end grenade to his left, and made a practiced movement with the SMG—a quarter of an inch to the right. He had to squeeze the trigger, swing to the right and duck behind the shed, practically all in the same motion. Within a microsecond! Or risk getting hit by a fragment! Not likely though because of the distance and because fragments tend to fly upward at a slant.

He made another practice movement.

"On the floor," he said loudly.

"Okay," he heard Camellion's voice from inside the shed.

Ferro aimed, pulled the trigger, jerked to the side of the shed and fell flat.

The blast was so loud that the explosion must have caused people in the south of Rome to look at each other in puzzlement. People in Campagna must have thought that some farmer had plowed into a World War II. shell and touched it off.

There was a bright and brief flash of fire, a wall of wavering dirt, then nothing but a fifteen foot wide crater—an inverted cone, the bottom of which was not quite a foot wide. Very slowly, dirt began to dribble from the center of the bottom area. Soon there was a tiny hole. Dirt began to drop faster and faster. The hole began to expand. . . .

Inside the metal shed, the Death Merchant pulled the ring of the smoke cylinder, tossed it through the trapdoor opening and reached for the two Auto Mags. At the same time, George McAulay and Tom Pierson tore out the door of the shed and ran toward the smoking crater. Jumping up from the ground, Ferro ran around to the front of the shed. He was inside by the time Pierson and McAulay reached the crater and Camellion was dropping through the square entrance in the middle of the floor.

The hole at the bottom of the crater was a yard wide, but the dirt had slackened and was not dribbling as fast. McAulay and Pierson jumped back when they saw the hole, fell flat and reached into the bags beside them. Twelve seconds later, an offensive grenade and an incendiary grenade arched over the crater, fell, and dropped through the hole at the bottom of the crater to the passage below.

The Death Merchant landed on the stone floor on the balls of his feet. He had thrown the canister of smoke at a forward angle, in such a manner that it had landed ten feet in front of where he now stood.

Throwing himself quickly to the right and going into a fighting crouch, Camellion could see only a fluttering wall of violet smoke. Six feet to his rear and fifteen feet on either side of him were large smooth stones of the walls—*By God! Marble! I was right! I'm in the ruins of an ancient Roman temple!* The floor slanted sharply, so that as he approached the wall of smoke and the floor became level, he found that he was twenty feet below the surface of the ground above.

Camellion was preparing to dart through the fluctuating wall of opaqueness when he heard the grenade roar a hundred feet ahead, slightly to his right. With the violent explosion came intense shrieks of agony. He knew why: the offensive grenade and the incendiary grenade had exploded together, and the offensive grenade had scattered the burning thermate over a wide area. A speck of the molten iron was enough to burn right down to the bone, then through the bone!

Thank God, Zeus, Jupiter, Buddha, Brahma, Jehovah, Allah, and Boonbooth, the warrior god of Xernoyxii, for Yoga deep-breathing exercises!

The Death Merchant took a very deep breath and ran through the wall of violet, moving in a crisscross pattern. A blink—and he saw that he had run straight into hell.

He caught a flash of a thirty foot wide chamber lighted by small electric bulbs and built of marble, pink marble. The room was gigantic—four times as long as it was wide. Running down the center of the enormous area was a row of black marble columns, each one of a kind called *cipollino*—"onion"—because of the wave-layer markings on the surface of the polished stone.

Toward the rear, from the direction in which he stood, Camellion saw a low, narrow passage, so low that one would have to stoop to enter it—*The tunnel from the cellar!* Ahead of this opening was a pile of rocks and earth, a narrow beam of sunlight slanting down from the bottom of the crater and half a dozen screaming figures, twisting and turning in a final fandango of death, making wild, frantic motions in an effort to extinguish their blazing clothing. Two more human torches rolled and burned and screamed on the stone floor. Two other blackened forms lay still.

Other men and women were behind wooden boxes and crates to Camellion's right, and among them were Bernardo and Angelina Moretti. The Death Merchant couldn't see their faces clearly, but he did catch sight of their two white smocks. With other *Brigatisti Rossi,* the Morettis opened fire the instant they spotted the Death Merchant, who fired two quick shots as he dove to the cover of a black marble pillar and heard enemy projectiles zinging off the other side of the five foot in diameter pillar. A moment later he heard another familiar sound: an Ingram submachine gun chattering furiously to the left and slightly behind him.

One of Camellion's .44 AMP missiles had missed human flesh. The second solid nosed bullet hit Federico Narni several inches above the right knee and 85 percent effectively ripped off his leg. Yelling, the bearded terrorist went down, blood spurting from the femoral artery and making an unsightly stain on the pink marble wall.

Robert Ferro—careful not to hit the Morettis—triggered off half a magazine, his streams of 9-millimeter missiles buzzing into two men with pistols and a woman firing an Italian BM59 assault rifle. The two men went down riddled across their chests, Isabella de Goldoni collapsing in a shower of blood from her torn out throat.

Camellion, down on one knee behind the black marble column, turned and saw a grimy, hawk-nosed Ferro shoving a full magazine into the Ingram. A rug of black hair showing through the V of his shirt, open to the waist, Ferro was behind an oblong block of black marble. A few feet from each end of the altar was a tall bronze candle holder. Ferro and altar were less than ten feet away.

"I order you to remain upstairs," Camellion said sternly.

Ferro presented the Death Merchant with one of his grins

that resembled a sideways sneer. "I seem to recall that you did. But aren't you glad I'm here?"

"You'd better believe it," conceded the Death Merchant. "Doing the job alone would have been rather Herculean." He coughed. The smoke was spreading and fouling the air, the staleness being increased by the black smoke and stink from the burning bodies, the latter a compound stench of burnt cloth, leather, metal, and what smelled like overdone pork.

"There's eight or ten of them up there," Ferro said with growing impatience. "They're all heavily armed. We don't have much time the way this smoke is drifting. Any ideas?"

There was another blast of slugs against the side of the pillar and the altar. Camellion shifted his thoughts into high gear. The terrorists were maybe forty feet away—*And I still have two smoke grenades.*

"Listen," he called to Ferro, "when I start firing, you scramble over here."

"Okay, but wait a sec!" Ferro finished the last swallow from the pint bottle, then flipped it over the marble altar.

The instant the bottle hit the floor and shattered, the terrorists set up a furious firing, their missiles chipping the sides of the marble altar and sending up an off-key racket of ricochets which the Death Merchant ignored. As flat on the floor as the belly of a bullfrog, he leaned around the right rounded side of the pillar and started firing both Auto Mags, his first round exploding the face of a terrorist cocking a Russian AK54 automatic rifle. A mess of brains and bones splattered the woman next to him as she and the other terrorists dropped to escape the .44 AMP projectiles. One man choked out a cry that would have been a scream if the .44 missile, which had torn all the way through a crate of cotton wadding, hadn't torn all the way through his upper chest and killed him.

By the time Camellion quit firing, the two Backpacker Auto Mags were empty and Robert Ferro was standing next to him by the pillar.

"A soft word turneth away wrath!" Ferro said, shoving a full magazine into the Ingram and cocking the SMG.

"Bless you, Brother." Camellion rolled over on his back, stood up and started reloading the two AMPS.

"I don't suppose we are going to turn the other cheek like the good book says?"

The Death Merchant pulled back the bolt-slide of the left AMP.

"You cover me with the Ingram. Once I'm twenty feet closer, I can toss the last two grenades in their laps. By the time they start choking, I'll be all set to rush in and polish them off, except for the teeth puller and his frau."

"It's a hell of a risk."

"So is crossing the street. Let me know when you're ready."

"Anytime, *amico mio.*"

Camellion moved behind Ferro to the other side of the pillar. Ferro glanced at him and Camellion nodded. Ferro leaned around the pillar on his side and cut loose with the Ingram, firing four-round bursts, the high cracks of the SMG ringing throughout the underground temple which, 2,300 years earlier, had known the lusting shouts of men and women worshipping Liber Pater, the god of fertility and fecundity. Now the temple knew only the Cosmic Lord of Death.

Camellion raced ahead, not even bothering to zigzag. He didn't have the time. He was only six feet from the pillar that was his objective when the Ingram stopped firing and three terrorists reared up from behind crates and carton. By the time they could swing up their weapons, Camellion had the desired pillar between them and himself and Ferro was tossing 9-millimeter projectiles from two Hi-Power Belgian Browning autoloaders.

Trying not to cough, Camellion sneaked a look around the pillar, to his left. The terrorists were less than twenty feet away—to the north—and one of them, a short narrow chested runt, wearing blue jeans and a turtle neck sweater—*And in this heat!*—had crept out from behind a box and actually . . . *Thinks he's going to creep up on me! Bye-bye, stupid! You're all guts but no brains!*

Camellion dropped the muzzle of the Backpacker a few inches, pulled the trigger and the weapon roared. The hard nosed projectile crashed into Peter Strombi's stomach, the slam bang impact lifting him off the floor, doubling him over and sending him crashing against the crate.

Camellion jerked back and pulled the smoke grenade from the clip on his belt—*Damn it, Ferro! Get that chatter box going!* Ferro didn't disappoint him. Once again the Ingram started to chatter, its 9-millimeter missiles sizzling toward the terrorists. Camellion went to the other side of the column, leaned out and tossed the smoke grenade. He had the last grenade off his belt and was pulling the pin when the first one landed and thick blue smoke began pouring out of the four emission holes at the top of the can and the single hole at the bottom.

Camellion threw the second smoke canister from the left side of the black marble pillar. Then, taking a deep breath, he charged forward, prepared to kill and prepared to die.

The two smoke grenades had landed in the middle of the remaining Red Brigadists. Natale Genina had picked up the first smoke canister and had attempted to throw it back at Camellion. All he got for his effort was to get his arm shot off by the keen-eyed Ferro. Genina screamed, blood from his butchered arm falling all over his face. He spun around and the grenade, hissing out thick clouds of smoke, fell several feet from the two Morettis and Giuseppe Marcello, all three of whom were coughing and having great difficulty breathing.

Christian Klar, the West German terrorist, who was a member of the old Baader-Meinhoff gang and who had been hiding out in the below ground temple, had a handkerchief dipped in wine over his mouth and nose, and was somewhat better off than his Italian comrades. He too was caught off guard when the Death Merchant was suddenly in the midst of them.

Peter Paul Bruno got off a shot with a Spanish Largo pistol, but the nine millimeter slug missed Camellion, who had seen Bruno swinging the pistol toward him and had ducked as he blew away Isacco Lotto, exploding the big man's chest with a slug. Lotto fell back and started to go down, falling heavily against a cursing Anna Bonnabertinni, who was coughing and trying to get the muzzle of her H & K 91 semi-automatic rifle in line with Camellion. To her right, Christian Klar, a hardened underground-savvy veteran of a movement pledged to the destruction of all existing institutions, was getting ready to snap off shots from the P-38 Walthers in his hands.

One of the Death Merchant's AMPs roared and Anna Bonnabertinni lost her right breast to the hot, chewing impact of a .44 missile that tore a bloody tunnel through her body. Her corpse sagged, forcing the nimble-footed Klar to jump to one side.

Four of them left! The two Morettis, the blond, no-chin freak wearing an SS officer's belt, and that other joker with black hair down to his shoulders. I don't want to have to terminate them. Four can make like parrots better than two. But only one has to speak!

Camellion fired two shots close to Klar's legs, the scream ricochets making the kraut jump and causing Joe Marcello's slugs to miss the Death Merchant. A 9-millimeter Parabellum projectile hissed by Camellion's left shoulder. Another 9-millimeter missile, from one of Klar's P-38s, tore through Camellion's shirt on the right side and left a burn line on his rib cage. Another shave of a moment and a 9-millimeter bullet from Joe Marcello's Beretta pistol missed the back of Camellion's neck by less than an inch, the chunk of lead tugging slightly at his collar in its passage to failuresville. Sprawled out on the floor, Bernardo Moretti and Angelina Moretti tried weakly to lift their autoloaders between fits of coughing. Neither of them could hardly see and they didn't want to take the chance of shooting either Klar or Marcello.

Camellion executed a high ball of the foot jump and slammed Klar with a snap-kick that wrapped Klar's stomach around his backbone, shook the foundations of his brain and dropped him into unconsciousness.

Joe Marcello, spittle dribbling from his mouth, tried desperately to get off another round from his Beretta. Coughing, he tried to see through the blue haze ahead. Coughing, Camellion landed lightly on his feet, close to Marcello, and the barrel of one Backpacker came down hard against the top of Marcello's right wrist. The Red Brigade leader howled in pain and the Beretta fell from his numb hand. His world quickly exploded into black velvet when Camellion slammed the barrel of the second Auto Mag against his head.

Camellion was on Dr. Moretti before the dentist realized he was the target. One kick and Moretti's Spanish Astra went flying. A second kick—aimed and delivered just so—against Moretti's temple and the man sagged against his wife, who was trying to use the German Luger in her hand. Angelina Moretti felt the Luger jerked from her hand, then the shock of a Backpacker barrel against her chin. Her consciousness snapped off with the rapidity of a light bulb losing its light.

The Death Merchant shoved one Backpacker into a holster and, wracked with a fit of wheezing, stumbled toward Christian Klar, who had been almost totally demolished by Camellion's snap-kick to his gut. Nevertheless, the German terrorist was trying to stand up.

Camellion, moving at an angle toward Klar, made out the

outline of Ferro, who had come in at an angle from the other side and would soon be directly in front of Klar.

"Bob—drop!" Camellion yelled hoarsely.

Fast reflexes saved Ferro's life. He dropped flat a split moment before Klar's right hand touched the top edge of the Nazi buckle around his waist. One section of the buckle snapped open, and there was a loud pop, the sound similar to a child's capgun being fired.

The Death Merchant thumbed on the safety catch of the right Auto Mag, reversed the weapon in his right hand, and threw it by holding the short barrel. He didn't miss Klar. The end of the butt slammed into Klar's upper lip, a smash that knocked out several teeth and pulled the German terrorist almost all the way into dreamland.

Ferro quickly rolled to one side, out of the line of fire, while Camellion raced over to the West German and delivered a karate side-hand chop to Klar's right temple. Out cold, the German sagged against the marble wall.

Camellion, staying to the right of the belt buckle, waited until Ferro was on his feet and standing to the left of Klar.

"Watch," Camellion said. He pressed one edge of the buckle and there were three sharp pops in succession. "Four barrels, the caliber slightly bigger than a twenty-two magnum cartridge."

Ferro, a handkerchief over his mouth and nose, noticed that it was the outside half of the buckle that had snapped open and that the four barrels, one above the other, were horizontal in this top half.

"How about that," said Ferro through the handkerchief. "A buckle that's a gun!"[1]

The Death Merchant picked up the Backpacker he had thrown at Klar and shoved it in a holster. His eyes burned, his lungs ached, and he could taste the phosphorous smoke filler in his mouth.

Ferro pulled the handkerchief from his face and fanned drifting smoke. "What a souvenir!" His excited face fixed itself into almost ecstasy. "Do you want it?"

[1] This device was invented by Herr Louis Marquis, Jr., of Wuppertal-Elberfeld. The Reich Patent Office granted him a patent, for a "cylinder revolver in the form of a belt buckle," on March 7, 1934. Later, Marquis converted the firing mechanism to that of a pistol.

"Take it. I'm going to get McAulay and Pierson, and we'll get these crumbs up to the surface."

With his peculiar talent for finding anything containing alcohol, Ferro had located seven bottles of wine in the temple. He had saved one bottle for himself. The other six he had poured over the four unconscious terrorists, who revived and were forced to crawl through the opening in the shed's floor, then stand against one side of the shed on the outside, their hands on their heads.

Bernardo Moretti had an expression of utter despair on his ugly face. To the south, his house was enveloped in flames and smoke. Within 15 minutes his carefully built dental practice had literally gone up in smoke and the grounds turned into a battlefield. He was convinced that his life and the life of his wife hung by a thread as slim as a hair. He didn't care. His life was wrecked and he wanted to die.

Angelina Moretti didn't try to hold back tears of fear and humiliation. Not that she would have been able to. Irritation from smoke was too great.

Torment from smoke also made rivers of tears flow from the eyes of Christian Klar and Joe Marcello, but from their defiant stance, Camellion was convinced that both men would die before they revealed as little as the day of the month— And there's not room in the car for all these extra people. The weak links in the chain are the tooth puller and his Mama Mia.

"The name 'Babuino' sure fits this dimwit!" McAulay switched from English to Italian and grinned at Doctor Moretti. "Fella, you're so ugly I'll bet when you were born the doctor slapped your mother!"

Moretti hung his head and stared at the ground.

Pierson looked from Klar to the Death Merchant. "You're sure it's him?"

"I don't make those kinds of mistakes in identification," Camellion said tersely, looking at the sullen German whose smoke-smudged face was a mess of dried blood. But Camellion admired him for his pride. Because of the pain in his face—swollen twice its size—and the agony in his gut, it was all the terrorist could do to stand with his hands on his head. But he was determined not to appear weak.

"Klar's poster is all over Europe. He's even wanted in Israel! He's one of sixteen 'super-elites' wanted by the West

120

German police. Go ahead. Tell them, Herr Klar. Tell them in either German, French, English, or Italian. I know you speak all four languages."

"Geh zu Hölle und Küss' mich am arsch!"[2] Klar spit out in German. He stared in hate at the Death Merchant.

Camellion shrugged and smiled broadly. "You'll get to hell before I do, friend. I'm sending you there right now. We don't need you, so *Leben sie wohl, dummkopf.*"[3]

The Auto Mag in his hand exploded, the .44 projectile striking Klar in the center of the chest and slamming him against the side of the shed and making the sheet metal vibrate.

Angelina Moretti screamed, jumped, and began to tremble uncontrollably. Giuseppe Marcello drew back, fear and surprise flickering in his dark eyes. But he instantly regained his composure, as much as was possible under the circumstances.

Lola Presswood turned away and tried not to vomit.

The dead Christian Klar toppled to the ground.

"I just figured out the true value of marriage," McAulay said cheerfully to Thomas Pierson, who was staring down at the dead German terrorist. "It gives a man something to do when his girl friend is out of town."

The Morettis are the weaker of the three. *I'll start with the long haired freak!* Camellion told himself. He turned his full attention to Joseph Marcello.

"I am going to ask you one question just once," he said in Italian. "Where is Maria Gondozatti?"

Marcello, in spite of the agony of his broken right wrist, didn't flinch. Camellion had seen that look time and time again, not the look of a brave man facing death, but the intense stare of a fanatic who would have dared God Himself to do His best.

"Meglio di stare a posto stuo, ed essere contato nell'inferno, invece di essere sconosciuto su i ginocchi tuoi, nel cielo! Sparamii—e sia maledetto!"[4] Marcello said with a sneer.

Camellion shook his head laconically. "Since you want to

2 "Go to hell and kiss my ass."

3 "Goodbye, stupid."

4 "Better to stand up and be counted in hell, then to be an unknown on your knees in heaven! Shoot—and be damned!"

121

join your German crackpot friend, I'll be glad to accommodate you!"

Tilting the barrel of the AMP upward, Camellion was about to squeeze the trigger when Angelina Moretti dropped her arms and flung herself in front of Joseph Marcello, much to the surprise of everyone, including an astonished and angry Joe Marcello.

"*Si ferma! Si ferma!*[5] Don't shoot him!" the woman screamed at Camellion, every muscle of her sweat and smoke smeared face convulsing.

The Death Merchant, on the verge of success, awaited developments. Patience is the companion of wisdom, but not in this case! He had contacted Wynn Rockford by walkie-talkie and had told the CI-nick to let him know the moment he sighted police cars coming down the road from the east, from Campagna.

Ferro laughed. "Lady, you've got your men mixed up! The baboon's your husband!" With the wine bottle in his left hand, he indicated Doctor Moretti, who seemed to be coming out of his trance and was glaring at his wife. Slowly he lowered his hands from his head.

"This man is one of my younger brothers, my youngest brother!" cried Angelina Moretti, her tearful eyes jumping from Ferro to the Death Merchant. "I helped take care of him when he was only a baby. There is no need to kill him."

Joseph Marcello, his embarrassment at being protected by a woman far greater than his fear of death, fastened his hands on his sister's shoulders and shoved her violently to one side, with such force that she almost fell. Angelina caught herself and spun on her brother.

"Tell them, Giuseppe," she begged, her voice rising hysterically. "Tell them or they will kill you!"

"*Silenzio,* woman!" raged Marcello. "I will tell these swine nothing. You will not tell them! We will die, but these pigs will never know where the *Brigate Rosse* is holding their precious saint."

Ho-ho! So she knows too! Camellion wanted to shout Hallelujah! Since she knows, it's a safe bet that her husband is privy to the same vital information.

Nonetheless, he did not squeeze the trigger and blow away

5 "Stop! Stop!"

Joe Marcello. Once the man was turned into a corpse, his sister might decide not to talk, to remain silent out of pure revenge.

Angelina Moretti looked helplessly and pleadingly at Camellion, then at her brother, her mind trapped in a paradox of indecision, between her desire to obey the wish of her brother and her urge to save his life.

"Well, Doc. The joke is on you," chided McAulay. "Your wife wants to save her brother and the hell with you!"

Camellion was about to say *"Arrivederci,"* raise the Backpacker and pretend he was going to put a slug in Marcello, confident that when he did, Angelina Moretti would talk. But it was Doctor Moretti who spoke.

"I will tell you what you want to know," the dentist said bitterly to Camellion. "I will tell you where Signorina Gondozatti is being held a captive. She is on—"

"Figlio di puttana! Keep your stupid mouth shut, Bernardo!"* snarled Costello in a rage. "Once they have the information, they can kill us!" Costello took a few steps forward, but halted when Ferro and McAulay shoved Browning automatics against his body.

"Not necessarily," Camellion said, sighing. "We want the information more than we want blood. But we'll kill all of you if we don't get it."

Bernardo Moretti stared at his wife and shook a finger at the distraught woman. "When death is near the truth comes out!" His voice was as full of malice as his weary eyes. "I know now why you married me—to escape the Trastevere slums. Love me? You slut! You used me!"

His dreadful accusing eyes fastened on Joseph Marcello—so full of hellish fury that Marcello involuntarily flinched. "And you, Giuseppe! You will die with the full knowledge that you and your murderous friends have failed!"

Shaking with fury, the smoke and stink of his destroyed house fresh in his nostrils, Moretti turned to Camellion and shouted, "Maria Gondozatti is at a farm five miles to the northeast of Anzio, at the farm of a Brigadista named Vittorio Salvi Duse."

"Damn you!" screamed Joseph Marcello. "God damn you!"

"A good try, but I don't believe you," Camellion said mildly, although he believed otherwise. Marcello's rage was genuine. No man could fake such fury and malignant disappointment. "The next thing, you'll be 'swearing' to me in the name of your 'sainted mother!' "

McAulay was lightning quick in furthering Camellion's test.

"Yeah, and I'll bet his mamma is alive and as healthy as a horse!"

"My mother has been dead for six years," Moretti said forlornly. "I don't have to swear to anything."

"He is speaking the truth," protested Angelina Moretti, a grain of hope dropping from her voice. "The Saint is at Duse's farm. There's a secret room under the barn and they—" She stopped speaking when the walkie-talkie on the Death Merchant's belt buzzed.

Camellion switched the set to full volume so that everyone could hear, even if they might not like what Rockford had to report. No one did, including Camellion.

"Police cars several miles down the road. I'm pulling out in four minutes. Get your tails over here—now!"

"We'll be there." Camellion switched off the walkie-talkie, shoved the device into its case, glanced at Ferro and said, *"Genickschuss."*[6] Then he turned and started running to the Pirelli in the front yard. McAulay, Pierson, and Presswood, gave a final look at the three Red Brigadists and started to follow as the Hi-Power Browning in Robert Ferro's hand exploded.

Ferro's first bullet hit Joseph Marcello in the chest and pushed him against the side of the shed. The second slug struck a wild-eyed Angelina Moretti, who was throwing up her hands and starting to scream, between her breasts. With a low moan, she slumped next to her dying brother.

Doctor Bernardo Moretti didn't even glance at his dying wife or her body. He only smiled at Ferro who slug-popped him in the chest and walked over to the three bodies as Moretti fell. As if stepping on cockroaches, Ferro matter of factly shot each body twice in the head. He took a long swallow of wine from the bottle in his hand, threw the bottle to one side, and started running toward the car.

---

[6] "Neck-shot," the technique of execution—or murder—made infamous by the German Gestapo during WWII. Such a shot severs the spinal cord and causes death, but not instant unconsciousness. Camellion used the word as a synonym for "termination."

Wynn Rockford stopped the Pirelli in the center of the narrow bridge, picked up a metal cylinder from the seat and got out of the car. He turned the timer on one side of the device to 2-M, placed the cylinder upright on the floor of the bridge, got back inside the vehicles and drove forward.

Moving at 60 miles per hour, the Pirelli was almost to the Camaldolese monastery when the cyclonite cylinder exploded and destroyed the bridge.

The Italian police would have to walk.

Many of the monks were outside their cells, staring toward the direction of the blasted bridge and at the billowing column of smoke, to the west, climbing skyward. They stared in fear at the Pirelli as it raced past and Rockford headed for the wheat field.

"How are we going to rescue Gondozatti without getting her killed?" McAulay lit a cigarette.

"I don't know," Camellion said simply.

"They can kill her before we can even get under way," Pierson said. "The news of what we did back there will be all over Italy within several hours. The Italians are big on television news."

Very soon, Rockford was turning the car into the clearing by the side of the wheat field, the tires screaming and skidding on loose rock and maquis scrub.

There sat the helicopter, a hundred feet out in the field, the ten passenger craft painted white, red, and green, the colors of the Italian flag. The three rotor blades were feathering.

Rockford slammed on the brakes and parked the Pirelli next to the Dodge. "Camellion, get your people on the chopper," he said. "Larry and I will take care of the cars."

The CIA pilot had lifted off, and the helicopter was at 340 feet when the explosive devices in the Dodge and the Pirelli exploded and scattered flaming junk all over the hot countryside.

The pilot sent the chopper upward, wanting to reach a twelve thousand foot level. The Death Merchant didn't wait. He opened the suitcases and glanced around. "Let's get changed and"—he looked at Lola Presswood and grinned a twisted smile—"don't get excited, doll. I've seen women in bra and panties. So have the others. If they hadn't, they wouldn't be here."

Reaching into one of the leather suitcases, McAulay chuckled and looked up in amusement at a poker-faced Lola Presswood. "And if you've never seen a man in shorts—golly, what you've missed!"

Lola did not comment. She didn't even feel embarrassed when she slipped out of the colorful Gypsy clothing and exchanged it for blouse and slacks. She was too emotionally drained. She had seen the most violent side of international intelligence operations, and she hadn't enjoyed the sight. She told herself again that the terrorists hadn't been murdered. Why, Christian Klar alone was responsible for scores of brutal murders, including a busful of Israeli schoolchildren. The terrorists had been executed; the terrorists had been killed because of sheer necessity. Yet she was still sickened at the way Camellion and Ferro had "terminated" the terrorists. *Terminated?* A stupid word! Why didn't they say *kill* and be done with it? One might as well call a grave robber a "resurrectionist!" She supposed that men like Richard Camellion—and even that vulgar Ferro—were necessary in a world that was only a sugar-coated slaughter house . . . men who were self-contained, men who needed nothing or no one and who would always be alone, even in a crowd. Without such men—would there be a United States of America?

Larry Kolswith came out of the control compartment, closed the small door and stumbled his way to the Death Merchant, who was buttoning a sky-blue sports shirt.

"I have news," Kolswith whispered in a low voice, yet loud enough for the others to hear. "About ten minutes ago the Red Brigades blew up several rooms on the third floor of our Embassy. They used some kind of rocket."

"Casualties?"

"Four secretaries. Essential personnel were not touched. Ambassador Trentham was at the Italian Trade Ministry when the rocket hit. And his family is safe."

"Another score for us to settle," Ferro said savagely.

"There's also a special message for you at the S-house," Kolswith said to Camellion.

"No doubt more bad news," McAulay commented, fastening his belt. He then reached for a rag and the solution bottle to wash his face and hands. "All we need now is to have Maria Gondozatti's corpse dumped in the middle of St. Peter's Square. . . ."

Chapter Twelve

By eleven hours of the following day, the plan had been completed, except for minor details. Conrad Derstine had assured the Death Merchant that the *USS Lafayette,* a submarine of the Trident class,[1] would be in position, fourteen miles west of Anzio, from twenty-three hours to zero-two hours. Yet no one was very enthusiastic about the special operations mission that, hopefully, would free Maria Gondozatti from the *Brigate Rosse* . . . no one, including Richard Camellion.

The main reason for the gloom was that the saintly mystic might be already dead and the probability that, if she were still alive, the terrorists would kill her the moment they realized they were under attack. There were other reasons, the origin of which lay in the message that Derstine had received the previous afternoon. Someone had told the brand new Italian intelligence agency that the American CIA was responsible not only for the deaths of Vito Camerini and the "West German" agents found dead with him, but also for the murders of Alfredo Bertini and the four Italian policemen at the roadblock on the Grande Raccordo Anulare, the "Ring

---

[1] The Trident submarines are armed with Trident missiles and represent the ultimate in American undersea weaponry. The Trident submarine is America's third generation of nuclear-powered boats. With a length of 560 feet, the Trident Class is 135 feet longer than the previous Poseidon subs. The Trident travels faster, runs quieter and can stay at sea longer than previous "boats."

Road." It was only logical that the Italians would believe that the CIA was also responsible for the shoot-out and burn-down outside of Campagna, even though the papers and the TV newscasters were saying that the destruction was the work of "Left wing terrorists."

Fortunately, the Italian government had not lodged a formal complaint with the U.S. State Department. Nor had the Italian press hinted at CIA involvement. Derstine had obtained the information from one of his agents—a plant—in the Italian intelligence service. As it was, the Italians were worried about the complaints of Ambassador Trentham, who demanded more and better protection for the U.S. Embassy— and the reason why the Italian police couldn't keep their home-grown terrorists under control.

Derstine's communique had also contained a report regarding Paul Campanella. The man had left his place of employment to go to lunch. He had not returned to the paint store and it was believed he had been kidnapped. By the KGB? Who else could have done the job? Who else could have tipped off the Italian intelligence service?

The clincher was that until Camellion and the CIA had proof that the KGB had put the grab on Campanella, they could not be positive about Marsilio Riggio. It was this not knowing, this uncertainty, that bothered Camellion and the people around him.

Riggio would keep. Maria Gondozatti would not.

Derstine had had more bad news—strictly personal for the Death Merchant. Part of Camellion's agreement with the CIA was that, while he was "in the field," the Agency would inform him of anything that might touch his personal life in the U.S.A. And something had, a week before. A close friend of his had been found murdered in Colorado. Retired, Everett Padden had been a professional deprogrammer for parents whose children had run away from home to become members of a "religious" cult.

Camellion was positive that Everett's last case—*He told me, only a week before I left the States*—involved the Universal Church of the Cosmic Reality, one of the largest cults in the United States. The sinister organization was controlled by a freak of nature known as the Rev. Hannibal Nigel Frimm, or as the brainwashed members of the cult referred to him, "His Oneness," and "His Onlyness."

The Universal Church of the Cosmic Reality had its national headquarters in Colorado. . . .

The Death Merchant knew that when he returned to the United States, he would have to find the murderer, or murderers, of Everett Padden. The worst boss anyone can have is a bad habit, and Camellion had a boss that was an absolute dictator—a passion for justice.

God help Hannibal Frimm and his damned goofy 'Frimmies' if I find they are responsible for Everett's death. 'Cosmic Reality?' Bunk! If they murdered Everett, there'll be a 'Cosmic Reality Kill!'

First things first.

Camellion shook off his disconsolate thoughts of Padden, sat up on the couch and looked at McAulay and Tom Pierson who were seated at a bridge table, McAulay teaching Pierson to play *sette e mezzo*, a popular card game.

"George, are you sure that the white suits will be delivered in time?" Camellion cleared his throat and stretched lazily.

"No later than one this afternoon," McAulay said confidently, all the while studying the seven card spread in his hand. "Kolswith is making the buy and he and Rockford are damned efficient."

"Those two aren't such hotdogs," said Ferro from across the room. "They were as nervous as the rest of us when that chopper came down on the cemetery grounds. After we switched cars and Rockford was driving, he made a wrong turn. An expert would have had that 'get-route' down pat."

Ferro, sitting on the floor, his back against the side of a captain's chest bar, resumed polishing his favorite weapon in hand-to-hand combat—a twelve inch long, handwrought stainless steel letter opener, its blade as sharp as a razor.

"At least we won't have the 'Iron Virgin' with us tonight," McAulay remarked cynically." He frowned when Pierson discarded two cards and grinned slyly at him.

"She was pretty good under fire," Ferro said, rubbing a rag back and forth across the blade of the highly polished letter opener. "She didn't make mistake one."

Camellion said, "Presswood's trouble is that she lets her morality get in the way of common sense. She belongs behind a desk, not out in the field."

Tom Pierson spread the rest of his cards face up on the table and regarded McAulay with a look of triumph. "George, it's all over. Unless you have a couple of aces up your sleeve?"

"Holy marimbas!" McAulay threw down his cards in good natured disgust. "I should have had more sense than play cards with a psychologist in the F.I.D." He looked over at the Death Merchant who had left the couch, was sitting on a flip-top footstool, and was spreading a map on the rug.

"Let's get organized," Camellion said, "and plan the final route."

The three men gathered around the map, which had a conic projection scale of 1;4,000,000 1 inch = 63 statute miles.

"Anzio is only thirty miles south of Rome, or about forty-eight kilometers as they say over here," McAulay said. He was stretched out on his stomach, his chin braced on his folded hands. "At least we won't be on the road very long. Just a leisurely drive."

"Not necessarily," interposed Ferro. "We could be stopped by the police at a roadblock. If the police don't think our Vatican passports are genuine and search the car, we'll be in hot water up to our armpits when they find the rockets and other equipment in the truck."

"We'll simply have to neutralize the police, should it come to that," said Pierson. "Of course, if we do that and we're still miles from Duse's farm, we could have a serious problem."

"You said it!" laughed McAulay. "Like the police catching up with us before we could get there."

Ferro passed a hand over his brow, glanced at McAulay, then grabbed the Death Merchant with his gaze. "We can't afford to be complacent," he said decisively. "The Italian secret service boys aren't all that dumb." He tapped a dozen or so large photographs that lay next to the map. "Duse's farm and its location is based on these photographs. How can we be sure the photographs are accurate?"

"Good point. Good point." McAulay agreed, sitting up. "I'm not too enthusiastic about putting our lives on the line merely on the say-so of aerial photography experts. If we hit the wrong farm, we won't get a second chance at the right one." He reached out and picked up one of the photographs that, taken at zero-one hours that same morning, was the product of a high resolution infrared camera. The photographs had been taken from a plane flying at eight thousand feet.

"But you have to admit that Derstine has a very efficient organization here in Rome. To have obtained those photographs so quickly and rushed them over to us—that's efficiency."

"Assuming the ground men didn't tip the pilot and the photographer to the wrong farm." Ferro ran the blade of the sharp paper knife through thumb and forefinger. "The hell of it is, we won't know until we get there." He looked to Camellion for some kind of support, but Camellion said without hesitation, "You're rowing up the wrong river, Bob. Derstine had the farm checked out, the same farm that was photographed. Vittorio Duse lives there. Derstine even sent us a rundown on the man. You know that. Duse's in his thirties and inherited the farm from his father."

"There aren't any guarantees, except about death and taxes," McAulay said with resignation. "Death is certain and taxes will rise."

"I can think of lots of things that could go haywire," Camellion went on. "The Impulsizer might not function. For that reason we're taking two of the devices with us." His tone became heavily jocular. "Tell you what, Bob. Why not worry that the pilots from the *Lafayette* might land at the wrong farm, or that one of the mini-helicopters might stall and crash in the Tyrrhenian Sea after we're lifted out? Or the sub's not even getting to the right coordinates?"

"Yeah, you're right, Mr. C.," Ferro conceded readily with a slightly shame-faced grin. "We've got to work with what we have. What time do we leave tonight?"

"Around twenty-forty-five hours," Camellion said. "I estimate it will take an hour to get through inner city traffic and out to the highway. If we get ahead of schedule, we'll stop along the way and kill time in some *trattoria*."

"The actual attack," Pierson said. "What's the time estimate?"

"Thirty minutes maximum," Camellion told him, sounding as if he were deliberating. "There's an army garrison about thirty miles to the east of Duse's farm and—"

"Forty-eight kilometers," thrust in McAulay.

"We can expect those fumble-bumbles to come calling when the racket starts, which will be with the first rocket. Before they get there, we'll have to rescue the hotline-to-heaven, get to the choppers and scram to the sub."

131

"What tactics do we use to keep her captors from blowing her away before we can get to her?" Ferro spoke with disarming frankness.

"We don't." Camellion was also blunt. "There aren't any we can use. I'm gambling that they won't have the nerve to kill her."

Tom Pierson stared at the Death Merchant with mute disbelief.

"God works in mysterious ways, but this is ridiculous!" McAulay said dramatically, his gaze searching Camellion. "The Brigades set bombs, rob banks, and kill anyone who gets in their way? So why shouldn't they pepper one old woman with slugs?"

Ferro said deferentially, "Bull and bunk! A man like you doesn't gamble with those odds, Mr. C. What's the gimmick?"

"Belief in the supernatural," Camellion said briskly. "Line up ten members of the *Brigatisti* and you'll find nine Catholics, men and women who've been a part of the church since the day they could walk." He glanced at Pierson. "As a psychologist, you know that a person continues to be a "prisoner" of his early childhood training, more or less. I don't think the Brigadists will kill her. I don't think they'll want to risk the wrath of God by blowing away one of His saints."

Pierson seemed undecided. Finally, he said, "Psychologically, your theory is half-sound. But"—he sighed—"who can say for sure. Terrorists have different motives. The Palestinians are supposed to be fighting for their 'homeland,' a homeland that didn't even exist before the Israelis took over. The Palestinians are really fighting because they believe in anti-Semitism."

"The Red Brigades are just as crazy and stupid," Ferro said.

"But with a difference. Many of the Red Brigadists come from upper-class families. In this respect, their acts of violence can be regarded, in part, as a reaction against their parents' preoccupation with materialism in rebuilding a war-ravaged Europe."

Disgust dropped over Ferro's face. "Bullshit! Analyzing the 'why' doesn't solve the problem. Bullets do. A dead terrorist is an ineffective terrorist."

"At least there's one thing we can count on," offered Mc-

Aulay. "There's going to be a hot time outside of Anzio tonight."

The Death Merchant smiled.

"A real barn-burner, like we say in Texas. . . ."

Chapter Thirteen

It was the Death Merchant's uncanny talent with cosmetics and Tom Pierson's acting that saved Camellion and his four men at the two roadblocks.

The Lancia was first stopped by Italian army troops outside of Locatto, a small hamlet seven miles south of Rome. While members of the squad kept their Beretta machine guns trained loosely on the car, a Lieutenant, accompanied by a Sergeant, approached the Lancia on the driver's side. In a respectful voice, the Lieutenant asked Camellion, who was the driver, for identification— "And may I inquire where the good Fathers are going?"

"Certo,"[1] Camellion replied politely. He took the Vatican passport booklet from the inner right breast pocket of his white coat, handed it to the Lieutenant and waited patiently, grateful that the safe house had been equipped with a photographic laboratory. Derstine had sent blank passport books. The Death Merchant had then made up each man's face, including his own, after which all of them had dressed in white suits, Roman collars and black bibs. Their photographs had been taken and the photos pasted into the Vatican passport books.

The Lieutenant, a young man with long sideburns, looked at the photograph in the book and the name *Reverend Louis E. Harengs,* of the Abbey of St. Benedict, near Antwerp. The Italian army officer looked at Camellion. Yes. The same face, the face of a man in his sixties. The Lieutenant leaned

---

[1] "Certainly."

134

closer to the window and peered at Robert Ferro, who sat in the front seat next to Camellion. "Father Monnaie" smiled tolerantly and held out his Vatican passport.

The Lieutenant looked at the three "priests" in the back seat—McAulay and Wynn Rockford on each end, Pierson in the middle. Pierson sat with his neck bent so far to the right that his ear touched his shoulder. His right arm was pressed against his chest, as if frozen, the fingers of the hand stiff and clawlike. His hair was snow white, his skin wrinkled. To all appearances, he was an old man in his eighties.

"What is wrong with the priest in back?" inquired the Lieutenant.

"Monsignor Glauert is partially paralyzed," Camellion said sadly. "He suffered a stroke a few years ago. He cannot speak. The Monsignor wanted to visit the abbey on Monte Cassino once more before he passes on to the judgment of our Lord."

Lieutenant Gibolda nodded in understanding. "Then you are on your way to Cassino, Father Harengs?"

"Yes, my son. We are most anxious to get there. Monsignor Glauert hid out for some time at the abbey during the war, hiding from the evil Nazis who would have executed him for helping the Belgian underground. But I am curious. Why are you and your men guarding this highway?"

"Terrorists, Father. We cannot be too careful. Only yesterday, terrorists murdered a number of people, including a dentist and his wife. They burned his house to the ground."

"How terrible!" Camellion pretended shock. "But surely, young man, you do not think we're terrorists?"

"Of course not, Father." With an embarrassed smile, Lieutenant Gibolda returned Camellion's passport. "Please proceed, Father, and have a pleasant journey. *Buona notte*, Father."

"God bless you, my son. *Buona notte*, Lieutenant."

The second stop was several miles to the north of Anzio. This time the car was halted by members of the Stradisti, the Italian equivalent of the American state police. The officer in charge was very polite but, more thorough than the Italian army lieutenant, insisted on inspecting all five Vatican passports; and even Camellion's heart skipped several beats when the officer asked if anything was in the trunk of the Lancia. At the time, Stradisti were on both sides and in front of the

car. For Camellion and the other men to have reached fo
weapons would have been tantamount to suicide.

"Si, our luggage," Camellion said, matter-of-factly. "Woul
you like to inspect the trunk, although I assure you we d
not have any terrorists hiding in our suitcases."

"I don't think you have either, Father," the officer said
smiling. "Please pardon our stopping you. We are only doin
our duty during these troubled times. Have a pleasant sta
at the abbey—and are you sure of the route? After you leav
Anzio, take the road that leads to the east. Cassino is onl
forty kilometers east of Anzio.

Camellion nodded. *"Grazie e buona notte."*[2]

The policeman touched his fingers to his cap. *"Buon
fortuna, Padre."*[3]

Once again they were in the clear, the car headed towar
Anzio.

"We're forty-five minutes ahead of schedule," Robert Ferr
said to Camellion. "I think we should stop in Anzio an
have a drink."

"Are you telling us you didn't bring a bottle with you?"
joked "Father Belgoin" with mock seriousness.

"Whether I did or didn't is none of your damned business
Rockford," growled Ferro, in no mood for jokes. "But w
are ahead of schedule, and we sure as hell can't pull off th
road and just sit."

"We'll stop on the south edge of Anzio," Camellion said.

Half a mile to the south were the lights of Anzio. Th
night was warm and muggy despite the strong sea wind blow
ing in from the west, from the Tyrrhenian Sea, that hug
body of water between the west coast of Italy and the eas
coasts of Corsica and Sardinia.

Other than the possibility that the *Brigate Rosse* might hav
killed Maria Gondozatti, or moved her to another locatior
Camellion was also worried about the weather. During th
afternoon the sky had been bare except for cirrus clouds
those thin wisps of high clouds blown into streaks by th
strong winds of high altitudes.

Gradually the sky had changed and thicker and lowe

2 "Thank you and goodnight."

3 "Good luck, Father."

136

clouds had moved in from the west. Now the air had become too humid for the water-vapor from aircraft engines to evaporate, so that vapor trails became persistent.

Slowly the heavy clouds had been replaced by rain clouds, which raced across the face of the white moon. Below the wide cloud base there were broken-up bands of even lower clouds. These indicated the real danger, for such a cloud pattern was often the forerunner not only of rain but of gale force winds, winds that would make the Bell YAH-63A helicopters impossible to control.

Those three choppers are our only lifeline to the sub. . . .

Traffic was not too heavy on the main thoroughfare of Anzio, and it didn't take long for Camellion to reach the south end of the town. Finally he parked fifty feet past an *osteria* housed in an ancient brick building whose facade was of Gothic design, and he wondered how the old pile had escaped the severe air and coastal bombardment of Anzio during World War II.

"Slip your autoloaders under the seats," Camellion ordered crisply. "In the light, one can detect the bulges."

Ferro leaned over and shoved a Hi-Power Browning under the front seat, saying, "Aren't you coming?"

"I'm staying with the car," Camellion replied. "All we need is for some punk to try to steal this heap. And I want to look at the map. Don't stay longer than a half hour . . . that's the max."

While the four men went inside the *osteria,* Camellion removed the map from his coat, spread it out on his lap and, with the aid of the glow from a nearby street light, studied the section of the map in the general vicinity of Vittorio Salvi Duse's farm. Earlier, that morning of the same day, CI-nicks had gone over the route very carefully and had made the map. Conrad Derstine had sent the map to the safe-house.

Camellion looked closely at the map. There was the main highway south of town. Two miles outside Anzio, the highway formed a Y, one section moving along the coast to the south, the other arm turning to the east. Camellion traced his finger along the line that branched to the east. He soon found what he wanted: a blue line that was the dirt road cutoff. There was a red X marked at the beginning of the dirt road and the penciled notation: *Turn off here. Follow blue line to next red X.*

The blue line moved to the north, then curved to the northeast. He found the next red X., and next to it: Stop here. A blue line and a red line, side by side, led from the X to a large green circle. Inside the circle were the word's *Duse's farm. Distance from last X to farm, 350 feet. Also: 3.6 miles from first red X, or turnoff point from main highway.*

Camellion folded the map and put it back into his pocket. Either the map was right or it was wrong. "I'll soon know!" he told himself.

Eighty minutes later, Camellion and the four men with him knew that the map was correct, the proof being in the farm they were passing. While Camellion drove at a moderate speed, Ferro and Rockford looked at the house and out buildings in the distance through infrared night sight devices and mentally compared what they saw with the photographs the CI-nicks, who had followed the same route, had taken that morning.

"No doubt in my mind." Rockford was the first to give his opinion. "It's the same layout in the photographs."

McAulay joked, "Now all we have to do is grab a plane to check out the pix made from the plane. One thing about Derstine, he covers every angle."

"It's Duse's place," Ferro said. "Let's just hope the Red Brigades haven't moved Maria what's-her-name."

"Or killed her," added Pierson. He said in a louder voice "We'll want to park as close to the farm as we can, won't we?"

"We'll park where the car can't be seen," McAulay said in a serious tone. "If we park too near the road and one of the Brigatisti, staying at the farm, comes in from the west and saw the car, he'd wonder what it was doing there. This isn't exactly 'lovers' lane' country."

The Death Merchant said, "According to the map, there's a field of rye half a mile to the west, but the map has to be wrong."

Surprised, Ferro swung around to the Death Merchant. "Well now, the map's been right so far. If you're worried about cover, there are plenty of trees to the west and north of the farm. We won't have any trouble sneaking in. Hell it's as black as a whore's heart over there."

"But why is the map wrong?" Pierson asked, directing his question at the Death Merchant.

"Rye can be planted in the fall or the spring," Camellion

138

explained. If Duse planted his rye in the spring, it would already be cut. Fall planting is in September."

"There must be something in that field!" McAulay declared firmly. "Or the CI-nicks would have marked it 'empty' on the map, or 'barren' or something."

Camellion turned the Lancia around a curve and there was the field, to the left. Camellion slowed and looked at the spikelets waving in the wind . . . rippling brown waves, three to four feet high.

"It's timothy!" There was a titillating quality to the Death Merchant's voice.

"What the hell is 'timothy'?" growled Ferro.

"Hay. Those other CI-nicks didn't know the difference between timothy hay and rye."

Pierson, who had turned and looked out the rear window, said, "I can't see the farm house from here."

Ferro had picked up the nightsight device and was looking out across the field. "Lots of trees on the other side of the field. Ash and maples. I estimate the distance from rear to trees to be from 365 to 400 meters."

"Let's say a quarter of a mile." Camellion turned out the headlights, stopped the car but kept the engine turning over. The road, in both directions, was deserted. "I'll make sure the ground in the field isn't muddy. It could have rained around here earlier in the day."

He got out of the Lancia, taking care not to slam the door, moved around the front of the car and went into the field. He walked twenty feet through the hay, bent down and felt of the ground with his fingers. The ground was dry.

He hurried back to the car. "This place is as good as any," he said, getting the car under way.

"Have you thought about how the tires are going to leave wide paths through the hay?" asked Ferro.

"We'll have to risk it." The Death Merchant gathered speed, said "Hang on," and started turning the wheel to the right, his foot pushing down on the gas. The Lancia bounced as it crossed the four foot wide depression between the edge of the road and the edge of the field; then the front of the car was pushing aside the hay and the vehicle started across the dark field.

The Death Merchant parked in an area that was shielded on the east and the south by white birch and chestnut trees whose trunks were decorated with the intensely fragrant pink flowers of trailing arbutus.

There was little conversation. The five men got out of the car. Camellion unlocked the trunk and he and Ferro took out heavy suitcases. The men exchanged their white suits for forest-patterned night-cover camouflage suits. Belts with holstered 9mm Brownings were strapped on and the walkie-talkies were attached to belts. They slipped the straps of canvas bags, filled with fragmentation and incendiary and tear gas grenades, over their shoulders. They attached gas masks to their belts and checked Ingram submachine guns. There were also two M16 rifles, to which were attached grenade projection adapters, and two bags of M31 Heat Rifle grenades.

"The *Lafayette* should be in position," Pierson said, completing the check of his Ingram. "My watch says eleven-fifteen."

The Death Merchant opened another suitcase, and lifted out an FM battery operated radio receiver and transmitter known as an AN/PRC-6vs, the last two letters a designation that a voice scrambler was a part of the short-range communicator.

While the men finished checking their kill-equipment, Camellion put on the headset, extended the antenna, switched on the set and picked up the mike. "Dove-2 calling Eagle-1. Dove-2 calling Eagle-1. Dove-2 calling Eagle-1."

The reply from the *USS Lafayette,* from the Agency case officer on board the sub, who was acting as coordination officer, was instantaneous. Affirmative: the three small helicopters could be assembled, lifted topside within half an hour. Affirmative: the three choppers would take off and land in accordance with Camellion's instructions.

"Transmit those instructions."

"I'll place two Impulsizers several hundred feet south of where we parked the car. The pilots should not have any difficulty homing in on the devices. I'll set them at full beam strength. Time check, please."

"23.22 hours."

"At 24.15 hours have the helicopters take off. We should be back here at the assembly point by the time they land. If we're not, have the pilots wait no longer than half an hour. Weather check."

"High winds expected in several hours, maybe sooner. Do you wish to cancel the operation?"

"Negative."

The Death Merchant put the radio back into the suitcase and returned the suitcase to the trunk of the car. He took the two Impulsizers from the trunk, carried them an estimated 150 feet to the south, got down on his haunches, and switched on the devices. He next raised the tiny face plates in each device and looked at the tiny red bulbs. Fine. The bulbs were blinking. Each Impulsizer was working. The Impulsizer was a very sophisticated omnidirectional range station, by means of which an aircraft could obtain omnibearings by homing in on the on-course signals generated by a special shunt-fed oscillator.

Camellion closed the face plates, put the two Impulsizers on the ground, and hurried back to where the men were waiting, the two Auto Mags bouncing against his legs as he ran.

"I'm not exactly enthused about how the wind is rising," Ferro said. "All we need to screw us up is a good blow."

"I never think of failure." Camellion slung the sling-strap of an M16 over his left shoulder, and the strap of a bag, filled with M31 HEAT rifle grenades, over his right shoulder. Each grenade weighed 25 ounces, and there were ten of them in the bag.

He picked up an Ingram machine gun and said cheerfully, "Let's go do it."

They moved in a southeast direction, over ground that was rocky, craggy in places, hostile everywhere, and filled with trees and various kinds of vegetation—all this a part of Duse's farm that had never been under cultivation.

Now and then they came to large man-cut stones which formed parts of crumbling walls or what had been a pavement at one time—ancient ruins, wrapped in the moss and ivy of time and ignored by archaeologists.

Halfway to the rear of the farm house and the other buildings, they skirted a large one hundred foot square area that had been, perhaps, an ancient marketplace. But only the paving stone and the stones of half-walled buildings remained. A few tall pillars still remained upright, vines twisted like green snakes around them. Other once stately columns lay broken in the square, in the center of which was a large fountain.

Only ghosts remained, pale phantoms of memory mouthing

141

silent screams. It was almost as if one could hear the echoes from that time when the marketplace was filled with people and vendors were selling their wares.

But now there were only ghosts and broken stones, with the hollow moan of the wind searching through the emptiness, an eerie and mournful sound, nature's dirge to the distant past and dead gods.

"I suppose you know we're doing the job you psychologists should have done?" Ferro poked Pierson playfully in the ribs.

"You're half right," Pierson said. "The company was going to send three parapsychologists to study Maria Gondozatti. But the Red Brigades beat them to the punch."

"Hey, look there!" McAulay whispered. "We're coming to an orange grove."

The five men passed through the small grove, brushing against trees whose oranges were chunks of gold the size of linebackers' fists. They had adjusted their sight to the darkness and could see that ahead lay a field filled with natural outcroppings of rock, some trees and small grass.

Camellion out in front, they crept across the field and moved as close to the farmhouse as they could, taking positions behind some rocks that were close to a clump of wild motherwort. The farm was less than 250 feet to the southeast. The only sounds were crickets in the distance, the croaking of bull frogs from a pond a mile to the west, and the cry of the wind.

"That bird Duse has a nice looking place," commented Lynn Rockford, who was studying the farm through an infrared night sight device. "It's well kept and prosperous looking. Here, Camellion." He handed the night-score to the Death Merchant. "See for yourself."

Camellion saw. The large two story farmhouse was covered with brick-siding. To one side of the house and behind the front section was a large patio with a fountain in the center. Camellion could see a large pigpen, what could have been a tool shed, a few other outbuildings, and the barn. At one end of the barn was a silo. The east side of the barnyard was fenced in, and there were horses within the enclosure. Tall oaks were scattered around the house.

"It's a big baby, that barn," Ferro said. "I figure a hundred-feet-by-sixty-feet. Did you notice, it's made of concrete blocks. That's something for Italy. Hell, that would be a nice barn back in the States."

142

The Death Merchant put down the nightviewer and slipped the strap of the M16 and the strap of the bag of rockets from his shoulders.

"There isn't much logic in all of us staying here while the house is blasted. Ferro, you and I will slip to the barn. Once we're there, the others can blow apart the house, then join us. You and I can set up cover fire."

"We'll save time that way," Ferro agreed, glancing up at the dark sky. He started taking off his M16 and the bag of rocket-grenades.

The Death Merchant glanced at the three other men. "Okay. Who wants to be a rocket man?"

"I don't even want to be here," McAulay said lazily. "But I was in Vietnam and know how to use a launcher." He reached out and took the M16 and the bag of rocket-grenades from Camellion.

"I was in 'Nam, too," Pierson said amiably, taking the rifle and grenades from Ferro. "I can level that house if you want me to."

"What I want you both to do is to blow the ground floor out," Camellion said. "Once enough of the first floor has been demolished, the rest of the house will cave in. Another thing, save six or seven grenades for Italian Army vehicles—just in case."

"Leave your walkie-talkies open," Ferro said, looking toward the house. "When you hear one of us say 'GO,' start blowing the house apart."

Lynn Rockford touched the Death Merchant on the arm. "I'm not going to stay here," he said with unnerving calm. "I'll go with you and Ferro."

The Death Merchant nodded and turned to go.

Hunched down, Camellion moved at an angle that would take him and Ferro and Rockford, on either side and slightly behind him, to the side of the silo at the north end of the huge barn. As far as they could see, there wasn't anyone around; yet lights burned on both floors of the house. Camellion and Ferro and Rockford soon found that the house was not deserted when a door opened on the east side and three men came out onto the patio. The men walked around to the front of the barn, but since Camellion and his men could not see the front, they didn't know if the men had gone inside.

143

"They sure didn't go out there to pull cows' teats," growled Ferro. "Not at this late hour."

"That damn barn is sure big," Rockford said. "We might have a difficult time finding the entrance to the underground room."

"If we can take two or three of them alive, one of them will tell us," Camellion said coldly. "But we can't do anything out here lying on our bellies. Let's go."

Like silent ghosts, they moved across the field, their feet crunching against grass and weeds and scattered gravel rock. Shortly they had reached their goal and were standing by the west side of the silo, listening intently to every sound and trying to watch all directions at once. Above them reared the tall silo and the second and third floors of the giant barn, the few tiny windows on the upper floor dark.

The Death Merchant pulled the walkie-talkie from his belt, but he didn't turn it on. Instead, he said to Ferro and Rockford, "From the northwest corner of the barn, we have a clear view of the east side of the house. There's only one problem."

"The other side of the barn." Ferro revealed his own expertise at clever strategy. "I'll check out the east side. From the southeast corner, I should be able to see the front of the house and terminate anyone who might come out the doors in the front of the barn."

He pulled a bottle of brandy from his hip pocket and unscrewed the cap.

Camellion thought for a moment, then said, "Rockford, go with him. I'll give you several minutes, then signal Tom and George to open fire."

Ferro finished his drink, recapped the pint bottle, shoved it back in his pocket and belched loudly.

"Damn it!" Rockford hissed angrily. "If anything tips off the terrorists ahead of schedule, it will be that damned belching of yours!"

After Ferro and Rockford had left, the Death Merchant started counting off the seconds, giving the two men an extra half minute for good measure. "148, 149, 150." He switched on the walkie-talkie, muttered "Shoot," then moved away from the silo and quickly to the northwest corner of the barn.

Directly to the west there were the pig pens, and he could hear the porkers snorting and smell them. The stiff wind brought more odors, the aroma of roses from the direction of the house; of lemons; and from the garden north of the patio, the tangy scent of garlic and tomatoes.

The first HEAT grenade struck the house on the north side and exploded with a roar that sounded like a case of dynamite going off. When the smoke cleared and the dust began to settle, there was a ragged twenty foot hole in the wall. Half the wall on the north end of the house had been destroyed, with some of the second story floor revealed, the end of the joists splintered and plasterboard ripped and torn. Rubble from broken concrete blocks and brick siding lay scattered over a wide area.

The enormity of the explosion did not surprise the Death Merchant. A high explosive antitank rifle grenade, the M31 had an explosive filler of 9.92 ounces of Composition-B, and the capability of penetrating 25 centimeters (10 inches) of homogeneous steel armor or 50 centimeters (20 inches) of reinforced concrete. What made the M31 so very deadly was that the antitank grenade achieved penetration by means of the Munroe Principle of the shaped charge. The Munroe Principle is governed by the following three principles of explosive reactions: (1) An explosive force reacts against the weakest force containing it. In the M31, this containing force was a thin sheet of copper which forms an inverted cone liner. This cone gives the filler its shaped effect. The grenade's hollow nose provides the proper standoff distance for the explosive forces to converge. (2) An explosive force reacts against the force containing it at right angles. In the case of the M31, the forces reacted against the copper cone at right angles and moved toward each other. (3) Converging explosive forces combine to form a third and greater force known as the explosive jet. In the M31, the jet is a combination of heat and force which will melt a path through armor and carry pieces of molten armor through it. These molten chunks then rapidly return to solid form. In the case of an armored vehicle, the jet penetrates the vehicle's body armor and also flakes off pieces of the inner side of the armored hull. This fragmented armor ricochets about the interior of the vehicle's body, killing personnel and detonating sensitive ammunition.

When the shell burns through concrete, it is the jagged chunks of concrete that act as fragments; and since concrete is much softer than armor plate, the radius of destruction is always four to five times larger.

The second and third antitank grenades, fired simultaneously by McAulay and Pierson, rocketed through the smoking hole in the north wall, struck a wall in the interior of the house and exploded into brief balls of red flame. This time there were high screams and more tinkling of glass from the upper and the lower windows, the two concussions, along with the severe vibration of the house, causing window panes to shatter.

The door toward the east rear opened and two men and a woman staggered out, coughing from fumes and smoke. The two men were in pants and undershirts, the woman in bra and panties. All three were barefooted.

The Death Merchant cured their coughing instantly with a six-round burst of Ingram fire, watching in satisfaction as the 9mm projectiles knocked the three terrorists to the debris-littered stones of the patio.

Blammmm! Blammmmm! Blammmmmm! McAulay and Pierson were demolishing the house, bit by bit, wall by wall, room by room. The time came when the top floor on the north side no longer had walls to support it. Gravity did the rest. The curb roof crumbled. Dormer-type windows in the roof of the attic dissolved. A chimney that had stood 180 years fell apart in a shower of bricks and mortar. With a loud grinding sound, as beams snapped and floor boards splintered, the north end of the upper story crashed to the first floor.

Blammm! Blammm! Blammm! McAulay and Pierson sent three more antitank grenades into the mass of wreckage, the ear-splitting explosions sending up enormous sprays of rubble, clearing the way for grenades to strike the front half of the house still standing.

The terrific blasts had done more than demolish half the farm house; they had also panicked the animals. The hogs began to squeal and run back and forth in their pens, while cows kicked out and tried to free themselves from stanchions. Horses, behind the fence to the east of the barn, whinnied, stomped the ground, and moved nervously in fear. Animals can "smell" death, and these animals were detecting the sweet scent of a massacre.

The Death Merchant had been doing a kind of a double duty, watching not only the farm house, but the small windows of the second and the third floors of the barn, some of which were lighted. Camellion suspected that something very special, other than Maria Gondozatti, was in the barn. The windows were closed. Ordinarily, since they were used for cross ventilation, the windows would have been open.

When Camellion saw three of the windows swing inward, he raked the openings with a chain of machine gun slugs, then retreated to the north side of the silo, debating whether to have McAulay and Pierson slam several grenades into the northwest corner of the barn. But suppose hay was stored on this end and the barn caught fire. Rescuing a roasted "Saint" would be a waste of time. Camellion concluded that the chances of a fire on the north end were remote. The silage in the silo was most probably corn. Hay was never stored in a silo. The hay door would be on the second floor in the front of the barn, and since the east of the barn was fenced in for animals, there would be a large entry door on the east side.

Hearing the roaring of Ferro's and Rockford's submachine guns, Camellion moved around the silo to the northeast corner of the barn, took the walkie-talkie from his belt, turned it on, held it close to his mouth, and said, "George! Tom! Put a couple of grenades into the upper floors of the northwest corner of the barn. I repeat, the northwest corner. But first count to thirty, slowly. That will give me time to contact Ferro and Rockford. Verify."

"Understood," Pierson said.

Rockford cut in, "We hear you."

"I'm at the northeast corner of the barn," Camellion said. "I'll wait for George and Tom to link up with me. The three of us will then join you and Ferro. Don't get trigger happy when you see us. Got it?"

"Affirmative," Rockford said.

"You heard, Tom, George?"

McAulay said over the walkie-talkie. "We put two grenades into the northwest corner, upper floors, then join you at the northeast corner. Will do 'Father.'"

"Right," Camellion said. "But forget the thirty count. Just do it."

"Get set for the big blast!" McAulay said.

The Death Merchant switched off the set, shoved it into its belt and waited. A few seconds passed. Then the first anti-tank grenade stabbed into the third floor, on the west side, at the northwest corner, of the barn. The explosion shook the entire barn and blew an eight foot hole in the concrete block wall, huge chunks of blocks shooting outward. Before the smoke could clear, the second grenade burst on the second floor on the north side. Another hole was suddenly there and fragments of concrete slammed against the west side of the silo, some chunks dropping around Camellion, who looked at his watch, then at the sky. They were right on schedule, but clouds now entirely obscured the moon.

Standing at the southeast corner of the big barn, Robert Ferro had a first row seat in watching McAulay and Pierson blast the farmhouse. The full evacuation started when Pierson and McAulay began destroying the forward section of the house. Five people, three men and two women, rushed out of the front door, one of the women and a man carrying automatic rifles. Two more men crawled out of a second story window and, hanging by the crooked sill, dropped to the ground. One man landed safely, but Vittorio Salvi Duse cried out like a kicked dog when his right leg snapped below the knee. Andrea Scrovegni, the other man, stopped and helped Duse to his feet while the other five Red Brigadists ran across the front yard toward four cars—two Fiats, an OM and a Volkswagen.

That's when a cold eyed Robert Ferro opened fire, moving the Ingram from left to right. The two women went down first, hair flying, screams dying in their throats. The man with the automatic rifle tried to swing around and get off a burst. He never got off the first round. A bullet hit him in the throat. Two more poked him in the chest. He hit the ground only a few seconds before Ferro raked the last two men with hard lead core slugs.

Interested only in saving his own life, Andrea Scrovegni pushed away Duse's left arm that was around his neck and tried to run to the Volkswagen. Caught off balance, Duse fell to the ground, gritting his teeth in pain and hating Scrovegni, who managed to run ten feet before Ferro raked him perpendicularly from left shoulder to thigh.

Duse rolled over on his stomach, and lay still, his arms out in front of him, thinking that his only chance of staying alive was to play dead. He screamed in fear and pain when a long burst of slugs raked the grass in front of him and four of the 9mm missiles cut off the tips of his fingers, three on his right hand and one on his left. He jerked in agony, rolled over on his back, and wondered why the enemy didn't finish him off.

Ferro reloaded the Ingram and turned around to make sure that Rockford—standing to one side of the big center door that opened and closed on an outside rail—was still watching the windows on the second and third floor. He was, although there wasn't too much danger that any of the *Brigatisti* would try to use any of them. The windows were not very large and anyone inside the barn had to lean out and look down to see Ferro and Rockford, who were against the side of the barn. Three men had tried it. Three men now hung draped over the window sills, stone dead from Rockford's slugs.

Ferro screwed up his mouth in satisfaction when he saw Camellion, Pierson, and McAulay hurrying toward him and Rockford.

Chapter Fourteen

The 25-by-40-foot underground room had become a prison, and Luigi de Santis and Francesco Alongi knew it. They had seen the end coming the day before, upon learning of the catastrophe that had befallen Joseph Marcello and the Morettis. Marcello would die rather than reveal any secrets. He probably had. But the *babuino* and his woman? Alongi and de Santis had to assume that either Bernardo Moretti or Angelina Moretti had revealed where Maria Gondozatti was being held prisoner. Accordingly, the two leaders of the Red Brigades had formed an emergency plan, since their only course of action was to move the "Living Saint" to a new location.

First, they had waited to see if the Italian police would raid the Duse farm, reasoning that if the attackers of the Morettis were connected in any way with the Italian government, the farm would be raided that same day, at least by nightfall. It wasn't. By the next day, Alongi and de Santis were positive that the enemy did not have any connection with the Italian government. Who then were they? The American CIA? the Russian KGB? If it was one or the other—why? There was only one answer that Alongi and de Santis could arrive at: either the Americans or the Soviet Union wanted to grab Maria Gondozatti from the *Brigate Rosse!*

Alongi and de Santis had gone about making arrangements to move the saintly prophetess to a house in Anzio. They had arrived that night at Duse's farm in high spirits and detailed the plan to Duse and the others in the house; the woman

150

would be transferred at dawn to a truck hauling produce to markets in Anzio.

The first shock had been when Duse had told them it would be impossible to transfer Signorina Gondozatti, and then had told them why!

Alongi and de Santis' second surprise came when they were in the underground room, came in the form of an anti-tank grenade. Besides the two Red Brigade leaders, there were only three other persons in the room, the nurse who had attended the Living Saint, Vincenzo Trazono, a policeman from Anzio, and Marco Negarre, who did the cooking and was the general custodian of the room. This lack of manpower was quickly remedied. There were 42 Red Brigadists hiding out from the police on the third and the fourth floors of the barn. Alongi and de Santis had ten of the Brigadists come to the underground stronghold. Another ten were posted on the first floor of the barn, some of the men and women, being from the city, scared stiff of the cows stomping around in their stalls. The other 14 terrorists fled to the first floor in panic when antitank grenades exploded in the northwest corner of the barn.

Suddenly the bombardment was over and there was only the firing of a single submachine gun. Within a minute it too stopped, and there was only silence.

Vincent Trazono, a German Luger in one hand, looked up at the low concrete ceiling. "Could it be that they have left?"

"Don't be an idiot!" snarled Alongi, raking him with a stare of disgust. His movie idol's face twisted in helpless rage, he glared at the back of de Santis, who was looking through a periscope that was built into a hollow square post whose bottom was on the first floor and whose top opened in a ventilator on the peak of the barn's roof.

"Luigi, this is stupid, this doing nothing but waiting!" raged Alongi. He put a heavy hand on de Santis' shoulder. "Why not go upstairs and fight them. We have the men, not only down here but upstairs."

De Santis turned from the periscope, his eyes furious, his hands knotting into fists. "Don't be a fool, Francesco. There are already men upstairs. Let them handle the fighting. We can't be positive that the enemy knows about this room. No! We wait down here!"

Standing a few feet ahead of Ferro, the Death Merchant looked out from the southeast corner of the barn. The front section of the farmhouse had sagged to the east so that the bottom floor was completely buried and two room of the upstairs, on the west side, were revealed, one bed hanging precariously over the splintered edge of the floor. The rest of the furniture in the two bedrooms had tumbled into the wreckage below. The wrecked house had begun to burn, although the flames, toward the northwest side, were just getting started.

He looked across the space at the terrorist still alive. The poor devil lay on his back, his arms propped up on his elbows, his bloody hands in the air.

"I thought it would be a good idea to take one alive," Ferro repeated, "and that jimbo over there was too good to pass up. He's got a busted leg so he can't run. To make sure he couldn't fire at us, I slug-punched him in the fingers."

Chewing on a sprig of rosemary, Camellion stuck his head around the corner and looked at the front of the barn, at the double doors and the hay door and gin pole above them. The double doors and the hay door were closed.

Poor animals! The hogs had broken out of their pen and were running across the field toward the north. A billy goat and four nannies followed them.

"Cover me," Camellion said.

"You are," grunted Ferro. "But make it snappy or we'll miss the next streetcar."

Bent low, Camellion ran a crisscross pattern toward the front yard, dropping down halfway beside a cultivator in front of the toolshed. No shots were fired from the windows in the front side of the barn. He jumped up, sprinted to Vittorio Duse, shouldered the Ingram, reached down, grabbed the moaning man by his bloody wrists and dragged him across the grass to the front of the wrecked house, to a position that hid them from the front of the barn.

"Who—who are you?" Duse's voice was a dry croak. He stared in fear as Camellion pulled an Auto Mag and pressed the muzzle against the side of his left leg, just above the knee.

"Come sta, pebble brain," Camellion said pleasantly. "We know that Maria Gondozatti is in a room underneath the barn. You are going to tell me where the entrance to that

room is, or I'll cut you to pieces with slugs." He slammed the barrel of the AMP across Duse's right leg. The man howled in agony.

"Talk! Right now!" Again Camellion raised the AMP.

"N-No! NO! I'll t-tell you. The last stall in the barn. There's a trapdoor in the floor. A ladder—you crawl down a ladder to the room."

"How many Brigatisti are in the barn?"

"Thirty-five . . . forty . . . something like that."

Camellion's face shone with alarm. "That many? Why?"

"Brigatisti Regolari,"[1] . . . h-hiding out from the *polizia.*"

"I suppose you know that if you're lying, I'll come back and break every bone in your body?"

Duse only stared at him.

The Death Merchant raced back to the corner of the barn and conveyed the information to Ferro, who was instantly suspicious. "You believe him?"

"I'd have shot his legs off if I hadn't."

Ferro scratched the end of his chin and looked over to where the five horses were moving nervously about. His eyes jumped back to Camellion. "Forty of the cruds, huh! All we need now is a pocketful of miracles. Grenades and teargas at both doors, right?"

"Wrong! Or rather half right. We're getting paid to take chances, not to commit suicide." Camellion looked past Ferro at George McAulay, who, halfway down the side of the barn, was inspecting the wedge of wood that Rockford had shoved into the hasp and latch of the large sliding door, to keep anyone inside from pushing it open.

In spite of the gravity of the situation, the Death Merchant couldn't help but smile. Disobeying Camellion's order, McAulay had brought along an M16 and a bag of antitank grenades. Camellion knew it would be an exercise in futility to ask George why. McAulay would only give the usual stock answer—I thought we might need them.

Ferro was quick to catch on. "Man! We'll blow that barn apart with antitank grenades." His ear-to-ear grin suddenly vanished. "You know how the hay will go?"

Camellion shrugged. "So we'll have to get her out before she and we are cremated. If not. . . ." His voice trailed off,

[1] Regular Brigadists.

and he made his way along the wall to McAulay and Rockford.

"I sort of figured we could use the antitank grenades," McAulay said with a lopsided grin. He patted the heavy bag on his hip.

"We certainly can." Camellion told McAulay and Rockford what he had in mind. Then, while McAulay moved along the side of the barn toward Ferro, the Death Merchant went to the northeast corner where Pierson was standing guard.

After a quick conference with Pierson, Camellion retraced his route. He stopped and whispered to Rockford, then hurried to Ferro, who was covering McAulay as George sprinted across the open space to the front of the wrecked house. By now, the entire rear section was a mass of hungry fire, the flames crackling, crawling toward the sky and illuminating the area with monstrous flickering shadows. Never one to take unnecessary chances, McAulay wasn't about to have a conscious enemy at his back, even if the man wasn't able to pick up a weapon. McAulay ran straight to Duse, snap-kicked the man in the head, turned and ran to the east corner of the house, where he had a clear view of the double doors in the front of the huge barn. He took out three antitank grenades. Two, he placed beside him on the grass; the third, he inserted into the launcher on the M16. Impatient to get started, he waited, aiming at the center of the doors.

The Death Merchant looked back at Tom Pierson and nodded. Pierson took a fragmentation grenade from his canvas tote bag and pulled the pin. He paused and measured the distance to the northeast corner of the fence enclosing the barnyard. He then threw the grenade and dropped flat to the ground. So did Ferro, Camellion, and Rockford.

The grenade blew a section of the wooden fence to match sticks, the explosion sending the terrified horses running to the south. Whinnying pitifully, the fear-crazed animals turned and stampeded in the opposite direction. They might have turned and slammed right into Camellion and the other men if the Death Merchant had not jumped up and fired a full magazine of Ingram projectiles into the upper windows of the barn. The horses turned once more and ran, and this time they stampeded through the blasted section of the fence and kept on going.

Growled Ferro, "We're about to have our tails shot off and

154

you have to worry about the damned horses—and what's that you're chewing?"

Camellion didn't mind. "It's not the horses' fault that they have to live on this planet with a pack of 'civilized' killers. I'm chewing rosemary. You've eaten it in dressing."

Pierson and Rockford now raced to the southeast corner and joined Ferro. All three dropped flat and pointed their Ingrams at the door while Camellion raced to the northeast corner, took out a fragmentation grenade, pulled the pin and expertly tossed it so that it landed only several feet from the center of the door.

There was a big bang, a flash of fire and part of the sliding door was blown inward. The smoke was still drifting when Camellion stepped out from the corner and tossed the second pineapple, which detonated and blew more of the door inward. His ears ringing, Camellion was pulling the pin of the third grenade as a dozen lines of slugs from automatic weapons zipped through the ragged opening where most of the door had been.

Not yet, you 'revolutionary' fools. We have more in store for you!

The Death Merchant lobbed the third grenade. No sooner had it roared off and cleared away what little was left of the door than McAulay sent the first antitank grenade through the front door of the barn. *BLAMMMMM!* A bright flash of red, and the door disappeared in thick shower of splintered boards.

McAulay sucked in his lower lip—*Seize the day and gather ye rosebuds while ye may!* As happy as a science fiction fan shaking the hand of Isaac Asimov or Andre Norton, McAulay sent the second antitank grenade into the barn. This one rocketed through the open space and struck a perpendicular twelve-inch square, solid oak beam. The brace, turned into a mass of enormous slivers, acted as a secondary missiles, the hundreds of wooden parings flying outward like an expanding universe, killing two cows and four members of the Red Brigades.

Five more terrorists were buried under tons of hay that tumbled from an upper loft which the shattered beam had supported. Several of the men and women, fearing that other lofts were about to fall, bumped into each other and tripped over their own feet in a frantic effort to retreat to the other end of the barn. They had a new fear when two canisters of

155

teargas sailed through the blasted east side opening, struck the stone floor and began hissing out clouds of gas. Two brave but foolish Brigadists made a futile effort to pick up the canisters and throw them back through the opening to the outside. They had not counted on the fragmentation grenade that the Death Merchant tossed in behind the teargas. It exploded almost in the faces of the two men, riddled them with shrapnel and pitched them up into the air. Concurrently, the third antitank grenade streaked into the barn, struck a Y-shaped brace in the center of the floor and exploded. Concussion killed six Brigadists instantly. Flying splinters from the blown apart Y-brace killed six more, four men and two women. One man went down with the end of an oak splinter protruding a foot from where his left eye had been, the point sticking out the back of his skull.

By now, the Death Merchant and his tiny force were ready, having put on their gas masks and in position. To the front of the barn, Rockford tossed in a fragmentation grenade at the same time that Tom Pierson lobbed a canister of teargas. On the east side, Ferro threw a grenade through the opening and Camellion followed with a canister of teargas.

For a shave of a second, Ferro and Camellion locked eyes through the glass of the gasmasks, Camellion thinking that while some men hunted helpless animals, he stalked the most dangerous game of all, game that could fight back, game that sometimes deserved to be destroyed. Man!

Do it! Go in and die! With full magazines in their Ingrams, the Death Merchant and Ferro streaked through the smoking hole into the smoking hell inside the barn.

Wishing they were any place but at Vittorio Duse's farm, Tom Pierson and Wynn Rockford charged through the front opening, their Ingram submachine guns spitting out short three-round bursts at the demoralized terrorist gangster ahead.

At the southeast corner of the house, a perspiring George McAulay got to his feet, ran over to the row of cars and put the M16 and the sack of antitank grenades under the Volkswagen. Ditto to the Ingram. An SMG wasn't worth yesterday's smile in a close-in firefight. George shouldered the Ingram, made sure the Puukko[2] knife was in place, pulled a Walther P-38—his favorite handgun—and a Hi-Power

2 The traditional Finnish sheath knife, designed by Tapio Wirkkala.

Browning from hip holsters, and began the run to the barn.

It was the drifting haze of teargas that saved the Death Merchant and his three men from being killed instantly. Not only did the opaque gas make it difficult for the enemy to see them, but it also stung the eyes and seared the lungs of the anarchists, causing them to shoot wildly.

A stream of gilded metal jacketed slugs sizzling in their direction, Camellion and Ferro zigzagged like men being jerked by invisible wires. One bullet plucking at his right sleeve and another barely missing his left holster, the Death Merchant saw that the barn was a tremendous rectangle of gas, confusion, and mangled bodies. Half-slipping on blood, he sprayed out the full magazine of Ingram cartridges, killing four of the revolutionaries, then jerked to the right in time to avoid a blast of projectiles from a woman firing a Polish AK-47 automatic rifle. Only seconds ahead of the stream of slugs, he jumped behind several dozen bales of hay that the Brigadists had stacked just before the first antitank grenade had struck the front of the barn. Concussion from grenades had thrown the bales of hay off center, but they were sufficient to stop high powered slugs.

It was a cow that saved Robert Ferro from being blown away in a blast of copper-coated lead. Two cows had dropped dead in their stalls from fright. Three more, jerking frantically within the stanchions imprisoning them, had choked to death. But two cows had managed to break free. Crazed with fear and bawling hideously, one of the cows ran in front of a man who was drawing down on Ferro with a Yugoslav M64B assault rifle. Instead of the 5.56mm projectiles hitting Ferro, they slashed into the side of the poor cow, killing her instantly. In the meanwhile, Ferro ducked to the left and dropped behind a heavy duty seed hopper that rested on the floor in an inverted position, the large, square mouth against the stones, the slanting sides upward.

Zing! Zing! Zing! Zing! Solid nosed projectiles cut through the 18-gauge steel of one side of the hopper, then, most of their power dissipated, ricocheted against the inside of the opposite plate. -

As a cyclone of slugs struck the hopper, Ferro glanced over at Camellion and saw that he, too, was pinned down, enemy projectiles, from machine guns, assault rifles, and pistols, chopping away at the hay. Ferro wondered why the inside of his mouth tasted like stale furniture polish. He stopped thinking about it when he and the Death Merchant heard a muffled but angry voice far to their right, toward the rear of the barn—*"Mettere sul conto loro, cretini!"*[3]

Ferro and Camellion each reached for a grenade.

Tom Pierson and Wynn Rockford met with almost no resistance, all of the terrorists having moved away from the front section of the barn. Only a man and a woman tried to level A-Rs at them, but died before they could get off any rounds, ripped apart by Ingram slugs.

The five terrorists buried by the hay weren't any more fortunate. Two of them were crawling out when Pierson and Rockford exploded their heads and necks with bursts of 9-millimeter projectiles, after which the two CI-nicks raked the pile of hay with the rest of the ammo in their Ingrams, listening to the cries of pain coming from underneath the hay and watching the top of the uneven pile undulate from the movements of the other dying revolutionaries.

Pierson, breathing heavily, darted inside a stall where a cow hung limp and bloody in its stanchion. It took a lot of effort, but Pierson succeeded: he didn't vomit. Oddly enough, he wasn't frightened.

Rockford, his face a mask of sweat behind the gas mask, leaped behind the end of a heavy wooden feed trough, put the sling strap of the Ingram over his left shoulder, and pulled both Browning automatics. He heard a noise behind him, turned and saw that the figure coming through the smoke, and outlined against the background of flames from the burning farmhouse, was a darting and weaving George McAulay. The next thing Rockford knew, a bawling mass of brown and white burst out of the smoke ahead and rushed by him. *A cow! A goddamned cow!* Like a juggernaut, the animal charged in the direction of McAulay, who jumped to one side. Kicking out its back legs, first one way and then the other, the deranged animal managed to find the battered gap where the front door had been and gain freedom to the outside.

"McAulay, over here!" yelled Rockford above the roaring of automatic weapons toward the center of the barn. McAulay reached Rockford as several grenades exploded more to the rear than to the center of the building.

---

[3] "Charge them, you dumb bastards!"

Rockford, McAulay, and Pierson, almost parallel to each other, hurried forward.

Richard Camellion and Robert Ferro knew that they couldn't permit themselves to remain pinned down. An instant after the grenades exploded, both men leaped out and darted ahead, the Death Merchant's hands full of Backpacker Auto Mags, Ferro's filled with AMT Hardballer .45 autoloaders. The two grenades had exploded in the midst of ten terrorists. Concussion had killed four, shrapnel three more; the other three were severely wounded. They lay like sacks of kicked cornmeal, moaning and in pain from broken bones. The other terrorists in the vicinity were in a state of momentary shock, their mental processes suspended in time. Camellion and Ferro had the advantage of lag time, and they used it to good advantage.

Hunched down, constantly weaving back and forth, never still for a single second, Ferro and the Death Merchant opened fire, the roars of the AMPs and the Hardballers almost as loud as a single grenade. Within three-point-zero-seven seconds, seven members of the *Brigate Rosse* were dead from the .44 and .45 jacketed hollow point projectiles. But when three men and two women began darting into stalls, all five carrying assault rifles, Camellion and Ferro realized it was time to seek cover.

I wish I had a roast beef sandwich! And also wishing he were someplace else, Camellion moved to the steel bed of a large tilt cart and got down behind the three foot high side farthest from the enemy. Ferro slid down beside him, his chest heaving like a bellows, his camouflaged ranger's suit wet with blood, at the rib cage on the left side.

"How bad is it?" asked Camellion, reloading the Backpackers, his voice muffled within the gas mask.

"A deep graze," Ferro said tightly. "Burns like hell, but it's not serious." He tapped his wristwatch and looked at the Death Merchant.

"Either we take them in a hurry and get down there to that old woman, or we move out. If we wait and see the cartoon twice and stop for popcorn, we'll miss the helicopters."

The Death Merchant didn't reply until the glancing slugs against the far side of the steel cart bed had sung their last screaming song.

"Keep throwing shots at them," he said and pulled the

walkie-talkie from his belt. "I have a plan. If it doesn't work, we'll pull out."

"If it fails we'll be stretched out beside them!" growled Ferro. He winced. "Damn the sonofabitch who gave me this cut!"

Camellion shook his head in frustration. The walkie-talkie in his hand was junk. A bullet had plowed through the set. He reached out and pulled Ferro's walkie-talkie from its case, switched it on and punched the signal button.

It was Pierson who answered. "We're all okay. I think we're thirty to forty feet to your left. Exactly, where are you and Ferro?"

"Behind a steel truck bed. Now listen. I want the three of you to direct machine gun fire at the stalls across from us. I repeat, across from us. While you fire, start moving in. Ferro and I will lob a couple of tear gas grenades and move in from this side.'

Cut in McAulay, "What about frag stuff?"

"Negative. We're too close. So don't get any bright ideas. Confirm."

"Affirmative, loud and clear," Pierson responded.

"That's it—do it!" Camellion switched off the walkie-talkie shoved it into the case on Ferro's belt and tapped him on the right shoulder. Ferro first fired three more shots around the left end of the bed before he pulled back.

"Let's give them another taste of gas," Camellion said.

Together, he and Ferro tossed two canisters of teargas in the direction of the stalls and heard the two cans start hissing at about the time that McAulay, Pierson, and Rockford began to advance and started firing, using the "fire-and-advance" technique. One man would fire and keep the enemy down while the two behind him advanced. One of the two, who had advanced, would then trigger off a short burst, giving the first man time to catch up.

The two .45 Hardballers and the two .44 Auto Mags reloaded, Ferro and Camellion took deep breaths and moved from the end of the bed. Hunched low, they moved in a darting, crisscross pattern, their firing timed and deadly methodical, although at times they pulled the trigger by instinct, not knowing whether their slugs had struck flesh or wood.

Within fifteen seconds, the other three members of the attack force had caught up and formed the other three-fourths of the loose semicircle that was suddenly within the last remnants of the Red Brigades within the large barn, including Luigi de Santis, Francesco Alongi, and Vincent Trazono. Determined to win or die, Alongi and de Santis had come up from the underground room to lend their firepower to the dwindling force upstairs. Another reason for their departure was their fear that, with all the grenades going off, the floor of the barn—the ceiling of the room—might fall in on them. Even Sophia Demone, the nurse, had climbed the ladder. As crazy as the rest of the Brigatisti, she carried one of the deadliest of all weapons, a *Lupara,* or sawed-off shotgun.

The only thing the two sides had in common was the grim knowledge that it was either kill quickly or be killed just as quickly. Nor did the people of either side have time to reload; each second was too precious. Those who did have a few cartridges left in their weapons hoarded them with a miserliness born of desperation, of an instinct to live. The exception was Richard Camellion. Even though he wasn't about to commit suicide, he did realize that life wasn't all that important. Living in the world of matter actually didn't matter, if for no other reason than the "past," the "present," and the "future" were all illusions. Mind, once created, could never be destroyed.

Outnumbered almost three to one, the Death Merchant and his force of four still had a slight advantage, in that they wore gas masks and were not burdened by burning eyes and fits of coughing. Had it not been for the stiff wind sucking the gas through the two blasted doors, the Red Brigadists would have been much worse off. As it was, they still had plenty of fight left in them. In that respect, it was as though Camellion and his men had escaped from a herd of bulls and had jumped into a pit of grizzlies!

Camellion shoved one AMP into its holster; it was empty. With two cartridges left in the right Auto Mag and with five terrorists closing in around him, he concluded that he had picked a dangerous occupation. *But maybe not!* He shot one wild-eyed, bearded goof in the face and watched the man's skull and gray matter fly off into space.[4]

---

[4] Don't believe all the nonsense that the "victim was shot between the eyes and died instantly." It is not wise to shoot between the eyes unless one is using a very powerful cartridge, such as a magnum bullet, in which case the brain will be.

The second man, trying to swing a Taurus .38 revolver toward Camellion, took the last .44 bullet in the chest. Camellion could have sworn that the man squealed the instant the big hollow nosed projectile entered his body. But Camellion was positive that Ferro and the other three men were struggling with other Red Brigadists. The Death Merchant couldn't help them; he had troubles of his own.

From the corner of his eyes, he detected a man coming at him from the right. As Camellion reached for the ice pick in the holster on the back of his neck, underneath his shirt, Paul Clementi raised the garden sickle in his right hand.

Eight feet in front of Camellion, Vito Gutitia was rushing at him with a long handled pitchfork, the five gleaming prongs pointed at his stomach. *My! My!* The Death Merchant knew that his timing had to be better than good; it had to be perfect.

Reaching him first, Clementi swung the deadly blade of the sickle at Camellion's neck. The Death Merchant ducked, heard the blade hiss over his head, and, not giving Clementi time to draw back for another swing, turned slightly to the left and kicked him in the stomach with a right-legged sword-foot kick, a dynamite slam that sent waves of shock up the man's spinal cord to his brain.

His eyes as big as two brown headlights, Clementi was going down as the Death Merchant sidestepped to the right, avoided the needle-sharp prongs of the pitchfork, wrapped his left hand around the handle, just above the prongs, and, with his right hand, threw the ice pick by its blade. Only a blur as it shot across the short distance, the rounded blade buried itself in Gutitia's chest, below the hollow of his throat. The terrorist acted as if he had run into an invisible wall. He made a gurgling noise. Blood started to trickle from his mouth. His body began to wobble, his hands and arms fluttering. Then his legs turned to melted rubber and he went down.

Camellion dropped the pitchfork and looked over at the man who had caught the ice pick. He was about to pull the ice pick from the goon's chest when he spotted a short-haired woman in red shorts and red halter raising a double-barreled *Lupara* in the direction of Tom Pierson, who had just cracked

---

destroyed by hydrostatic shock. A target can be shot in the head with a bullet of moderate power and still survive long enough to get off several shots.

the skull of a terrorist with the barrel of his Browning and was struggling with another man.

The Death Merchant's right hand streaked toward the center of his chest, toward the slim holster that contained a rugged sheet metal punch with a solid metal handle and an all-steel, eight and a half inch blade that had a probe-hardened point. Camellion pulled the punch by its handle and threw it by instinct, worried that he might be a second too slow to save Pierson's life.

He wasn't. The blade stabbed into Sophia Demone's back, going in between her shoulder blades. She screamed, jerked and reared back, the quick stab of agony causing her to raise the *Lupara* and her finger to pull against one of the triggers. The shotgun exploded, but the widely dispersed shot struck only the ceiling. The woman half twisted around, her mouth opening and closing in disbelief, her eyes staring. The *Lupara* fell from her hands. Her eyes closed and she sagged to the floor, only a short distance from Wynn Rockford who, fighting like a man possessed by Satan himself, was using an empty Browning pistol and his favorite chopper, a five pound meat cleaver with deadly efficiency. One terrorist went down with his skull cracked from the side of the Browning. Another terrorist tried to grab Rockford with his left hand. Rockford chopped off the hand at the wrist, ducked the blow of a third goof, then slammed the blunt top of the big blade against the man's neck. Another man who came at him got a high karate round house kick in the chest that sent him staggering all the way back to George McAulay, who stabbed him in the side of the neck with his already bloodied Puukko knife.

An expert in Savate, the art and technique of leg and foot fighting, McAulay had previously slammed three Bragatisti into unconsciousness with vertical, horizontal, and side kicks. Now he went after Carlo Deledda and Monica Policarpa, both of whom were swinging empty assault rifles toward George, Deledda trying to bash his head in, Policarpa aiming for his ribs. The two terrorists might have succeeded if Tom Pierson hadn't scooped up a two foot length of splintered two-by-four and thrown it at Deledda and Policarpa, the end of the piece of wood striking Deledda in the right hip. Deledda yelled in pain and dropped the AK-47. Deledda's yell had interrupted the woman's swing and she hesitated for a few seconds and turned her head to him. Those few seconds were all McAulay "The Swift" needed. He jumped up and his right leg shot out like a monstrous piston, in a spinning twist kick that broke Monica Policarpa's nose, knocked out her front teeth, and fractured both jaws.

A large, lumbering man, Deledda tried to recover, tried to pick up the AK-47 he had dropped. He was bending over at the same time that McAulay's Puukko knife was coming up. Blade and neck connected. McAulay pushed sideways on the handle, then jerked out on the knife, jumped back and regarded his work.

Deledda gurgled out a quart of blood, sank to his knees and fell forward flat on his face.

McAulay quickly shoved a full magazine into the P-38, jerked back the slide and sent the first 9mm cartridge into the firing chamber. As always, McAulay was using "Dutch loaded" magazines, and the first shell was a hollow-nose.

George was turning to the left when he saw, twenty feet ahead of him, a brutal looking man, with a short beard and a half-bald head, trying to get in a shot at Camellion with a German Luger. The only reason baldy couldn't fire was that Lorenzo Pulci—so short he was almost a midget—was moving between him and the Death Merchant.

McAulay didn't waste time raising the P-38. Instead, he fanned[5] the trigger of the P-38, emptying the magazine in less than two seconds. Four 9 millimeters missed. Two projectiles—one a hollow nose, the other a solid slug—stabbed into Vincent Trazono's right side and pitched him over. He tried to pick himself up, groaned, then fell flat on his face.

The other slugs missed—except the one that hit Lorenzo Pulci in the small of his back. A solid nosed projectile, the bullet broke his back, glanced sideways from a vertebra, went through his body to the right and lodged in his liver.

Satisfied with his efforts, that he had saved Camellion's life, McAulay moved to link up with Ferro. He had moved only a dozen steps when a terrorist tackled him by the legs

[5] This technique is very useful when you are facing several opponents at once and works best with an autoloader which has a large magazine capacity. Brace your hand against the hip and wiggle the index finger of your other hand against the trigger. The technique—also called the "Alley Broom" technique—can be mastered with practice. But it is only useful close up, as it is a very inaccurate method of shooting.

and pulled him down. Quick as chain lightning, McAulay tried to rap the goon over the head with the empty P-38, but the man grabbed his wrist with one hand and smashed him in the chin with the other.

Robert Ferro, who was not far from Camellion, had let Francesco Alongi twist the long steel letter opener from his hand and then knock him backward with a savage blow to his head. Ferro, angry at himself because his timing and reflexes were off because of the burning pain in his side, became even more enraged when he tripped over a pile of rubble and fell heavily to his back.

Alongi, thinking he had the upper hand, rushed in to stomp Ferro in the stomach, never for a moment considering that Ferro might be the better man in technique. Ferro was. Waiting until Alongi's right leg was coming down, he grabbed the Brigade leader's right foot, twisted with all his might and snarled "sonofabitch" as Alongi lost balance and crashed to the floor. Alongi was also fast. He scrambled to his feet at the same time that Ferro jumped up and swung a straight right jab at Ferro's beak of a nose. Ferro, grinning evilly, ducked, grabbed Alongi's wrist, jerked on his arm, pulled him off balance, and kicked him in the belly.

"UHHHH-uhhhhhhh!" The wind jumped out of Alongi's round mouth. His eyes protruded from their sockets. He knew he had made the biggest mistake of his life, but, paralyzed from the pain in his gut, he was helpless to do anything about the hands coming at him in karate stabs and chops. Ferro's left hand speared him in the solar plexus. The right hand came down against Alongi's neck in a sword-ridge slam. His mind drowning in blackness, Alongi sank to the floor.

Luigi de Santis had also made a fatal mistake. He had reached out and grabbed the strap of the Death Merchant's grenade bag and had jerked Camellion back toward him in an effort to get his arm around Camellion's neck and to pull off his gas mask. Surprisingly, the Death Merchant did not resist. De Santis found out why when Camellion stabbed him in the gut with a terrific elbow jab. Pain streaked through de Santis and he released his hold on the canvas strap. Yet desperation gave him a superhuman strength. Camellion spun around and de Santis attempted to slam him in the face through the gas mask and mash him in the stomach with a fist. Camellion ducked the fist aimed at his face and, with a knee lift, blocked the blow aimed at his stomach.

Not giving de Santis time to form a new plan of attack, he stepped forward, threw his right arm over de Santis' head and over his right shoulder, so that his arm encircled the *Brigate Rosse* leader's neck. Camellion brought his right elbow under de Santis' chin and pushed the man's head under his armpit. Now he had de Santis in a "Stocks" hold. Still, de Santis threshed around. Again, de Santis tried to slam a fist into Camellion's stomach. He didn't because Camellion stomped on his left instep, then kneed him in the groin.

The Death Merchant next pushed his left arm between de Santis' right arm and right rib cage; he reached down across the man's back, grabbed de Santis' left wrist and jerked the arm upward, securing the man in an arm-bar lock. The Death Merchant tightened his right arm around de Santis' neck, flung both his legs upward, twisted again with his right arm and threw himself to the right. As Camellion and de Santis fell, there was a sound like a piece of wood being broken.

The Indian Death Roll had broken de Santis' neck. . . .

Camellion pushed the corpse from him and got to his feet. He liked what he saw. The floor was littered with bodies, and none of them were his men.

Six feet ahead of him, Ferro was putting the finishing touches to Joseph Macca, a fat terrorist who had been stupid enough to think he could beat out Ferro's brains by first smashing in his gas mask with the butt of a Bernardelli auto pistol. With one foot planted firmly on the handle of the pitchfork, Ferro had broken Macca's nose with a karate chop, had stabbed him in the stomach with a spearhand thrust and was now tripping the half-unconscious man backward. Macca fell on the end of the pitchfork, crying out in brief agony as the upturned prongs entered his back. Blood flowed out of his mouth. His eyes rolled back in his head and his body went limp.

Thirty feet from the Death Merchant, Wynn Rockford was reloading his Brownings. Not far from Rockford, Tom Pierson was coughing and picking up his gas mask. His left arm hung limp. The sleeve was rippled from a knife slash and was bloody.

McAulay staggered to his feet. He adjusted his gas mask,

bent down and pulled the Puukko knife from the back of a corpse.

Camellion went over to Vito Gutitia and pulled the ice pick from the dead man's chest, wiped the blade carefully on the pants of the corpse and shoved the ice pick into its holster. The Death Merchant next walked to Sophia Demone, who lay crumpled on her left side. He pulled the metal punch from the dead woman's back, wiped it clean of blood on her shorts, and carefully placed it in its holster.

"All this to rescue a nutty old woman who thinks she has a hotline to the Almighty!" McAulay said in a tired voice. He moved closer to Camellion and pulled back the slide of the P-38, sending a cartridge into the chamber.

The Death Merchant surveyed the area. The smell of blood and the sweet clawing odor of death could be detected even through the gas masks.

"Don't worry, George," Camellion said. "The company will give you a gold watch for this mission."

"Huh! By the time the company starts giving out watches, I'll be too damn old to care about the time!"

Nine terrorists—six men and three women, including Francesco Alongi—were still alive, all of them suffering from either cracked skulls or broken bones. Forced to sit on the floor, their hands on their heads, they stared miserably at the five men in gas masks, convinced that soon they were be killed by the mysterious enemy.

Finding Maria Gondozatti was no longer the problem. The trap door was wide open in the last stall. But was there an explosive device set to go off if the wrong people crawled down the ladder. The *Brigate Rosse* was notorious for such treachery.

"Kill us and be done with it!" Francesco Alongi spit out hoarsely, his raspy voice full of pain from the blows Ferro had given him.

The Death Merchant, analyzing the faces of the terrorists, assessed the nine for weaknesses. The man who had just spoken was tough. He'd never crack. So were several of the other men, and one of the women, judging from the way they stared defiantly at him. The other two women and the rest of the men were terrified.

"I believe you people refer to it as 'kneecapping,' " Camellion said affably. He had pulled a High Standard Sports-King autoloader from a shoulder holster inside his suit and waved it back and forth. "I think I'll use a bit of kneecapping."

Ferro pointed a thumb toward the floor. "Down there," he growled. "How's the bomb triggered to go off? A pressure mechanism?"

He stared at the nine terrorists sitting butt-flat on the floor. No one answered.

The HS Sports-King cracked twice. One of the men yelled and both his legs jumped. The man fell to his back, moaning. Camellion had placed a .22 long rifle bullet in each knee. Silvester Golessi, the man next to the terrorist who had just been kneecapped, jerked to one side, deep fear on his dirty face.

Twice more the Sports-King barked. Golessi screamed. The Death Merchant had shot him in the fleshy part of the right arm and in the right side of the left foot.

The Death Merchant estimated that he had created enough horror for shock effect and one of the women should be more than anxious to talk. He swung the slim barrel of the Sports-King toward Silvana Fieramosca, a rather pretty young woman in her twenties. She drew back, her eyes as wide open as possible.

"NO! No!" she shrieked. "I have never been to the room below. Ask Alongi. He knows! He is one of the leaders!"

"Leaders?" Camellion said gently.

"The other one was Luigi de Santis. He's dead."

"Who's Alongi?"

Silvana Fieramosca leaned forward and pointed at Alongi sitting at the end of the line.

The Death Merchant turned the Sports-King to Alongi, who surprised Camellion by showing fear— *He's cracking.*

"First your arms, then your legs," Camellion began. "I think then that I'll—"

"There isn't any bomb down there," Alongi said quickly. His eyes shone with dread and his voice faltered. "And we didn't kill the Living Saint."

"You were right, Mr. C!" Ferro turned to Camellion. "They didn't have the nerve to kill the poor old woman."

"We didn't kill her, but s-she's dead!" Alongi said and braced himself for the bullets he expected.

The Death Merchant walked over to Alongi and placed the

168

muzzle of the .22 autoloader against the man's left temple.

"She . . . she died of natural causes," muttered Alongi. "Earlier in the day. We t-think she had a heart attack."

"But there isn't any bomb?"

"N-No. There's no bomb."

"If there is, you'll go straight to hell with us."

The wind had blown away the tear gas and Camellion and his men removed their gas masks. While Ferro, Pierson, and Rockford kept weapons trained on the battered and bruised terrorists, Camellion and McAulay pushed a trembling Francesco Alongi toward the trapdoor in the floor of the last stall.

"You're going down first, Alongi," said Camellion, who had drawn one of the Auto Mags. "Wait at the bottom of the ladder. Try to run and I'll put a bullet in your head."

Alongi only nodded. He stepped onto the ladder, climbed down and waited at the bottom as instructed. When Camellion and McAulay joined him in the musty room—lighted by only a single bulb—he led them to a cot in the far corner.

The woman, wearing a simple black dress, lay on a faded brown blanket, her arms at her ide, her eyes closed. A rosary was entwined within the fingers of her left hand. The expression on her wrinkled face was one of peace.

"We didn't kill her." Alongi's voice rose in panic. "She just died. We had a nurse with her, and the nurse found her like that, the way she is now. She must have died in her sleep."

"Where's the nurse?" demanded McAulay.

"Dead. You people killed her."

Camellion stared at the woman on the bed— *Our luck has been double bad!*

With a motion so swift that even McAulay didn't expect it, the Death Merchant slammed the barrel of the Auto Mag against Alongi's temple. The Red Brigade leader crumpled to the floor and lay still.

McAulay was surprised. "Why didn't you shoot him?"

"Why waste a bullet? He'll never leave this room."

McAulay's gaze went back to the cot. "What about her? What are we going to do?"

Camellion walked to the side of the cot, bent over and felt for a pulse in the woman's throat. There wasn't any. Her skin was cold and clammy.

"She's not just drugged?" McAulay said. "She is dead?"

"As dead as she can get. And don't ask me if she's a 'ringer.' She isn't. She's the real Maria Gondozatti."

"I know," replied McAulay. "We were both shown large photographs of her before we left the States. I was only wondering what we are going to do now. There's no point in taking a dead body with us. So I guess we leave her here."

"You guessed right, George. Even if we wanted to take her with us, we couldn't. We've got to move fast or miss the helicopters. Let's move it."

The Death Merchant and McAulay went back upstairs. While McAulay went after the M16 and antitank grenades he had stashed under the Volkswagen, Camellion and the other three men marched the rest of the captives to the trap door and forced them to climb down the ladder. Camellion then closed the trap door and wedged a large wooden splinter into the hasp.

McAulay was waiting for them at the east side entrance. With the rest of them, he too tossed in an incendiary grenade and watched as the fire bombs burst into intense white fire.

"I'm surprised that the antitank grenades didn't set the hay on fire," Pierson commented.

"It was just one of those things that they didn't," Rockford said.

"Listen—all of you," Camellion said. "We have only eighteen minutes to reach the three choppers. Cut out the chatter and run. Those helicopters won't wait."

They reached the northeast corner of the barn, then scurried across the field, each man wondering if they would reach the choppers in time. Drops of rain hitting their faces, the men also thought of the doomed terrorists trapped in the underground room, and they were grateful that they had not met the same horrible fate and were still alive. Whether or not they kept on living depended on their getting to the helicopters.

Behind them, the barn was engulfed in flames that crackled and clawed higher and higher into the dark, windy sky.

Setting a fast pace, the Death Merchant was at the point, the others strung out behind him, all five exerting all their strength as they pushed through grass and around trees and shrubbery. Now and then, one of them would stumble and fall. The man would pick himself up, renew his efforts and keep on going.

Their lungs screaming for air, they heard the idling rotor blades before they saw the helicopters. In another few minutes, they were running among white birch and chestnut trees whose branches were being pelted by rain, now coming down harder, and twisted by wind getting stronger and stronger.

With the Death Merchant still in the lead, they raced past the Lancia into the field.

There sat the three Bell YAH-63A helicopters, spaced out in the form of a triangle. A small attack craft, powered by two 1536-hp General Electric T700 turboshaft engines, the YAH-63A had room for only the pilot in the front seat and the co-pilot/gunner in the seat behind him. But when the rear seat was removed, two men could squeeze in behind the pilot. Stripped of its 40-mm grenade launcher in the nose, six Tow missiles, and the 30-mm cannon in the barbette below the rear fuselage, the small bird would be able to carry the extra man with ease.

Camellion barked orders. Robert Ferro and Tom Pierson, stripping off their weapons and grenades as they hurried along, ran to the first helicopter at the point of the triangle. Wynn Rockford dashed to the bird at the left corner of the triangle. He threw off his gear and climbed in awkwardly behind the pilot. The two pilots didn't linger; they cycled up the rotor blades and lifted off.

The pilot of the last YAH glared at the Death Merchant through the canopy, pointed at his watch, then up at the sky. Camellion motioned for him to open the canopy.

"What the hell is the other guy doing?" yelled the pilot as Camellion climbed into the back space. "Goddamn it! There's a blow coming, and we've got to land this baby on the deck of a sub!"

To the right, a hundred and fifty feet to the northeast, there was a big *whoommmmm*. McAulay had exploded the Lancia with an antitank grenade.

"He's on his way," Camellion said. Taking off the two Auto Mags, he hoped the pilot hadn't noticed the string of vehicle lights coming down the road.

"He had better get the lead out," the pilot said grimly. "See those lights on the road? I doubt if they're friends of ours."

McAulay was soon back at the helicopter, but he stayed

out of range of the downdraft of the blades. Instead of running up to the cockpit, he fixed a grenade in the launcher of the M16, aimed carefully at the headlights of the first troop carrier and pulled the trigger.

A terrific explosion! A flash of red flame! The sound of steel being ripped apart!

McAulay tossed the M16 to one side, took off the bag of grenades, dropped them to the ground, ran to the helicopter, climbed in and squeezed down beside the Death Merchant.

The pilot closed the canopy and started to cycle up the blades.

"The blazing junk that was the first carrier should hold the Italian army for a while," McAulay said in a loud voice. Feeling as though he had swallowed a pound of confusion, he braced himself by holding onto the back of the pilot's seat as the chopper rose rapidly into the air. "Man, this is a tight fit, but it beats pushing a plow through a turnip patch."

Buffeted by wind and slashing rain, the helicopter headed west in the blackness, water pounding against the canopy.

The Death Merchant called out to the pilot, yelling to make himself heard, "Do you think you can make it back to the submarine?"

"Got to!" the man called back. He looked as young as a high school senior. "I sure as hell am not going to put us down in Italy. Don't get your balls in an uproar! The full storm won't hit for another half hour. By then we'll be inside the boat. But I don't think the hanger crew will have time to secure these babies inside the boat. They'll have to go over the side into the drink. Man, SUB-COM-2 will have a hemorrhage when it hears about it."

"About the woman back there," McAulay said to the Death Merchant. "I don't suppose the world will ever know what happened to her, unless we tip off the Italians."

"They'll be tipped off," Camellion said. "The floor of the barn will burn through, and they'll find her charred corpse. But they'll be able to make a positive ID through dental charts."

"If she's been to a dentist!"

"According to the CIA file I read on her, she has," Camellion said. "She also suffered from a heart condition. That's why she died. The strain became too much for her."

"We did it all for nothing," McAulay said, anger crossing his face. "It was one monumental exercise in futility. . . ."

"Look at the bright side," Camellion said. "We wiped out a lot of high-powered Red Brigade people. And we're alive and in good health. That's ninety-five percent of life, George."

In the dim green glow of the cockpit light, Camellion noticed that an odd expression was crossing McAulay's face.

"Let's have it, George. What's driving tacks into your brain?"

"I just remembered," McAulay yelled in reply. "You never did pay me the twenty bucks you lost in the bet over Cerridwen's name. . . ."

**Out of the American West rides a new hero.
He rides alone . . . trusting no one.**

SPECIAL PREVIEW

EDGE

BY
George G. Gilman

Edge *is not like other western novels. In a tradition-bound
genre long dominated by the heroic cowpoke, we now have
the western anti-hero, an un-hero . . . a character seemingly
devoid of any sympathetic virtues. "A mean, sub-bitchin,'
baad-ass!" For readers who were introduced to the western via
Fran Striker's Lone Ranger tales, and who have learned about
the ways of the American West from the countless volumes
penned by Max Brand and Zane Grey, the adventures of Edge
will be quite shocking. Without question, these are the most
violent and bloody stories ever written in this field. Only two
things are certain about Edge: first, he is totally unpredicta-
ble, and has no pretense of ethics or honor . . . for him there
is no Code of the West, no Rules of the Range. Secondly, since
the first book of Edge's adventures was published by Pinnacle
in July of 1972, the sales and reader reaction have continued
to grow steadily. Edge is now a major part of the western
genre, alongside ol' Max and Zane, and Louis L'Amour. But*

Edge *will never be confused with any of 'em, because Edge is an original, tough hombre who defies any attempt to be cleaned up, calmed-down or made honorable. And who is to say that* Edge *may not be a realistic portrayal of our early American West? Perhaps more authentic than we know.*

George G. Gilman created *Edge* in 1971. The idea grew out of an editorial meeting in a London pub. It was, obviously, a fortunate blending of concepts between writer and editor. Up to this point Mr. Gilman's career included stints as a newspaperman, short story writer, compiler of crossword puzzles, and a few not-too-successful mysteries and police novels. With the publication in England of his first *Edge* novel, *The Loner,* Mr. Gilman's writing career took off. British readers went crazy over them, likening them to the "spaghetti westerns" of Clint Eastwood. In October, 1971, an American editor visiting the offices of New English Library in London spotted the cover of the first book on a bulletin board and asked about it. He was told it was "A cheeky Britisher's incredibly gory attempt at developing a new western series." Within a few days Pinnacle's editor had bought the series for publication in the United States. "It was," he said, "the perfect answer to the staid old westerns, which are so dull, so predictable, and so all-alike."

The first reactions to *Edge* in New York were incredulous. "Too violent!" "It's too far from the western formula, fans won't accept it." "How the hell can a British writer write about *our* American West?" But Pinnacle's editors felt they had something hot, and that the reading public was ready for it. So they published the first two *Edge* books simultaneously; *The Loner* and *Ten Grand* were issued in July 1972.

But, just *who* is Edge? We'll try to explain. His name was Josiah Hedges, a rather nondescript, even innocent, monicker for the times. Actually we meet Josiah's younger brother, Jamie Hedges, first. It is 1865, in the state of Iowa, a peaceful farmstead. The Civil War is over and young Jamie is awaiting the return of his brother, who's been five years at war. Six hundred thousand others have died, but Josiah was coming home. All would be well again. Jamie could hardly contain his excitement. He wasn't yet nineteen.

The following is an edited version of the first few chapters, as we are introduced to Josiah Hedges:

* * *

Six riders appeared in the distance, it must be Josiah! But then Jamie saw something which clouded his face, caused him to reach down and press Patch's head against his leg, giving or seeking assurance.

"Hi there, boy, you must be Joe's little brother Jamie."

He was big and mean-looking and, even though he smiled as he spoke, his crooked and tobacco-browned teeth gave his face an evil cast. But Jamie was old enough to know not to trust first impressions: and the mention of his brother's name raised the flames of excitement again.

"You know Joe? I'm expecting him. Where is he?"

"Well, boy," he drawled, shuffling his feet. "Hell, when you got bad news to give, tell it quick is how I look at things. Joe won't be coming today. Not any day. He's dead, boy."

"We didn't only come to give you the news, boy," the sergeant said. "Hardly like to bring up another matter, but you're almost a man now. Probably are a man in everything except years—living out here alone in the wilderness like you do. It's money, boy.

"Joe died in debt, you see. He didn't play much poker, but when he did there was just no stopping him."

Liar, Jamie wanted to scream at them. *Filthy rotten liar.*

"Night before he died," the sergeant continued. "Joe owed me five hundred dollars. He wanted to play me double or nothing. I didn't want to, but your brother was sure a stubborn cuss when he wanted to be."

Joe never gambled. Ma and Pa taught us both good.

"So we played a hand and Joe was unlucky." His gaze continued to be locked on Jamie's, while his discolored teeth were shown in another parody of a smile. "I wasn't worried none about the debt, boy. See, Joe told me he'd been sending money home to you regular like."

"There ain't no money on the place and you're a lying son-ofabitch. Joe never gambled. Every cent he earned went into a bank so we could do things with this place. Big things. I don't even believe Joe's dead. Get off our land."

Jamie was held erect against this oak, secured by a length of rope that bound him tightly at ankles, thighs, stomach, chest, and throat; except for his right arm left free of the bonds so that it could be raised out and the hand fastened, fingers splayed over the tree trunk by nails driven between them and bent over. But Jamie gritted his teeth and looked back at Forrest defiantly, trying desperately to conceal the twisted terror that reached his very nerve ends.

"You got your fingers and a thumb on that right hand, boy," Forrest said softly. "You also got another hand and we got lots of nails. I'll start with the thumb. I'm good. That's why they made me platoon sergeant. Your brother recommended me, boy. I don't miss. Where's the money?"

The enormous gun roared and Jamie could no longer feel anything in his right hand. But Forrest's aim was true and when the boy looked down it was just his thumb that lay in the dust, the shattered bone gleaming white against the scarlet blood pumping from the still warm flesh. Then the numbness went and white hot pain engulfed his entire arm as he screamed.

"You tell me where the money is hid, boy," Forrest said, having to raise his voice and make himself heard above the sounds of agony, but still empty of emotion.

The gun exploded into sound again and this time there was no moment of numbness as Jamie's forefinger fell to the ground.

"Don't hog it all yourself, Frank," Billy Seward shouted, drawing his revolver. "You weren't the only crack shot in the whole damn war."

"You stupid bastard," Forrest yelled as he spun around. "Don't kill him. . . ."

But the man with the whiskey bottle suddenly fired from the hip, the bullet whining past Forrest's shoulder to hit Jamie squarely between the eyes, the blood spurting from the fatal wound like red mud to mask the boy's death agony. The gasps of the other men told Forrest it was over and his Colt spoke again, the bullet smashing into the drunken man's groin. He went down hard into a sitting position, dropping his gun, splaying his legs, his hands clenching at his lower abdomen.

"Help me, Frank, my guts are running out. I didn't mean to kill him."

"But you did," Forrest said, spat full into his face and brought up his foot to kick the injured man savagely on the jaw, sending him sprawling on to his back. He looked around at the others as, their faces depicting fear, they holstered their guns. "Burn the place to the ground," he ordered with low-key fury. "If we can't get the money, Captain damn Josiah C. Hedges ain't gonna find it, either."

Joe caught his first sight of the farm and was sure it was a trick of his imagination that painted the picture hanging before his eyes. But then the gentle breeze that had been coming from the south suddenly veered and he caught the acrid stench of smoke in his nostrils, confirming that the black smudges rising lazily upwards from the wide area of darkened country ahead was actual evidence of a fire.

As he galloped toward what was now the charred remains of the Hedges farmstead, Joe looked down at the rail, recognizing in the thick dust of a long hot summer signs of the recent passage of many horses—horses with shod hoofs. As he thundered up the final length of the trail, Joe saw only two areas of movement, one around the big oak and another some yards distant, toward the smouldering ruins of the house, and as he reined his horse at the gateway he slid the twelve shot Henry repeater from its boot and leapt to the ground, firing from hip level. Only one of the evil buzz that had been tearing ferociously at dead human flesh escaped, lumbering with incensed screeches into the acrid air.

For perhaps a minute Joe stood unmoving, looking at Jamie bound to the tree. He knew it was his brother, even though his face was unrecognizable where the scavengers had ripped the flesh to the bone. He saw the right hand picked almost completely clean of flesh, as a three fingered skeleton of what it had been, still securely nailed to the tree. He took hold of Jamie's shirt front and ripped it, pressed his lips against the cold, waxy flesh of his brother's chest, letting his grief escape, not moving until his throat was pained by dry sobs and his tears were exhausted. . . .

"Jamie, our ma and pa taught us a lot out of the Good Book, but it's a long time since I felt the need to know about such things. I guess you'd know better than me what to say at a time like this. Rest easy, brother, I'll settle your score. Whoever they are and wherever they run, I'll find them and I'll kill them. I've learned some special ways of killing people and I'll avenge you good." Now Joe looked up at the sky, a bright sheet of azure cleared of smoke. "Take care of my kid brother, Lord," he said softly, and put on his hat with a gesture of finality, marking the end of his moments of graveside reverence. Then he went to the pile of blackened timber, which was the corner of what had been Jamie's bedroom. Joe used the edge of the spade to prise up the scorched floor boards. Beneath was a tin box containing every cent of the two thousand dollars Joe had sent home from the war, stacked neatly in piles of one, five, and ten dollar bills.

Only now, more than two hours since he had returned to the farmstead, did Joe cross to look at the second dead man.

The scavenging birds had again made their feast at the man-made source of blood. The dead man lay on his back, arms and legs splayed. Above the waist and below the thighs he was unmarked, the birds content to tear away his genitals and rip a gaping hole in his stomach, their talons and bills delving inside to drag out the intestines, the uneaten portions of which now trailed in the dust. . . .

Then Joe looked at the face of the dead man and his cold eyes narrowed. The man was Bob Rhett, he recalled. He had fought a drunken coward's war, his many failings covered by his platoon sergeant Frank Forrest. So they were the five men who must die . . . Frank Forrest, Billy Seward, John Scott, Hal Douglas, and Roger Bell. They were inseparable throughout the war.

Joe walked to his horse and mounted. He had not gone fifty yards before he saw a buzzard swoop down and tug at something that suddenly came free. Then it rose into the air with an ungainly flapping of wings, to find a safer place to enjoy its prize. As it wheeled away, Joe saw that swinging from its bill were the entrails of Bob Rhett.

Joe grinned for the first time that day, an expression of cold slit eyes and bared teeth that utterly lacked humor. "You never did have any guts, Rhett," he said aloud.

* * *

From this day of horror Josiah Hedges forged a new career as a killer. A killer of the worst kind, born of violence, driven by revenge. As you'll note in the preceding material, Edge often shows his grim sense of irony, a graveyard humor. Edge is not like anyone you've met in fact or fiction. He is without doubt the most cold-bloodedly violent character to ever roam the West. You'll hate him, you'll cringe at what he does, you'll wince at the explicit description of all that transpires . . . and you'll come back for more.

DEATH MERCHANT
by Joseph Rosenberger

the EXECUTIONER by Don Pendleton

| Over 22 million copies in print! |

☐	40-027-9	Executioner's War Book		$1.50
☐	40-299-6	War Against the Mafia	#1	1.50
☐	40-300-3	Death Squad	#2	1.50
☐	40-301-1	Battle Mask	#3	1.50
☐	40-302-X	Miami Massacre	#4	1.50
☐	40-303-8	Continental Contract	#5	1.50
☐	40-304-6	Assault on Soho	#6	1.50
☐	40-305-4	Nightmare in New York	#7	1.50
☐	40-306-2	Chicago Wipeout	#8	1.50
☐	40-307-0	Vegas Vendetta	#9	1.50
☐	40-308-9	Caribbean Kill	#10	1.50
☐	40-309-7	California Hit	#11	1.50
☐	40-310-0	Boston Blitz	#12	1.50
☐	40-311-9	Washington I.O.U.	#13	1.50
☐	40-312-7	San Diego Siege	#14	1.50
☐	40-313-5	Panic in Philly	#15	1.50
☐	40-314-3	Sicilian Slaughter	#16	1.50
☐	40-237-6	Jersey Guns	#17	1.50
☐	40-315-1	Texas Storm	#18	1.50
☐	40-316-X	Detroit Deathwatch	#19	1.50
☐	40-238-4	New Orleans Knockout	#20	1.50
☐	40-317-8	Firebase Seattle	#21	1.50
☐	40-318-6	Hawaiian Hellground	#22	1.50
☐	40-319-4	St. Louis Showdown	#23	1.50
☐	40-239-2	Canadian Crisis	#24	1.50
☐	40-224-4	Colorado Kill-Zone	#25	1.50
☐	40-320-8	Acapulco Rampage	#26	1.50
☐	40-321-6	Dixie Convoy	#27	1.50
☐	40-225-2	Savage Fire	#28	1.50
☐	40-240-6	Command Strike	#29	1.50
☐	40-150-7	Cleveland Pipeline	#30	1.50
☐	40-166-3	Arizona Ambush	#31	1.50
☐	40-252-X	Tennessee Smash	#32	1.50
☐	40-333-X	Monday's Mob	#33	1.50
☐	40-334-8	Terrible Tuesday	#34	1.50